House Reckoning

Also by Mike Lawson

The Inside Ring

The Second Perimeter

House Rules

House Secrets

House Justice

House Divided

House Blood

House Odds

Rosarito Beach

House Reckoning

MIKE LAWSON

Atlantic Monthly Press
New York

Published simultaneously in Canada
Printed in the United States of America

FIRST EDITION

ISBN: 978-0-8021-2253-7
eISBN: 978-0-8021-9253-0

Atlantic Monthly Press
an imprint of Grove/Atlantic, Inc.
154 West 14th Street
New York, NY 10011

Distributed by Publishers Group West

www.groveatlantic.com

14 15 16 17   10 9 8 7 6 5 4 3 2 1

To Jamison Stoltz, senior editor at Grove Atlantic.
Thanks to his hard work, his astute comments, his attention
to detail, and his insights, the published version of my novels
is always significantly better than the original manuscript.

Part I

1

"We got a problem," Enzo said.

Carmine Taliaferro was feeding his fish. He'd never figured himself for a fish guy, but he was in a pet store with his granddaughter one day, looking at the puppies, and saw the aquarium there. He didn't know the names of the fish then; he just liked the colors: the bright yellows, the iridescent blues and greens. His favorite was a little black one about two inches long with a red stripe on each side, like the racing stripes on an Indy car. So he bought the aquarium and put it in his den and he'd sit there, watching the fish, thinking about nothing, just relaxing. It was like watching baseball on TV with the sound turned down.

"What kind of a problem?" Carmine asked, glancing over at Enzo.

When Enzo Marciano was younger, he'd looked like the hood he was. As he'd gotten older, hard muscle pooled into layers of fat, he lost most of his hair, and started wearing glasses. Now all he needed was a mustard-splattered apron and he could be the guy behind the counter at the corner deli—but that didn't mean he wasn't still a hood.

"It's DeMarco," Enzo said. "He identified the guy who killed Jerry Kennedy. He's gonna kill him."

"Goddamnit," Carmine muttered. "I knew this was going to happen."

"He came to ask permission but he wasn't really asking, if you know what I mean. I told him I was gonna have to talk to you and he said he understood, but he's not gonna let it go, no matter what you say. You know how he is."

When Carmine shook his head, Enzo misinterpreted the gesture and said, "Yeah, I know. We can't let him do it. We don't need that kind of heat."

Carmine laughed. "Heat? There won't be any heat if DeMarco kills him. The kid will just disappear and nobody will have a clue what happened to him."

"What are you saying? You're gonna let him do it?"

Carmine lit a cigarette and started coughing as soon as he drew smoke into his throat. Fucking cigarettes were the thing that was going to kill *him* one day.

"No. That kid's young, but he's smart and he's connected. What I'm saying is, I need him more than I need DeMarco."

Carmine picked up a plastic bag sitting next to the aquarium. It was filled with water and contained about twenty small fish, each fish maybe a quarter of an inch long. The fish were almost transparent and if you looked closely you could see their tiny hearts beating. He took a switchblade out of his pocket—he'd killed a punk with the knife when he was sixteen—and split the bag and dumped the fish into the aquarium. Then he just watched, not realizing there was a little smile on his face, as the other fish attacked the new fish. They wiped them all out in about two minutes. Those brightly colored fish didn't look like predators—but then neither did guys like him and Enzo.

"Damnit, Enzo," Carmine said. "It's really too bad about DeMarco. It just breaks my heart."

2

Maureen DeMarco glanced into the living room. Again.

He was still sitting there in the big recliner they both thought of as *his* chair. He was probably, almost certainly, brooding over Jerry Kennedy. He'd been brooding about Jerry ever since the funeral. When he'd first sat down it was just starting to get dark outside and now it was completely dark, and he hadn't even turned on the light next to his chair. He'd been sitting there for an hour.

She felt like screaming at him. She wanted to say, "You just forget about Jerry! He was a useless, drunken bum. You got your own family to think about." But she knew screaming at him wouldn't do any good. Screaming at Gino DeMarco was like screaming at a rock. He didn't get mad. Well, he probably did get mad—but he never did anything. He'd never raised a hand to her in the twenty-seven years they'd been married. For that matter, she couldn't remember him ever raising his voice to her. If she started yelling at him, he'd just leave the house and not come back until after he was sure she'd gone to bed. And in the end, he'd do what he wanted, no matter what she said.

She was making a pie because Joe was coming home from school for a visit tomorrow, and she was making as much noise as she could, banging dishes around, kneading the dough like she was hitting a punching bag. She knew she was just ruining the piecrust and would have to make another one. She also knew Gino could hear her and he knew, with all the noise she was making, that she was mad. But would he turn around and ask what was bothering her? No, not him. Not ever. He was a rock.

She was a junior in high school when she met him at a St. Patrick's Day dance. Even now, when she was mad at him, she still smiled when she thought about that night. He was there with a bunch of other Italian boys who'd snuck into the gym and he kept looking at her, but then he'd look away as soon as she looked at him. She could tell he wanted to ask her to dance—and she knew he wouldn't.

She still couldn't believe it, all these years later, how she'd walked up to him, tapped him right on his big chest, and said, "I like this song. Why don't we dance?" Her girlfriends had been mortified, but she didn't care. She knew she had to make the first move because he never would have. Yeah, she knew what he was like before she even knew him at all.

He'd gotten a bit heavier as the years had passed but he wasn't fat and he was still a handsome man: dark hair not thinning a bit, a big nose that fit his face, the cleft in his chin, the muscles in his arms. She'd always loved his arms. She always felt safe in them.

Her father had pretended not to like him at first. He'd say things like "You going out with that dago kid again?" Irish fathers felt obligated to say things like that back then. And she'd respond by saying, "Don't you go calling him that. That's prejudice. Plus, he's Catholic. That should make you and ma happy."

The fact was, her father had actually liked him right from the start. He had three daughters and had always wanted a son, and he and Gino used to go to Mets games together all the time before her father died. And when Joe got old enough to go with them . . . Her father had lived for those Sunday afternoons, sitting there in the cheap seats in the upper deck, telling his grandson what bums the Yankees were.

When they got married, her mother had basically told her to be subservient to him, although her mother had never used a word like *subservient* in her life. "Your job," she said, "is to be a good wife and make a good home for him. You take care of his house and his children. You learn how to cook. And you don't be a nag. I know you, Maureen. You got a mouth on you. Don't you turn into one of those sharp-tongued harpies and drive him into another woman's bed."

She'd taken her mother's advice for a while, for as long as she could. She'd been the sweet little wife, going along, not questioning things, but at some point she'd said to hell with it and began to assert herself. The only problem was she waited too long because by then he was already working for Carmine.

That was the worst thing about their marriage: it wasn't just what he did, it was that he wouldn't talk about what he did. When they first got married, he was working on the docks, over in Jersey. It was a union job, a good job, and she was proud to tell people her husband was a longshoreman. He didn't make a lot of money, and the work wasn't always steady, but he made enough—enough to make the down payment on the little house they still lived in. Then two things happened: she got pregnant and he got laid off—and that's when he went to work for Carmine.

In those days the neighborhood in Queens where they lived was like a little village where everybody made it their business to know what was going on. Who was cheating on his wife; who'd been fired for drinking on the job; whose kid had just been expelled from school . . . The neighborhood, like a living organism, always knew. It was a vast network of gossiping wives, old ladies with nothing better to do than sit on the porch all day and watch, butchers and bartenders and waiters always listening as their customers talked. So the neighbors knew her husband was working for Carmine Taliaferro maybe even before she did.

Every once in a while, one of the wives, one of the unhappy ones who wanted everyone to be as miserable as she was, would ask: "So,

Maureen, what's Gino doing these days? I heard he got laid off, you poor thing." She could tell by the gleam in the woman's eyes that she knew who her husband was working for.

Maureen DeMarco had heard the term "property manager" some-place, and that was the lie she always told. She'd say that Gino worked for a man who owned a lot of property—and Carmine did own a lot of property—and that Gino collected the rents and fixed stuff that was broken, that sort of thing. She told the lie so often she almost believed it herself; she knew nobody else did. Eventually, the only women she confided in was a lady down the block whose husband was in prison and her best friend, Connie, who lived all the way up in Albany.

It had been a strange and stressful marriage, the three of them all pre-tending they were a normal family. Gino would go to work, although he didn't work normal hours, and when he came home, he never said what he did that day and she finally stopped asking. It actually became easier after Joe was born because then they all had something to talk about: they talked about Joe.

He'd been a great father; she had to admit that. He went to his son's games and went to the school with her to meet the teachers. He made Joe do his homework and always stressed the importance of a good education. It was really Gino, more than her, who insisted Joe go to college, and it was Gino who encouraged him to get a law degree. What a laugh that was: her husband working for Carmine Taliaferro and her son on his way to becoming a lawyer.

She'd tell herself—all the time, she'd tell herself—that she should count her blessings instead of complaining all the time. Gino had al-ways taken care of her and Joe. They'd never been rich, but they'd never gone hungry and her son never went to school with holes in his shoes. The mortgage on the house was paid off and they'd been able to send Joe to Catholic schools. And somehow—God only knows how—Gino had been able to make enough to pay Joe's college tuition. So maybe she wasn't proud of what her husband did, but he was an earner and he'd never spent even a day in jail. There were a lot of women she knew who couldn't say that about their men.

The other thing about him was that he wasn't like those goombahs he worked with—guys like Jerry Kennedy, who was Irish but was still a goombah. Gino DeMarco wasn't a drunk, he didn't have a girlfriend stashed away in the city, and he didn't go down to Atlantic City to gamble. He was a family man, and when something needed to be repaired around the house, he always did it himself and seemed to genuinely enjoy the work. And when Joe was old enough, he let him help so Joe would know what to do when he owned a house.

But, damnit, he made her mad. Then it was like she couldn't help herself, like she was possessed or something. She slammed the rolling pin into the dough and yelled, "Well, for Christ's sake! Are you just going to sit there in the dark the whole damn night?"

Of course, he did just what she'd known he would do. He got up and put on his jacket and a old gray tweed flat cap and said, "I'll be back in a while."

Jesus! Why couldn't she ever learn to keep her mouth shut?

3

The tavern was a neighborhood dive called Angelo's, although Angelo had sold it three years ago and retired to Florida. It was small—ten seats at the bar, four booths along the wall—and dimly lit to better hide the shabbiness of the place. The jukebox hadn't worked since Angelo left, which was a good thing as far as Gino was concerned. On a shelf over the bar was a ten-inch Sony with bent rabbit ears showing a West Coast game: Seattle against Oakland, and Gino had arrived just in time to see Ken Griffey Jr. park one in the bleachers of the Kingdome in Seattle. Gino had never liked indoor ballparks and was glad Shea Stadium didn't have a dome.

He took a seat at the bar as far as he could get from two squabbling old drunks at the other end, and ordered a beer. As the bartender placed the drink in front of him, he said, "Now don't make me have to cut you off tonight." That was the bartender's idea of a joke; he knew Gino would sit there sipping the one beer until he left.

Tomorrow, Enzo was going to tell him that Carmine didn't want him to kill the kid. Enzo would say killing him was bad for business. But Gino knew, even if Enzo didn't, that Carmine was glad Jerry Kennedy was dead. The kid had actually done Carmine a favor. Gino needed to decide—he'd been trying to decide ever since Jerry's funeral—if he was going to disobey an order from Carmine. Was Jerry Kennedy worth what it might cost him? And what would Carmine do if he went through with it?

Maybe Carmine would order a hit on him. Maybe—but he didn't think so. For one thing, Carmine knew he'd be hard to kill and if Carmine tried and failed, he'd have no choice but to go after Carmine. He also knew that even if he killed Carmine, they'd get him in the end. He couldn't fight off the entire Taliaferro family.

But he didn't think Carmine would kill him. Most likely he'd just stop giving him work. He'd ostracize him. Exile him. He wouldn't have any money coming in unless he could find a straight job, which would be hard to do after what he'd been doing the last twenty-some years. The good news was that he had a lot saved up, the house was paid off, and this was Joe's last year of law school. They could go a long time before he and Maureen would need money. Then after a while, maybe a year, Carmine would need him for something his other guys couldn't handle, and then Carmine would chew him out, make him swear he'd never disobey another order, hug him, and things would go back to normal. At least, that's the way he thought it would play out. The thing was—and Carmine knew this—he didn't really have a choice when it came to the kid.

———◆◆◆———

Jerry Kennedy was the first person Gino DeMarco ever got into a real fight with, the kind of fight where you threw punches and didn't just roll around on the ground wrestling, afraid to hurt the other guy because he might hurt you back. They were both in fourth grade and when the fight was over he had a bloody nose and Jerry had a black eye and a cut lip, and their shirts were torn. Sister Catherine Mary had screamed at them, spraying spittle everywhere, which made them laugh, and the nun smacked them both. They became best friends after that.

They were altar boys together. They stayed over at each other's houses. They played on the same teams, although Jerry rode the bench more than he played. Jerry stole the booze the first time they got drunk, and Jerry was the guy who got him laid the first time, too, these Polish sisters who would go to bed with anybody in the neighborhood if you bought them a six-pack of beer. Jerry was the best man at his wedding and he was the godfather of one of Jerry's kids. Jerry had loaned him money when times were tough. And Jerry was the guy who got him the job with Carmine Taliaferro.

After he and Maureen got married, he stopped hanging out with Jerry except for a beer now and then. For one thing, Maureen had never really liked the guy and working on the docks was hard and the hours were sometimes brutal; after work all he wanted to do was go home and sleep. But he didn't mind the work and was grateful to have a job, and he and Maureen put money down on the house.

Right after that, right after he made the down payment and signed the mortgage, it all went to hell. He didn't understand what was going on with the economy: on the news they talked about inflation and deregulation and foreign trade imbalance, and a lot of other shit he didn't understand. All he knew was they cut back his hours, then sometimes he'd get work only a couple of days a week, and finally, because he didn't have seniority and wasn't related to anybody important, they laid him off. And when they did, Maureen was three months pregnant.

Jerry asked him out for a beer one evening after he'd spent the day going to a dozen places looking for work. The first thing he noticed was that Jerry looked flush. He was wearing a good suit and his shoes had a shine. He paid for the beer with a fat roll he pulled from his pocket, tipping the waitress like he was a Rockefeller.

He knew Jerry worked for Carmine Taliaferro, and he knew what Carmine was. He figured Jerry got the job because he married a Sicilian girl who was related to Carmine, but he didn't know for sure. He also didn't know what Jerry did for Carmine, and he never asked. He found out later, after it was too late, that Jerry didn't make all that much and the roll he flashed that night came from one of his infrequent, lucky days at the track.

When Jerry asked how things were going, Gino told him: no job and a pregnant wife.

"You want me to ask my boss if he might have some work for you? I mean, just until you find something else."

Gino shook his head. He'd seen other guys go down that path and most of them ended up in jail. A few of them ended up dead.

"Then how 'bout a loan to tide you over?"

This was what Maureen didn't understand about Jerry: he'd give you the shirt off his back if you were his friend.

"Nah, that's okay," Gino said. "I'll find work soon."

Two weeks later—he still hadn't found a job—Jerry called. "I have to go down to Florida and drive a truck back up here without stopping. I need a wingman. You'll make five hundred bucks."

In those days, when gas was fifty cents a gallon, five hundred dollars was a lot of money. Five hundred dollars was enough to pay the mortgage for two months.

"What's in the truck?" Gino asked.

"I don't know, and I'm not asking."

Gino thought at the time that he'd be a fool to take the job. The cops could be watching Carmine's guys. Or they could be watching the guy whose stuff was in the truck. If it was guns, whoever was driving could go away for five years and crossing state lines made it a federal charge. But the thing was, the mortgage payment was due at the end of the month and he was going to have to ask somebody for a loan: his father, his father-in-law, maybe Jerry. Begging friends and relatives for money would be humiliating, particularly as he didn't have any idea when he'd be able to pay them back. Then what would he do the month after that?

He told Maureen he had a job driving a truck and would be gone a few days. When he saw her eyes light up, thinking he'd gotten on with the Teamsters, he told her it was just a one-time thing, that a guy just needed a backup driver. He didn't tell her the guy was Jerry. He didn't exactly lie to her—but it felt like a lie.

And that's how it all started. The next job came a couple of weeks later when Jerry said he needed someone to go with him to collect from a guy who owed Carmine money. "This guy's big, bigger than both of us put together, and he's kind of a nut. I just want someone backing me up in case he wants to fight."

"Okay, but I'm not carrying a gun."

"You won't need a gun."

"And I'm not gonna pound on this guy if he won't pay you."

"He'll pay. Like I said, I just need you to pull him off me if he goes nuts."

In the beginning, he was always drawing lines in the sand, lines he said he'd never cross—and then he ended up crossing almost all of them.

———◆◆◆———

The first time he killed a man, it was basically the same sort of thing.

He'd been working for Carmine for nearly three years and by that time he could no longer pretend to himself—much less his wife—that he wasn't one of Carmine's hoods. He drove more trucks filled with things he knew were stolen. He was part of a crew that emptied out an appliance warehouse in Danbury, Connecticut. One night, he and Jerry went with a guy to a dealership on Long Island and stole twenty brand-new Buicks off the lot because the guy had keys for all the cars. Gino always acted calm when he did these things but on the inside he was quaking. He realized after a while that he wasn't really afraid of going to jail; he could handle jail. What terrified him was the way Maureen would be humiliated if he was arrested. And what would she tell Joe when he was old enough to wonder where his father was?

He just sort of slipped into it. It wasn't like he made a conscious decision to become a criminal. He told himself he didn't have a choice—that he had to take care of his wife and kid—but the truth, if he was honest with himself, was that he'd taken the path of least resistance. He tried finding legitimate work, but after beating his head against a wall, getting rejected time and time again, it was just easier working for Carmine than to keep looking for a straight job.

It didn't take long before Carmine and Enzo Marciano, the underboss, started giving him more responsibility and it wasn't hard to figure out why. A lot of the men Carmine employed weren't all that reliable and some were just plain stupid. They drank too much. They got into fights in bars. They gambled. They ran around with women who weren't their wives. Jerry Kennedy, he had to admit, was basically that kind of guy. Carmine appreciated the fact that if he needed Gino, all he had to do was call his house; if he called Jerry's house, Jerry was likely to be out at the track or sleeping with a cocktail waitress he'd met in some joint.

Carmine started to use him as a bodyguard when he felt he needed one. Gino paid attention, he didn't lose his temper and let things get out of hand, and he didn't run his mouth. But he suspected maybe the main reason Carmine used him was the way he looked. Gino DeMarco had a face that could back people down; he *looked* like a guy that would shoot you if he had to. And when he was Carmine's bodyguard, he had to carry a gun. Carmine insisted on that—and another line got crossed.

But there were things he wouldn't do, like beat up a witness who saw one of Carmine's thugs break into a jewelry store. The witness was a baker and his shop was across the street from the jewelry store, and he arrived at about four in the morning to start making his dough. When Carmine's guy, so drunk he could barely walk, broke the jeweler's window and grabbed a bunch of cheap stuff that was on display, the baker heard the window break. He saw Carmine's guy stumbling back to his car and got the license plate number because the idiot had parked right under a streetlight.

Everybody agreed some time in the can might be good for the thief, but he was related to Enzo Marciano. Everybody seemed to be related to everybody else in Carmine's crew. Enzo told Gino and Jerry to go see the baker, a man in his sixties, and rough him up so he'd get the message that he wasn't to testify. Gino refused to do it.

"He's a nice old guy who runs a bakery," he told Enzo. "My mother buys her cannoli from him. I'm not gonna beat him up."

"Hey!" Enzo said, puffing up like a rooster, "you're gonna do what the fuck you're told."

"No, I'm not," Gino said and left, figuring he would soon be unemployed again.

In the end, Jerry and someone else smacked the baker around a little, not too bad, and Enzo chewed Gino out but kept him on the crew. Enzo said the only reason he did was that Gino was smarter than most of the other dummies Carmine employed, but if he ever disobeyed an order again . . .

By this time, he and Maureen were fighting all the time. Well, *they* weren't fighting; *she* was fighting. She cried. She screamed. She begged him to quit. She threatened to take Joe and leave him—which he knew she would never do. She ranted how he was going to end up in jail and how she'd be left alone with a son she couldn't provide for, which, of course, made him feel like shit. He endured days of stony silence and it seemed as if he slept more on the couch than he did in their bed.

The worst part was, he wasn't making all that much money. If he'd been able to get steady work as a longshoreman, put in forty hours a week with a little overtime now and then, he would have made more on the docks than he was making working for Carmine. But he couldn't find work. He tried to tell Maureen this but she didn't want to hear it. So he did what a man does: he provided for his family, which meant he kept working for Carmine.

Every week he got paid what amounted to a base salary, but it varied and he could never tell if it varied due to the mood Carmine was in or how much cash the outfit took in that week. If he took part in a job, then he'd make more—like a commission—but how much more wasn't tied to anything specific, like how much risk was involved or how much money they made on the job. There were a few months when he wasn't sure he was going to be able to make the mortgage and he had to go to Enzo and beg for an advance, but he never told Maureen that.

Everything changed the day he killed Mario Colombo.

Mario Colombo—no relation to the Colombo family in New York—showed up in Queens one day with a dozen guys, mostly men he'd met in prison. Colombo was insane, a violent psychopath who for some reason thought he could just muscle in on Carmine's operation. Carmine had a reputation for avoiding violence because violence was bad for business. He'd kill if he had to, but only as a last resort. So maybe Colombo thought Carmine was soft or unwilling to risk losing a bunch of his troops in a major war. But how could he possibly think that Carmine would give up without a fight? It made no sense.

Whatever the case, Colombo roughed up a guy who owned a bar in Carmine's territory, threatened to rape the guy's daughter, and took over the bar to use for his headquarters. All the drinks were now on the house. A couple of days later, Carmine heard about this and sent two men over to find out what the hell was going on. They just went to talk to Colombo, to let him know he was making a serious mistake, but Colombo's guys beat Carmine's guys so badly they both ended up in the hospital. That same night, Colombo's crew hit a numbers operation that Carmine's cousin ran. They pistol-whipped his cousin and stole almost six grand in cash.

Carmine held a meeting the next day with his senior guys. Gino was only there because he'd been assigned as Carmine's bodyguard until things were settled with Colombo. The purpose of the meeting was to discuss taking Colombo out; it was apparent he wouldn't listen to reason. Carmine wanted it done quietly. He didn't want guys using machine guns, leaving a dozen dead bodies lying in the street. He said he didn't want to read in the papers any nonsense about gangland massacres because then, the next thing you know, the FBI is assigning some cockamamie task force.

As they were all grousing about the best way to do the job, Gino said, "How much will you pay the guy who kills him?" Carmine looked at him for a long time before he said, "Three grand. Why? Are you volunteering?" Everybody else in the room laughed. They laughed because Gino already had a reputation for not being willing to take part in the rough stuff. Carmine ignored the laughter. He had always seen something in Gino the others hadn't.

"Yeah, I am," Gino said.

"Why?" Carmine asked.

"Because of what he did to Pauly."

Pauly was Pauly D'Amato, one of the guys Colombo's people had put in the hospital. He was a little guy who made everyone laugh.

Gino liked Pauly, but Pauly wasn't the reason he volunteered. Joe was three years old and growing out of his clothes and he was embarrassed that his son wore hand-me-downs from Maureen's sister's kids. Maureen hadn't bought a new dress for herself in probably a year and he couldn't remember the last time they went out to dinner to a nice place, just the two of them. But the big thing was, Maureen was pregnant again. He could barely provide for one kid; he had no idea how he was going to provide for two. Three grand meant that he and Maureen wouldn't have to live from day to day.

"How you going to do it?" Carmine asked.

DeMarco said, "You don't need to know that."

To which Enzo Marciano had said, "Hey! Who the fuck you think you're talking to?"

Carmine held up a hand to silence Enzo. "You're right. I don't. You got a week to make it happen. If it doesn't happen, I don't wanna ever see your face again. You understand?"

Gino nodded.

He watched Colombo for three days. Whenever he moved around the city, he always had four men with him, and when he was at his bar/headquarters, there were at least twice that many guys with him. The only time he was alone was when he went back to his hotel, and even then all his men stayed down the hall from him. Some nights he'd have a woman with him, but never the same one. The women would show up after he got back to the hotel and Gino figured if Colombo was in the mood, he'd call a pimp and have a girl sent to him. Like he was ordering out for pizza.

Gino took all the money he'd saved up to pay the mortgage, borrowed some more from Jerry, and bought a piece with a silencer. He went down to the basement when Maureen was out of the house and fired the gun a couple of times into some phone books. It was louder than he'd expected but not that loud, and it didn't exactly sound like a gunshot when it was fired. It would do.

On the fifth day, he went to Colombo's hotel while Colombo and his guys were out having dinner. He took a guy with him who knew how to pick locks, and after he had Colombo's door open, he sent the lock picker away. The lock picker was a guy Carmine had used before and he could supposedly be trusted. Gino didn't like using the lock picker but didn't have a choice.

Four hours later, Colombo walked into his room and Gino stepped out of the bathroom and shot him once in the chest. And that was it. Colombo's guys left town two days later.

———— ◆◆◆ ————

Before he killed Colombo, the only thing Gino had thought about was how to kill him and not get caught or killed himself. He didn't let himself think about how he would feel about taking another man's life. He thought he would experience some sort of remorse—that he would feel guilty, maybe even depressed—but he didn't. He didn't feel much of anything—and that bothered him more than anything else.

He suspected the main reason why he didn't feel bad was because of who Colombo had been: a killer and a criminal and a lunatic, and the world was a better place without him. But Gino also wondered if maybe there was something wrong with him, being so cold and unfeeling about ending the existence of another human being. He finally decided there was nothing to be gained by dwelling on his lack of remorse or guilt or whatever a normal person would feel. A man did what he had to do, he didn't whine if things didn't turn out right, and he didn't brood on the past.

Two weeks after he killed Colombo, Maureen lost the baby she was carrying and the doctors said she wouldn't be able to have another. Now that depressed him. Neither he nor Maureen ever really got over it.

———— ◆◆◆ ————

Four or five months after he killed Colombo, Enzo escorted him to Carmine's office, saying Carmine wanted to talk to him—except Carmine didn't want to talk in his office. Carmine wanted to walk down to a park a couple of blocks away that had swings and teeter-totters and where good-looking young mothers would come to let their little ones play.

They wasted some time at a store near the park so Carmine and Enzo could get cups of coffee. The store owner practically genuflected when he saw Carmine, telling him how honored he was that Carmine would stop in his humble shop, insisting the coffee was on the house. They wasted more time when Carmine recognized one of the mothers at the park, a friend of his daughter's. He asked how the girl's folks were doing—was her dad still having problems with his hip?—and made a fuss over the baby, saying how beautiful the little girl was—who you could hardly see as she was so wrapped up in blankets and a tiny stocking cap. Finally, they took seats at a picnic table and Carmine got down to business.

"I want a guy named Leon Washington taken out," he said to Gino.

"Why?" Gino said.

Enzo started to say something—most likely, that it wasn't none of Gino's fuckin' business why—but Carmine shook his head. "Washington's a colored guy," he said, "and he and his brother sell heroin to the coloreds in Bed-Stuy. I've been their connection for years. I get the dope from a guy I know, sell it to the Washington brothers for thirty percent more than it costs me, then they step on the shit and sell it to the junkies. It's a good deal for everyone.

"Well, Washington and his brother came to see me last week. He says he doesn't need me anymore, that he's got his own connection. I can tell his brother—he's the one with the brains—knows this is a bad idea. I tell Washington, you think you can just cut me out? And he says, yeah. What are you gonna do? And I tell him, I'm gonna kill you is what I'm gonna do and find some other spook to distribute my dope for me. You know what he says to me?"

Gino shook his head.

"He says, well you can try. So I want Leon taken out, then I'll deal with his brother and if that don't work, I'll find somebody else. The main thing is, I need to send a message. People need to understand that this isn't the sort of thing you do."

"How much?" Gino asked.

"What do you mean, how much?" Carmine said.

"How much are you going to pay me for the hit?"

Enzo practically came across the picnic table at him. "Goddamnit, I'm sick of you, you fuckin' prima donna. You work for this outfit. You got paid for Colombo because it was your first time and he was a special case. But you're not some goddamn outside contractor. The boss just gave you a job to do, and you're gonna do it, and after it's over, maybe you'll get a little extra come payday. Maybe."

Gino shook his head. "No," he said. "I'm not going to kill a man and risk spending the rest of my life in Sing Sing without knowing how much I'll make."

Enzo said, "Get the fuck out of here."

When Carmine looked away and didn't say anything, Gino left.

Two days later, he heard that one of Carmine's other guys, a guy he didn't know very well, tried to kill Washington and got shot. Carmine called Gino into his office the day after the funeral, Enzo sitting there with a scowl on his fat face, and Carmine said, "A grand."

"It's going to be harder now," Gino said, "now that you sent some moron to kill him."

Enzo looked like he was going to explode, but Carmine said, "Yeah, you're right. Two."

"Okay."

It took Gino three weeks to do the job, but in the end Leon Washington became part of a strawberry field in Jersey and Carmine started doing business with his brother.

And that's the way it went for more than twenty years. He worked as a bodyguard and as a regular guy on Carmine's crew, meaning he stole things and collected from people who owed Carmine money. He was a bagman, delivering money to judges and cops. When Carmine had drugs to sell, Gino made sure whoever was buying didn't try to steal the dope instead of paying for it. And when Carmine wanted someone killed he would do it, but only if the price was right and only if the guy he was being asked to kill was another criminal.

The killings changed him, however. He'd always been a quiet man but after he became Carmine's enforcer—and that's who he was— there was no point kidding himself about that—he became even quieter, hardly ever talking when he didn't have to. A shrink might have been able to explain it—how the guilt or the shame or whatever it was had altered him—but all he knew was that he felt separate from other people. He was no longer the man he used to be; he'd become a man he didn't want to be.

After he killed Washington, he stopped going to confession— there was no point telling a priest he'd killed someone when he knew he was going to do it again—and since he stopped going to confession, he stopped taking communion, too. He still went to mass with Maureen and Joe—Maureen never asked him why he stopped taking communion—it was like she knew—and when he was in church, he would just go to some place deep inside himself and whatever the priest was saying became nothing more than white noise to him.

The only time he was ever really happy was when he was working on the house or doing something with Joe. Those were the best times— tossing a football to Joe in the park or becoming totally immersed in fixing something around the house. He remembered one time when he spent an entire week one July putting a new roof on the house, up there with his shirt off, sweating in the sun, Joe climbing the ladder to bring him lemonade Maureen had made. When it was done, he and Joe sat up there on his new roof together looking out over the neighborhood. That had been a great week.

So life went on and he continued to work for Carmine. What he wouldn't do, however, was kill a citizen—some ordinary schmuck who'd pissed Carmine off or who was going to testify against one of Carmine's thugs or somebody Carmine just wanted out of the way so he could muscle in on something. When Gino refused to do what Carmine wanted, Enzo would scream at him and Carmine would get pissed and give the job to somebody else. But he didn't fire Gino. Instead, he gave him the silent treatment. It seemed that between his wife and his boss, somebody was always giving him the silent treatment.

4

As Gino DeMarco sat in a bar mulling over his past and future, waiting for his wife to go to sleep, Carmine Taliaferro sat in his den watching his fish swim around in the tank. One of the little yellow fish was moving kind of slow, turning in small circles. He hoped it wasn't dying. He'd always liked that little fish.

His four-year-old granddaughter was with him, jabbering nonstop about anything that popped into her head. The girl was a talker, just like Carmine's daughter. And just like his wife, for that matter. He could hear his daughter and his wife in the kitchen going on and on about something son-in-law had done, and at the same time his granddaughter was wondering out loud if grandpa had a cat and would the cat eat all the fish. It felt like his head was gonna explode.

"Sweetie," he said to the little girl, "why don't you go tell Grandma to give you some ice cream."

"I don't want any ice cream," she said.

"Sure you do. Go on. Go see Grandma. Go get some ice cream. Grandpa's gotta make a phone call."

"I know how to make a phone call."

Jesus. "Stephanie!" he yelled. His daughter, who looked just like his wife when she was her age, stuck her head into the room.

"Yeah, Pop?" Stephanie said.

"Take Katie into the kitchen, will you? I gotta make a call."

"I *told* him I know how to make phone calls," Katie said, standing now, little hands on her little hips, glaring at him—another gesture that reminded him of his wife. His wife, daughter, and granddaughter were like those Russian boxes: you opened one box, and inside it was an identical smaller box. Then you open that box, and . . .

Finally he gets them both out of the room and shuts the door.

He didn't need to make a phone call. He just needed to think.

Like he'd told Enzo, he needed the kid; the kid was an investment in the future whereas DeMarco, as good as he was, had too many scruples and was a hard guy to control. The other thing, and nobody knew this but him, was that he'd ordered the kid to kill Jerry Kennedy. If DeMarco ever found that out . . . Well, he couldn't take the chance.

Kennedy had always been a drunk, but most of the time he kept the drinking under control. The gambling, however, got way out of hand. Kennedy was a compulsive gambler, the kind of guy who couldn't control the urge—the kind of guy who would bet on a cockroach race—and he ended up owing a bookie in Atlantic City more than twenty grand.

Then, a week ago, Kennedy gets nabbed by the feds. Unbeknownst to Carmine, Kennedy had been transporting dope for a guy in Trenton, trying to make enough money to pay off the bookie in Atlantic City, and the dumb shit sells the dope to an NYPD undercover. The feds immediately took over the case for interstate trafficking, but according to Carmine's source, the feds really took it over because they thought they might be able to force Kennedy to testify against Carmine. The feds didn't even arraign Kennedy—they didn't want Carmine to know they had him—and they were hiding him somewhere, trying to make a deal with him. And, by the way, they were offering him Witness Protection if he agreed to cooperate.

Carmine wouldn't even have known about Kennedy's arrest if it wasn't for his source in the Bureau, who was just a secretary. Carmine had thought that Kennedy was off on a bender or shacked up with some broad, and that's why he hadn't seen the damn guy in a while. But the secretary heard about Kennedy getting arrested and she knew Kennedy worked for Carmine.

The secretary worked for a big shot down at Federal Plaza, near Foley Square, and she kept her ears open for things that might concern Carmine. The only reason she helped him was that she had a daughter with a weird skin disease and couldn't afford the cream and shit her daughter needed. If the government had paid her better, she probably wouldn't have told Carmine anything. The problem, however, was the secretary didn't know where they were keeping Kennedy and she couldn't find out—and Carmine needed to know because he needed Jerry Kennedy dead.

Carmine figured that Kennedy's nuts were in a three-way vise. The guy from Trenton whose dope he'd lost probably wanted Kennedy to pay for that, the Atlantic City bookie definitely wanted his money back, and the feds were going to put Kennedy in jail for years if he didn't cooperate. Witness Protection would solve all of Kennedy's problems. He'd be a fool not to make a deal.

So Carmine needed Kennedy dead, but he couldn't use DeMarco because DeMarco would never agree to kill his best friend. He didn't really want any of his other guys to kill Kennedy, either. For one thing, none of them was as good as DeMarco but the main thing was, people could never keep their damn mouths shut. If he used one of his own people, the word would eventually get back to DeMarco.

He finally decided to force the kid to kill Kennedy.

The kid's name was Quinn. Brian Quinn. He was a cop. He was a tall, slim, good-looking young guy who would eventually end up with the kind of face you expected generals and presidents to have. He fit in well at the NYPD, which was a lot like the Catholic Church in America, where all the bishops and cardinals were wops and micks. Quinn's dad had been a well-liked NYPD detective, two of his uncles were cops, and Quinn's rabbi—his mentor in the department—was currently the chief of D's.

Quinn also married above his station. His wife was a good-looking woman but more important, her father was a federal judge and her mother was the daughter of serious Wall Street money. Quinn's mother-in-law was beaucoup rich and she was Quinn's ticket into the inner circle of the people who really ran New York. She was most likely disappointed her daughter had fallen for an Irish cop, but over time she would become quite impressed with her son-in-law.

So Quinn was going places. He was getting a law degree at night and Carmine figured that within a year he'd have a detective's shield, and after that, as bright and connected as he was, the sky was the limit for young Officer Quinn.

But as smart as he was, Carmine owned Quinn because being smart doesn't help when it comes to bad luck.

———◆◆◆———

Brian Quinn had done one stupid thing in his life, maybe the only stupid thing he ever did or would ever do again: he shot an unarmed man and lied about it.

He was working the graveyard shift in Queens when he and his partner—an overweight, not-too-bright Polack named Dombroski—got a call from dispatch saying a man just tried to break into a woman's house. The burglar was white, over six feet tall, wearing a black jacket and a blue or black stocking cap. The attempted robbery happened less than three minutes before they got the call, and Quinn and Dombroski were right there in the neighborhood.

Dombroski drove around hoping to spot the burglar on the street, and Quinn caught a glimpse of a man walking down an alley. (Quinn found out later the alley was a shortcut the guy sometimes used.) Quinn told his partner to drive to the other end of the alley to block off the guy's escape, and Quinn went into the alley on foot after the man. Quinn's version of the story was that he yelled at the man to put his hands up, the guy spun around, pointing a gun, and Quinn had to shoot him. What actually happened was the guy was holding a can of beer and when Quinn yelled, the guy was startled, he swung around fast, and all Quinn saw was something metallic in his hand so he fired.

He ran to the man to see if he was still alive. He wasn't. Quinn wasn't a particularly good shot but he had hit the guy right in the heart. Then he saw the beer can and realized he had just shot his career in the heart. He now had about five seconds to make a decision because Dombroski was jogging down the alley toward him, so he did what he knew other cops had done. He pulled his backup piece out of his ankle holster, placed it in the man's hand, and tossed the beer can under a Dumpster.

Quinn's story stank right from the start, and everybody knew it.

The man he'd killed was a drunk named Connors who worked in a paint store. The good news, at least from Quinn's perspective, was that Connors had a record. When he was eighteen—which was twenty years ago—he and another dumbass broke into an old lady's house, stole a few things, and then tried to pawn the shit to the only honest pawnbroker in New York. He did seventeen months for that. But that was the only good thing about Connors in terms of him being a viable suspect.

Connors had never owned a gun in his life. He was five foot seven and fat, not over six feet tall. The jacket he was wearing the night he was killed was red, which might have looked black in the right light, but he didn't have a stocking cap. NYPD detectives—guys who worked for

Quinn's rabbi, the chief of D's—showed the woman Connors's picture and the detectives got her to admit that yeah, Connors was *maybe* the man she saw for three seconds trying to jimmy open her window. It was strange that Connors didn't have a jimmy on him; he must have tossed it, they concluded, when he tossed the stocking cap.

In the end, thanks to his rabbi and his father-in-law, the federal judge, and a call from Quinn's mother-in-law to the mayor, it was deemed a good shooting and a fat drunk who worked in a paint store became a sly cat burglar who'd been ripping off houses in the neighborhood for the last five weeks. The department stopped short of giving Officer Quinn a commendation for ridding the city of this menace.

But this was when Lady Luck entered Brian Quinn's charmed young life.

When Quinn shot Connors, bad luck really had nothing to do with that. Quinn was practically a rookie, he was probably scared chasing a man he thought was a burglar down a dark alley, and he reacted without thinking when he saw something flash in Connors's hand. It was just a case of bad judgment combined with inexperience and too much adrenaline—but it wasn't a matter of luck.

Nor did luck have anything to do with Quinn's decision to try to cover up the killing. That was just Quinn thinking he was smart enough to get out of the situation, and lying about what really happened was better than admitting he'd made a mistake that could blemish his spotless record. Where Lady Luck walked into the picture was in the form of another lady named Janet Costello, who had insomnia.

Janet taught fifth grade at a public school in Queens. She also had twenty-twenty vision. Janet, in other words, was a good citizen and a reliable witness. When she couldn't sleep, which was almost every night, she liked to sit on her balcony—a balcony the size of a doormat with a view of an alley—and smoke and drink white wine. Her landlord wouldn't allow her to smoke in her apartment.

Janet was also the girlfriend of a man named Sal Anselmo. Janet had been raised in Queens and she knew Sal from grade school and dated him all through high school. She was heartbroken when he married another girl—and he was still married to the other girl and had three kids—but he came around one time when Janet was feeling lonely and vulnerable and she was now his mistress.

Janet saw Quinn put his backup gun in Connors's dead hand that night; she saw him toss the beer can under the Dumpster. If Quinn or his partner had ever looked up—instead of down at the dead man— they would have seen Janet sitting two floors above them, her hand clamped over her mouth. A couple of days later, Janet sees in the papers that Quinn is now some sort of hero for killing an unarmed man. She thought about going to the police and telling them what had really happened but was afraid to because she knew how the NYPD protected its own. So she called Sal and asked what he thought she should do. Sal said, "You keep your mouth shut, you fuckin' dummy," and then Sal told his boss, a guy named Tony Benedetto, who then told his boss— Carmine Taliaferro.

Carmine had several NYPD cops on his payroll. They kept him informed of investigations that might hurt him, kept him up to speed on problems his rivals were having, and, most important, they didn't usually arrest his people. But he could always use another cop, particularly if he could purchase him with blackmail instead of cash.

Carmine didn't approach Quinn right away, though. Patience was possibly Carmine Taliaferro's greatest virtue and the thing that distinguished him more than anything else from the gonzos who worked for him. Instead, he took a week and did his homework on Quinn and learned about the cop's father-in-law, the judge, his rabbi, the chief of D's, his richer-than-God mother-in-law, and the fact that he'd already passed the sergeant's exam and was getting a law degree. Now Carmine *really* wanted this cop.

Ten days after Quinn killed Connors, Carmine set up a meeting with Quinn and explained the facts of life to him, the main fact being that he now worked for Carmine. Carmine admitted that Quinn might be able to impugn an eyewitness but he told Quinn that this particular witness was a prosecutor's dream. He didn't, of course, give him Janet Costello's name. When Quinn said he didn't believe there was a witness, Carmine said, "Then how do I know exactly what you did, pulling your gun out of an ankle holster and tossing the beer can under the Dumpster? Plus I had a guy go down there and photograph the beer can—there's some graffiti on the wall behind the Dumpster so you can tell it was really in that spot. And when my guy took the photo, he put a copy of the *Times* against the wall so you can see the date. I now have the can and I'm about a thousand percent sure it will have your fingerprints on it.

"There's one other thing you need to think about, Officer Quinn," Carmine said. "When this witness comes forward and tells what you did, you ain't gonna be the only guy who gets in trouble. Whoever investigated the shooting and helped you hide the truth is also going to have their dicks lopped off. Think about that, Officer Quinn. How's that going to look, you getting the whole department in trouble because you lied your ass off?"

At first Quinn tried to bluster and bullshit his way out, saying how his pals on the force would come down on Carmine's operation like a ton of bricks, but in the end he caved.

"So what do you want?" he asked.

"Just information," Carmine said. "You keep me informed of things that can help me. And if you don't produce, then I don't need you, and my witness talks to the press and Connors's widow gets a big-mouth lawyer to sue the department."

A month goes by and Carmine gets nothing out of Quinn. He knows what Quinn's trying to do: he's trying to find the eyewitness and trying to find something he can use against Carmine. And this was about the time that Jerry Kennedy gets nabbed by the feds. Carmine called up

Quinn and told him: "You find Kennedy for me and if you don't, I'm gonna end your fuckin' career."

———————————◆◆◆———————————

Carmine walked through the bingo room in the basement of St. Sebastian's, a hundred crazy women there, shrieking every time a number was called. The grand prize that night was fifty bucks and the women acted like they were playing for a million.

Quinn was waiting for him in a little room that looked like a workshop, a bunch of tools hanging off a pegboard, a broken cradle they used for the Nativity scene sitting on the floor. Carmine had donated all the statues and shit for the Nativity scene.

"So where is he?" Carmine said.

"I don't like meeting with you," Quinn said. "Why couldn't we do this over the phone?"

"A, I don't give a shit what you like, and B, I don't like talking on the phone. So where is he?"

Quinn told him: a crummy motel outside Poughkeepsie, more than an hour's drive from New York.

"Are they protecting him?" Carmine asked.

"No," Quinn said. "I mean they don't have agents or federal marshals guarding him. They figure as long as only a couple people in the U.S. attorney's office know where he is, he's safe."

"Aren't they afraid he might split?"

"No. He doesn't have any money and he doesn't have a car and he's got too many people looking for him. He's safer in that motel than he would be on the street."

"How did you track him down?"

"I took a couple days off work and started following the most likely attorneys."

Carmine nodded. Smart guy.

Carmine didn't say anything for a long time. He just stared at Quinn while Quinn glared back at him. The young cop really hated him.

"I want you to kill him," Carmine said.

"Forget it," Quinn said.

"Quinn, if you take care of Kennedy, you'll be all paid up with me. I'll never contact you again."

"And I'm supposed to just take your word for that?"

"No. I'll give you the name of the witness who saw you shoot Connors. I'll also give you the beer can with your fingerprints on it. But the main thing is, you'll have the name of the witness. You can whack her for all I care. She don't mean shit to me. But the easiest thing to do is just scare her if she becomes a problem. You're a smart guy. You'll figure something out once you have her name."

Carmine could now see the gears spinning inside Quinn's handsome head, analyzing the pros and cons of killing Jerry Kennedy. He was most likely thinking that once he knew the name of the witness, he could do just like Carmine had said and find a way to neutralize her. He was probably also thinking—or maybe *rationalizing* was a better word—that Jerry Kennedy was scum, not an honest citizen, and he could justify Kennedy's death at least to himself if not to a judge.

"Okay," Quinn said, "I'll do it. But I don't ever want to hear from you again."

"You won't," Carmine said, but he was wondering if it was a bigger sin if you lied inside a church.

———◆———

Brian Quinn not only got a law degree from St. John's University; he also received an MPA from Harvard's Kennedy School of Government.

He spent time on high-profile assignments, including a couple of task forces where the NYPD partnered with the feds. He rose through the ranks even faster than Carmine had thought he would. But that was all in the future.

When the lives of Brian Quinn, Jerry Kennedy, Gino DeMarco, and Carmine Taliaferro crossed, Quinn was only a couple of years older than Gino's son, Joe.

5

Gino didn't understand why Jerry wanted to see him, but he couldn't refuse. All Jerry had told him was that he was in big trouble and needed to talk and couldn't talk on the phone. He told Gino he was staying in a run-down shithole near Poughkeepsie. He also said he was a dead man if Gino told anyone where he was.

"Oh, and one other thing. Can you bring me a bottle of bourbon? I don't have a car and there's no place near here to buy booze. I'm about to crawl out of my skin, I need a drink so bad."

The first thing Jerry did as soon as DeMarco stepped into the motel room was take the booze out of his hand and pour himself a drink. After he'd swallowed the first drink, he poured another and said, "You want one?"

Gino shook his head; he could tell Jerry didn't want to share the booze, not sure when he'd be able to get more.

Jerry looked like hell. He was the same age as Gino but looked ten years older because of all the alcohol and cigarettes, and because the only exercise he got was shuffling cards. But now he didn't just look older than he was, he looked like he might be sick, his face that pasty gray color you see in guys who've just had heart attacks.

"Why did you want to see me, Jerry?" Gino asked. "And what are you doing in this place?"

He told Gino the story, about the bookie he was into for twenty grand and the gangster in Trenton whose heroin he'd lost when he was arrested. The feds were now offering him Witness Protection if he'd tell them everything he knew about Carmine's operation, and he was going to take the deal.

"I'll never be able to pay back the guys I owe money to. And the guy in Trenton . . . He'll kill me."

"Carmine will kill you if you rat him out," Gino said.

"Yeah, if I was in a prison he would. Or if I hung around New York. But if the feds set me up in fuckin' Idaho, Montana, someplace like that, he'll never find me."

Gino wasn't too sure about that. "What about your family?" he asked.

Jerry shrugged. "Me and Arlene, we've been through for years and my son's an asshole. I won't miss him at all. But my daughter, she's a different story. That's one of the reasons I called you, Gino. I want you to look out for Julie after I'm gone."

"I don't have the money to take care of your family," Gino said.

"I'm not asking you to take care of them. I'm just asking you to keep tabs on Julie, and if she needs something and if you can do it, I'd like you to help her out."

"Sure," Gino said. He was the girl's godfather, after all.

"The other thing I wanted you to know, and it's the main reason I called you, is I swear I'm not going to tell the feds anything about you."

"What are you saying, Jerry? Are you worried I might kill you?"

"Yeah, I am. I mean, I know you wouldn't want to but if you thought I was going to give them something that would land you in jail, then I think you probably would. You wouldn't have a choice. So I'm telling you, right now, I'm not going to say a word about you. You're safe."

"But Carmine isn't," Gino said.

Jerry shrugged again, that New York shrug that said: *Hey, what can you do?*

Before Jerry could say anything else, there was a knock on the door and Jerry jumped like a firecracker had gone off in the room. He hissed at Gino, "Did anyone follow you here?"

"No."

Jerry went to the door and yelled, "Who is it?" The motel room door didn't have a peephole.

"John Tallman. Clerk for Assistant U.S. Attorney Andrew Mayhew."

"What do you want?"

"I just want to give you some papers from Mr. Mayhew. It's about your relocation, Mr. Kennedy. Mr. Mayhew wanted you to have them tonight so he could talk to you about them tomorrow. Now please open the door."

Jerry waved Gino toward the bathroom, and Gino went inside and closed the door. A moment later he heard a shot.

Without thinking, Gino pulled his .38 and jerked open the bathroom door. Jerry was on the floor and a man was standing in the doorway holding a revolver, also a .38. As soon as the man saw Gino, he fired at him and Gino fired back. They both missed.

The man who'd shot Jerry took off running. Gino went to his friend and knelt down and checked for a pulse. Jerry was dead. He stepped over the body and went after the shooter, but the shooter had already reached his car. Gino fired again and blew out the back window of the shooter's Dodge but missed the driver. He did get the last four digits of the license plate.

Gino looked around to see if any of the motel's other lodgers had come out of their rooms to investigate, but none of them had. The crummy motel only had six units and he didn't see a light on in any of them. He wondered if the feds had rented all the rooms to protect Jerry. Whatever the case, he didn't see anybody who might have seen him. He went back to Jerry's room, wiped his prints off the bathroom doorknob, and picked up the bourbon bottle, which was the only other thing in the room he'd touched.

On his way back to Queens, he stopped at a pay phone and called Carmine. "I need to talk to you. Tonight."

"Why?"

Carmine had to know that whatever Gino wanted to talk about had to be damn important because protocol demanded that he go through Enzo Marciano if he had something to pass on to the boss.

"Not over the phone," Gino said.

"Okay. I'll meet you at the place with Sinatra's picture."

There were a million places in New York with Sinatra's picture, but Gino knew where he meant.

Gino was sitting at a table with a beer in front of him but it didn't look as if he'd taken a drink. He'd probably just ordered the beer to keep the waitress from bugging him. Carmine ordered a sambuca, and after it arrived, he said, "So what is it?"

"Somebody killed Jerry Kennedy tonight and I want to know if you ordered the hit."

"What!" Carmine said. He wasn't pretending to be shocked—he *was* shocked. First that Quinn had dealt with Kennedy so quickly, but even more shocked that Gino knew Kennedy was dead. "What the hell are you talking about?" he said. "Who killed him? I haven't seen the damn guy for a while, but I figured he was on a bender. And how the hell do you know he's dead?"

So Gino told Carmine what Carmine already knew: that Kennedy owed money to a bookie, lost two kilos of heroin belonging to a gangster in Trenton, and the feds had stashed him in a motel outside

Poughkeepsie, where they'd been trying to sweat information out of him. The part that was a surprise to Carmine was that Kennedy had called Gino and asked Gino to come see him.

"Why did he want to see you?" Carmine asked.

"Because he wanted me to look out for his daughter after he went into Witness Protection. And because he was afraid I might kill him if I thought he was going to testify against me, and he wanted me to know that he wouldn't."

"Then some guy just knocks on the door and shoots him?" Carmine said.

"Yeah, a young guy, a kid in his twenties. And I want to know if you sent him."

Carmine pretended to get pissed. "Hey! If I had decided to kill him—and I would have if I'd known he was gonna rat me out—then that would be my business. I've put up with a lot of your shit over the years, but don't you go forgetting who I am."

DeMarco, the bastard, just stared at him.

"Anyway, I didn't order the hit. I already told you I had no idea Kennedy had been arrested. Maybe the guy who killed him worked for the guy whose dope Kennedy lost. You know, the guy from Trenton."

He watched Gino absorb the lie—and he thought Gino believed him.

"Okay," Gino said, "and I apologize for . . . for insulting you."

Bullshit, he was apologizing.

"But I'm gonna find out who it was," Gino said. "I saw him clear as a bell and I got most of his license plate. I'll find him."

Goddamnit, Carmine had thought at the time. *He probably will find him.* Gino didn't own a bunch of cops and bureaucrats the way Carmine did, but he was smart, stubborn, and resourceful. Yeah, he'd probably find him.

Carmine drove back home thinking that Brian Quinn might be the unluckiest fucking Irishman on the planet.

When Carmine got back home after meeting with Gino, his wife told him a man had called, said it was urgent, and to call him back. He called the number, which turned out to be a phone in a restaurant. He didn't identify himself. All he said was "A guy told me to call this number."

"Yeah, I know who you want." A moment later, Quinn was on the line.

"I need to talk to you. Right away," Quinn said.

Shit. He told his wife he had to leave the house again and she said, "What's going on? How many girlfriends you got?"

It was kind of a running joke with them, his wife acting like he had girlfriends all over town, him pretending he did. The truth was, he'd stopped caring about sex years ago.

He met Quinn at an Indian restaurant near the Queensboro Bridge, a place Carmine was confident nobody he knew would ever visit. Quinn was sitting there drinking some kind of stinky tea, pretending to be calm. He liked that about Quinn, the way he could control his emotions. Quinn got right to the point and told Carmine he'd killed Kennedy, but another man had been with Kennedy.

"I recognized him," Quinn said. "I've looked at the files our organized crime people have on you . . ."

Carmine almost smiled at that, picturing Quinn poring over the files, studying him the way he'd studied Quinn.

". . . and I know I saw his face in the file. I have a good memory for faces. Tomorrow, I'll get his name and call you. I need you to make sure he doesn't talk."

Carmine didn't say anything for a moment. For one thing, Quinn was starting to piss him off, telling him what he *needed,* like Carmine should give a shit what he needed.

"I already know who he is," Carmine said. "I met with him half an hour ago. He came to tell me Kennedy had been killed and that he was going after the guy who killed him."

"What did you tell him?"

"I did my best to convince him that whoever shot Kennedy probably worked for the guy in Trenton whose dope Kennedy lost."

"Good."

"No, it's not good. He saw your face, too, and he got part of your license plate, and Jerry Kennedy was his best friend. I figure in a few days, less than a week, he'll know who you are. Then he'll kill you."

Quinn didn't say anything immediately but Carmine saw him squeezing the teacup so hard he was surprised it didn't crack.

"What's his name?" Quinn finally asked.

When Carmine didn't answer the question right away, Quinn said, "I'll get his name from the files tomorrow, so you might as well tell me."

"It's DeMarco," Carmine said. "Gino DeMarco."

And five days later, Enzo came to Carmine's house while he was feeding his fish and told him that Gino had identified the man who had killed Jerry Kennedy: a young cop named Quinn.

6

Joe DeMarco walked into the house and the odor of whatever was cooking in the kitchen made him smile. His mother, an Irish girl who barely knew how to scramble an egg when she first got married, was one of the best Italian cooks in Queens. She was so good that Joe rarely went to Italian restaurants because he knew the food wouldn't be as good as his mom's.

He dropped his bag on the floor by the front door and walked into the kitchen. His mother hadn't heard him come in, and she was standing at the counter, whacking an onion into small chunks with a big knife, like she was mad at the onion. He could also see her lips moving, talking to somebody who wasn't there, which would have made him smile if she hadn't looked so angry. Which meant the imaginary person she was talking to was most likely his father.

"Hey, Ma," he said.

She jumped. "Oh, my God! You're gonna give me a heart attack, sneaking up on me like that."

She put down the knife and rushed over and hugged him. "Are you hungry?"

It seemed like that was the first question she asked every time she saw him, like he'd walked from D.C. to New York, foraging for food on the way.

"You want me to make you a sandwich?"

He held her for a moment and looked at her. She was slim but not frail, and there wasn't that much gray in her hair. But she was starting to look old, older than his dad looked, and they were both the same age. He figured it was fear etching the lines into her face: fear that her husband was going to be arrested one day, fear that he would be killed one day, fear that she wouldn't be able to support herself when he was gone. And maybe the biggest fear: fear that her only son might be sucked into his father's world.

He had seen pictures of her when she was young, before he was born, and she looked like . . . well, like somebody who would be *fun*. Now there was nothing fun about her, nothing joyful, nothing playful. Now she looked like who she was, a person always knotted up inside, perpetually angry at the man she married, maybe angry at the whole damn world.

But Joe knew she would never leave his father. Being Catholic was one reason why; the other reason was that she came from a class and generation that equated divorce with failure. More than anything else, however, he knew she still loved his father; he knew this even if she didn't. No, she'd never leave Gino DeMarco—she just wouldn't ever forgive him for being who he was.

Joe didn't feel the way she did about his dad. He loved the man unconditionally.

When he was young, like when he was eight or nine, he'd ask his mom what his dad did at work and why he didn't come home some nights, and she'd put him off saying things like "Oh, you know, he just works for a man. He fixes things for him, like the way he fixes things here around the house. And sometimes things have to be fixed at night. Now go clean up your room like I told you."

He was ten when he found out his dad worked for Carmine Taliaferro and who Taliaferro was. A kid named Jimmy Moskovey had asked him if his dad was a gangster and if he had gun. "What?" Joe had said. "What are you talking about?" "Well, he works for old man Taliaferro and everyone knows Taliaferro's a big gangster." The only thing Joe knew about Mr. Taliaferro at that time was that he was rich and he donated the uniforms for his Little League team. "My dad's no gangster," Joe told Jimmy, "and if you ever say that again, I'm gonna punch you."

But when he got home from school that afternoon, he asked his mom, "Does dad work for Mr. Taliaferro? Jimmy Moskovey said he's a gangster." His mom closed her eyes, like she'd been dreading this moment all her life. Finally she said, "Yes, he works for him but nobody knows for sure what Mr. Taliaferro does. People make up stories about him. And your father isn't a gangster." "But what does Dad do for him?" Joe persisted. "He just does stuff, but he doesn't do anything bad. Now quit pestering me. I've got work to do." His mother had never been much of a liar—she was too blunt and almost always said what was on her mind without caring what the consequences might be—but Joe, even at the age of ten, could tell she was lying. And that night, after his parents thought he was asleep, he could hear his mom yelling at his dad in the kitchen.

By the time Joe was in his teens, he knew from the neighbors, the newspapers, and the kids in school exactly what Taliaferro did. He was involved in loansharking, prostitution, and drugs. His guys shook down store owners for protection money, hijacked trucks, and fenced stolen goods. He bribed politicians and cops to stay out of the can. He also had his hooks deep into the garbage haulers' union, meaning everyone in Queens was basically paying him to take away their trash.

But no matter what people said about Taliaferro, Joe couldn't picture his father smacking around some little shopkeeper for protection money or beating up some guy who owed Taliaferro's sharks. He couldn't imagine him sneaking into some place and ripping stuff off. If anyone had ever said to his face that his dad was a thief or a drug dealer, Joe would have taken the guy's head off.

He eventually developed his own theory about what his father did. He didn't have any facts to back up this theory, but it was one that fit his perception of the man he knew. He decided his dad probably provided protection for Taliaferro. Taliaferro had to have enemies, and his dad made sure they didn't kill him. He could see his father's broad form, like in a movie, standing in the shadows behind Taliaferro, silent and unmoving, arms crossed over his chest, being Taliaferro's bodyguard. He probably also made sure that Taliaferro's men—who really *were* thieves—didn't steal from their boss. Plus Taliaferro, as everyone knew, had a lot of legitimate businesses: an auto body place, a company that painted houses, and half a dozen others. He had property all over the five boroughs. Joe could imagine his dad involved in some hazy way in those businesses, taking care of things, managing things, doing like his mom had told him when he was little: fixing things that were broken.

Joe knew that his perception of what his father did for Taliaferro might be wrong and some might even consider him naïve, but he knew one thing for sure: Gino DeMarco was, and always had been, a great father to him. Gino didn't just love him—he cherished him, he doted on him, he was always there for him—and Joe had never lacked for anything important. He knew one other thing about his dad that was hard for him to articulate but that he knew to be true: his father might do things that were illegal, but he'd never do something that was dishonorable.

Joe really had only one complaint about his dad, and it was the same complaint his mother had: Gino DeMarco was a man who never opened up to anyone. Joe had tried countless times to get him to talk about what he did for a living—or if not *what* he did, then just how he *felt* about what he did. He just wanted to understand why a man like him would be associated with Carmine Taliaferro.

But every time he tried to draw his father out, all he usually got in the way of a response was a head shake. The most his dad ever said to him was "Look, Joe, you need to quit asking me about what I do because I can't tell you. All you need to know is that I've made a lot of mistakes in my life. I didn't even graduate from high school. I ended up where I am now because I'm stupid and because I thought I didn't have a lot of other choices."

Joe knew his father wasn't stupid but he could tell he was ashamed about what he did.

"The main thing is, you stay away from the people I work with. You don't go near them. You get an education, then you move away from here, and you make your mother proud."

He had no idea, not then, that his father was a killer.

Maureen DeMarco smiled as she watched her son eat a meatball sandwich. She had a secret recipe for her meatballs she wouldn't share with anyone, not even her sisters. She laughed when he said, with his mouth full, "God, Ma, this is delicious." It felt good to laugh.

She was always amazed how much he looked like Gino, particularly now that he was a young man. He had the same powerful build, the same dark hair, the prominent nose, the cleft in his chin. The only difference between him and Gino was his eyes. They were blue like hers instead of brown like Gino's. His eyes, as near as she could tell, were the only physical characteristics he'd inherited from her.

When it came to his personality, he wasn't much like either her or Gino. He wasn't serious about much of anything—especially school—and was usually easygoing and in a good mood, although God help you if you made him mad. But with sports, he was different. He was very competitive when he played in high school and had been an outstanding catcher; he hated to lose. Gino said that if Joe had been able to hit a curve, he could have a gotten a scholarship to college.

She liked that he was nice to people, too, and he'd never been cruel to the type of kids other kids were cruel to when he was in school. She remembered his sophomore year in high school, how he went to a dance with this incredibly homely girl because she asked him and he couldn't bring himself to say no and hurt her feelings. She loved that he had the courage to do that.

There was one thing he had in common with her husband beside his looks, however: he never confided in anyone when something was bothering him—and just like with Gino, that pissed her off.

"How's school going?" she asked.

"Great," Joe said.

Maureen DeMarco rarely swore out loud; she thought women who cursed were cheap and tacky. So all she said was "Well, that's good to hear." But she was thinking: *Bullshit*.

He looked tired, with dark smudges under his eyes, and she knew what was going on. He was cramming like crazy to pass his final exams, trying to make up for goofing off when he should have been studying. He'd been like that as an undergrad, and would never have come close to getting into law school if it hadn't been for Gino. His junior year, Gino sat him down and told him that if his grades didn't improve, he was going to stop paying his tuition and make him enlist in the army. She didn't think Gino was serious about making him enlist—Gino loved him too much to ever put his life at risk—but Joe believed him and finally knuckled down. Or maybe he just grew up and realized if he wanted a good life he needed to apply himself. Whatever the case, he was now paying the price, having to study his butt off.

"You decided yet what kind of law you want to practice?"

The only lawyer she knew personally was Mr. Clemente, down the block. He made up wills and sued people whenever he could, but his family didn't live any better than the DeMarcos. Clemente's wife was always complaining about how little money they had.

"I'm going to apply to prosecutors' and public defenders' offices in cities near D.C. You know, Arlington, Alexandria, Fairfax, places like that. I have to pass the bar first, but I'm hoping to land a job with some prosecutor's office. I'd rater prosecute than defend; it's like playing offense instead of defense."

She wanted to say, *You gotta be shittin' me!* What she said instead was, "You're kidding."

"No. What's wrong with that?"

What's wrong with that? Your father's a gangster, for cryin' out loud! You should become a defense lawyer so you can defend him when he winds up in jail. And what happens when the prosecutor's office finds out who your father is?

Instead of saying what she was thinking, she said, "Well, I guess there's nothing wrong with that, a good city job, but is that where the money is?"

"No. The money is in tax law or corporate law or with big firms that represent white-collar crooks. But the truth is, I don't have the grades to land those kinds of jobs right out of school. I'm thinking if I do well in a city or a state job, then maybe I can get something better."

"You want to stay down there in Washington, and not come back to New York so you're closer to home?"

"Yeah, I like it there."

But there was this flicker in his eyes when he said this, and she knew what he was thinking. He was thinking that in D.C. they might not know who his father was, but here in New York, they'd find out for sure.

"D.C.'s not that far away, you know. It's not like I'm moving to California."

California. God forbid! Fruitcakes live in California. And what if he gets married and has kids? How will I ever see my grandchildren if they live out west? Which reminded her. "I suppose you're gonna see Marie while you're here." She tried not to sound disapproving.

"Yeah, maybe, if I got the time. I have to do some studying while I'm here."

Bullshit, again. She knew the real reason he'd come up from D.C. for a visit was to see Marie, not her or his father.

He'd been dating Marie off and on since high school and he was hooked on her. And she couldn't blame him, in a way. The woman was gorgeous, had a body like a movie star. But she wasn't all that bright and would probably end up working in a beauty salon, if she worked at all. The other thing was, Maureen had never trusted Marie. She seemed like the type who wouldn't remain faithful if times got tough. She knew, however, there was no point telling her son that.

"Oh, I forgot to tell you," she said. "Your Aunt Connie will be coming for dinner tomorrow."

Connie wasn't really his aunt; she was his godmother. She was also Maureen DeMarco's oldest friend. She lived up in Albany now, had a state government job up there. When she was younger, she'd worked in D.C. for a congressman from Boston and in those days, Connie had looked like a movie star, too. She'd looked like Sophia Loren. She didn't look like Sophia anymore, though. She'd gotten fat as she'd aged but it didn't seem to bother her. And in spite of her size she always seemed to have a boyfriend. She loved Joe like he was her own son.

"You should tell her about wanting to get on with some prosecutor's office. She might be able to help."

"Yeah, maybe I'll do that," Joe said.

Well, if he didn't tell Connie, she would. The thing about Connie was she had connections. Connections from when she worked in Congress and more connections now, working for the state of New York. Joe didn't know it, but it was Connie who had really gotten him into law school. He never would have been admitted with his grades if she hadn't pulled a few strings.

"Tomorrow, you go down to the florist and buy her some flowers."

"Yeah, good idea," Joe said.

She knew he'd forget by tomorrow and she'd have to tell him again.

She heard the front door shut. Gino was home. When he walked into the kitchen and saw Joe his eyes lit up, and Joe stood up and they hugged.

Gino DeMarco wasn't a hugger. Italians, they were almost always huggers, Maureen had noticed, always hugging and kissing each other on the cheek. Not Gino. And not Joe, either. The only men those two hugged were each other.

"So how you doin', hotshot?" Gino asked, a smile on his face. He smiled so infrequently that when he did it always reminded Maureen of the sun coming out after a storm.

"Great," her lying son said.

7

Carmine needed to talk to Quinn but he wasn't going to talk to him on his own phone.

The young cop had assured him that nobody was tapping his phone, but Carmine wasn't sure Quinn would know, particularly if the feds were the ones doing the tapping. And after Jerry Kennedy was killed, Carmine figured the feds must be taking a hard look at him, figuring he might have ordered the hit on Kennedy. For all he knew, those sneaky sons-a-bitches could be following him, so now he was even afraid to meet with Quinn.

Finally, he gave Enzo a note in a sealed envelope and told him, "Find a kid and give him a few bucks to take the note to the doorman in Quinn's apartment building. Deliver it before Quinn goes to work." The note told Quinn, no matter what he was doing, to be at a pay phone on a certain corner at eight o'clock that night. Carmine would call him from another pay phone.

"DeMarco knows who you are," Carmine said as soon as Quinn answered the phone.

Carmine figured Quinn would curse, say *shit, son of a bitch, goddam-nit*, something like that. But he didn't say anything at all for a moment, and when he did speak his voice was calm. "Do you think he might tell the FBI that I killed Kennedy?"

Carmine laughed. "He's not going to talk to the FBI, Quinn. I already told you what he's going to do. He's going to kill you because Jerry Kennedy was his best friend."

"Can't you stop him?"

"Nope. But maybe what I can do is set him up for you. That is, assuming you got the balls to take him out yourself. But I gotta warn you. He's good."

"Why don't you have one of your people take care of him?"

"Why the hell would I do that? Why would I risk one of my guys? And like I said, DeMarco's good. If my guy missed, DeMarco would kill me. You got yourself into this shit. You need to get yourself out of it."

Again there was a long pause. "So what's your idea?" Quinn said, no emotion in his voice at all.

It was kind of funny, Carmine thought. Here was this cop, this college-educated cop, who'd probably always thought of himself as one of the good guys. But he'd killed one innocent man and lied about it, killed Kennedy to get out from under Carmine, and now he was considering killing DeMarco. The way he sounded, it was like he was looking at a chessboard, trying to decide if he should castle his rook. If Quinn stayed this cold and ruthless, he was definitely going places.

———◆◆◆———

Carmine called Gino next and said, "We need to talk. Where we met last time. Make damn sure nobody follows you."

As he waited for Gino to arrive, he looked up at Sinatra's autographed picture behind the bar. Carmine couldn't figure it out. The fucking guy was from New Jersey, then he sings "New York, New York" and everybody acts like he's the king of Manhattan.

Gino sat down across from him.

"You wanna drink?"

Gino shook his head.

Those were two more things that Carmine was going to miss about him: he didn't talk except when he had to and he wasn't a drunk like that bum Kennedy, whose fault it was that everyone was in this mess.

Carmine took a sip of his drink, then started lying.

"I was gonna have Enzo tell you I didn't want the cop killed, that I didn't want the heat that would follow, and I especially didn't want to lose you if you got arrested. But I understand how you feel about Jerry, so I did some checking on the cop.

"I told you I thought maybe he worked for the guy whose dope Jerry lost, the guy down in Trenton. Well, I was wrong. He's connected to the bookie in Atlantic City, the one Jerry owed money to. The bookie knew he was never going to get his money back from Jerry, so he wanted an example made of him, and he made the cop kill him. You see, the cop owes the bookie, too; he owes him a lot. He's a degenerate gambler and Internal Affairs has been looking at him, too."

Carmine hoped he wasn't laying it on too thick.

"Anyway, what I'm saying is, this is a dirty cop, and if something was to happen to him, nobody's gonna give a shit. I mean, they'll give him the usual funeral, bagpipes and bullshit, but they're not gonna go to war over him."

Gino just sat there, his face like one of them Easter Island statues. Carmine could tell he didn't care how hard the NYPD would try to find the cop's killer.

"The thing is, and the reason I wanted to see you tonight, is I found out the cop is playing poker Saturday night at a warehouse down on the waterfront in Red Hook. It's a high-stakes game and he plays almost every Saturday, even though he loses almost every time. The warehouse will be the perfect place to take him out."

"I'm not going to kill him with half a dozen people around," Gino said, looking at Carmine like Carmine was nuts.

Carmine knew that Gino always worked alone and always picked a spot where there wouldn't be witnesses. He would plan a hit for days, sometimes weeks, to make sure the setup was right.

"You don't understand," Carmine said. "I know the guy who owns the warehouse. He's one of my connections for bringing dope into the country and he stores the dope in the warehouse before we move it out. I already called him and told him I don't want them playing the game there this week."

Carmine really did know the guy who owned the warehouse and he really was one of his dope connections, but the warehouse was never used for poker games.

"I also told him," Carmine continued, "that I don't want anyone to call the cop to tell him the game's been canceled. So Saturday night, about ten, the cop's going to walk into this big warehouse, then walk down to the office in the back, and there won't be anyone else there. You get there first and when he walks in, you take care of him."

Before Gino could object, Carmine went on: "The other thing is, it'll be noisy down there. They're offloading a ship and there'll be trucks driving around, forklifts, cranes, all that shit. This is good because nobody will hear a shot. But that means, of course, you have to make sure nobody sees you going into the warehouse."

When DeMarco just sat there staring at him, looking skeptical, like he wasn't enthused by Carmine's idea, Carmine said, "Hey, you got two days to check the place out. If you don't like it, then don't do it there. I'm just trying to help you out here, but do what you want."

8

———◆◆◆———

Joe met Marie at a bar near her mom's house. She was wearing a red sleeveless blouse—she always looked good in red—and white shorts and sandals. Her lipstick was bloody red to match her blouse. She had laughing dark eyes, incredible legs, and her dark hair was longer than when he'd last seen her; he liked it when she wore her hair long. He couldn't help but notice the top two buttons of the blouse were unbuttoned and showed off a little cleavage. The first time he'd touched her breasts, he thought he'd died and gone to heaven.

He was hoping that after he bought her a drink or two, they could go back to her house and have sex. Her mother was usually out in the afternoon, shopping or playing canasta with her girlfriends. But wouldn't you know? Not this afternoon.

As they sat there, he was seriously thinking about proposing to her but decided that this wasn't the sort of place where you proposed, not to mention that he didn't have a ring. Also, maybe it would be good if he had a job before he proposed. Instead of proposing, he just talked about the future, which he hoped would be *their* future.

"I'll be graduating in another couple of weeks, then I'll have to spend the summer cramming for the bar exam, but I'm hoping come fall I'll have a job down there in D.C. Virginia, actually."

"You want to live in D.C.?" She said this like Washington was an Eskimo village near the North Pole.

"Yeah. There're a lot of opportunities there." Then realizing that maybe his career opportunities weren't at the top of her list, he added, "You've always had a good time when you've been there before. It's an exciting place with all the politics, and there are a lot of great places to eat and drink."

Now she made this face like New York was the only place where they knew how to cook.

"Anyway, I was thinking you could come down this summer, stay a week or two, get to know the city better. And by then, maybe I'll have a place of my own." He hoped.

"What would I tell my mother?"

Before he could tell her that her mother wasn't all that bright and he'd come up with an acceptable lie, his damn cousin walked into the bar. What the hell was he doing here? Why wasn't he working?

His cousin, Danny DeMarco, was maybe the handsomest son of a bitch in Queens. Ask any girl in the borough. Joe also knew the bastard would screw anything in a skirt, and naturally he found Marie attractive. He didn't think, however, that Danny would be such a rat as to ask his own cousin's girlfriend out. He hoped.

They spent the next hour drinking beer, Marie laughing her ass off at almost anything Danny said. Danny was, Joe had to admit, a funny guy. It also seemed like she had to touch his arm or grab his hand every time she wanted to make a point. Joe was almost glad when she said she had to go home.

"I'll call you tomorrow," Joe said.

He was going to be really pissed if Marie's mom wasn't out of the house tomorrow.

He called Marie the next morning, and she told him to come over around two, that her mom was playing canasta that afternoon. He showered, shaved extra close, and splashed on some cologne he'd given his father five years ago, which his dad never used. But when he gets to Marie's house, her damn mother's there. She told Joe she had a headache and had decided to skip her canasta game but it was okay if Joe stayed for a little while and visited with Marie. Joe almost screamed at her: "So take a fucking aspirin!"

At least dinner that night was fun, mainly because his Aunt Connie, his godmother, was there. She was a hoot. She even put his mother in a good mood. His dad, who usually didn't say much anyway, was even more silent than usual, and Joe got the impression he had something on his mind.

His mom mentioned at one point that he wanted to get a city job, working for a prosecutor's office.

"Really?" Connie said.

"What's wrong with that?" his father said, like he was coming to Joe's defense.

"Well, nothing, I guess," Connie said. "That kind of job is a good way to launch a career." But Joe noticed the look she gave his mother.

"Anyway," Joe said, "I'm hoping to get hired by some outfit near D.C. I like it there. I'm taking the bar exam in the fall."

"I know a lot of people down there," Connie said. "I'll see if I can do something to grease the skids for you, sweetie."

Then she started telling stories about this man she used to work for, this John Mahoney, a congressman from Boston who was now Speaker of the House. Connie said the guy drank like a fish, was probably getting money under the table from all kinds of people, and cheated on his wife every chance he got. The way she talked, though, Joe could tell she was actually fond of the guy and he couldn't help but wonder, back then when his Aunt Connie had a waist, if she and Mahoney might have been an item. Whatever the case, Mahoney sounded like your typical D.C. politician, the kind of guy Joe didn't ever want anything to do with.

Connie left about eight and Joe was thinking he should spend at least a couple of hours studying before he went to bed. That was when his father said, "I gotta go out for a while." His mother gave him a look that would blister paint off the wall but didn't say anything.

Joe was sitting at the dining room table when his father left the house. He was trying to make sense out of some case he was told would be on one of his finals, some convoluted, incomprehensible thing having to do with property law. Before his dad walked out the door, he gave Joe's shoulder a little squeeze. "I'm proud of you, kid. You're gonna be a great lawyer."

Gino DeMarco turned out to be really wrong about that.

9

The front of the warehouse in Red Hook faced the waterfront. It had big sliding doors, like an airplane hangar, and next to the sliding doors was a smaller, normal-sized door. Above the small door was the number one in faded red paint, about two feet high.

At the pier was a Japanese ship carrying a bunch of big construction equipment that had to be offloaded a piece at a time and later reassembled where they were doing the job. Running parallel to the ship were railroad tracks that were used by the cranes and there were a dozen flatbed trucks in a queue waiting to be loaded.

There were people everywhere—longshoremen on the ship and on the pier, truck drivers, customs agents, and members of the ship's crew. Forklifts were zipping all over the place and it was a miracle they hadn't run over somebody. It was noisy with men yelling and the engine noises produced by the forklifts and trucks, and lights on the ship and the pier had the whole pier lit up like Yankee Stadium for a night game.

Gino walked past the warehouse sliding doors, which were locked with a padlock. He didn't sneak by the warehouse but moved like a man with a purpose, a man who belonged where he was. He was dressed in a black denim jacket, blue jeans, and boots. On his head was a hard hat. In other words, he looked like most of the men on the pier. He turned when he reached the end of the warehouse and walked along the side of it, in the alleyway created by an adjacent warehouse.

There were half a dozen doors on the side of the warehouse and he walked until he came to a door with the number five painted above it. Gino had a key for the door. He figured Carmine had obtained the key from somebody connected to the warehouse or the poker game. Carmine said that the guy who ran the game normally unlocked the number-five door at nine thirty so the players could get in. He told Gino that after he let himself in he was to leave the door unlocked so the cop could get in as he normally did when he played poker there Saturday nights.

Gino had been to the warehouse the night before, at the same time, to check the place out. There was no way he was going to make the hit there, no matter what Carmine had said, without examining the place in advance. Last night, just like tonight, there had been men all over the pier and trucks and forklifts zooming around. Nobody had noticed him last night and they didn't notice him tonight; he was just another longshoreman doing his job.

He unlocked the number-five door, stepped into the warehouse, and pushed down a little button on the doorknob to make sure the door stayed unlocked. The first thing he noticed after he was inside was that the warehouse was fully illuminated from big overhead lights in the ceiling—and that wasn't good. When he'd checked the place out the night before, the overhead lights hadn't been on. He'd been able to see, however, because the warehouse had big windows set up high in the walls, and all the lights on the pier had provided enough illumination for him to see where he was going. He figured whoever was in charge of the game told the warehouse guys to leave the overhead lights on on Saturday night so the players could make their way back to the office where the game was played. Whatever the case, he was now worried about how well he'd be able to conceal himself with the place lit up like an operating room.

The warehouse was about a hundred feet wide on the side that faced the waterfront, and almost two hundred feet deep. The office where the game was played was at the far end, away from the waterfront. Wooden crates and barrels filled the place, stacked on pallets, and the pallet loads were stacked on top of each other as high as a forklift could reach. Some of the crates looked like they'd been there for years. There were aisles between the crates wide enough for a forklift and the center aisle going back to the office was the widest aisle, wide enough for a semi with a flatbed trailer.

The warehouse had one other feature that Gino had considered when he was planning the job. There was a big steel I-beam that spanned the width of the warehouse and attached to the I-beam was a chain fall—a hand-operated, electric crane—that was used to pick up heavy items and load them onto trucks. The I-beam had wheels on it that ran in rails so the I-beam could be moved back and forth along the length of the warehouse and the chain fall could be moved back and forth across the I-beam. A catwalk ran around the perimeter of the warehouse at the same height as the I-beam. The catwalk was needed to be able to get at the chain fall—to grease it, and perform any other maintenance required—and the catwalk also had a lot of crap stored on it: coils of rope and tarps and cargo nets the warehouse guys didn't use very often.

Gino had thought about lying down on the catwalk, under a tarp, and when Quinn walked down the aisle, he'd shoot him from there, figuring Quinn would have no reason to look up. He finally rejected that idea since he'd be shooting downward at a moving target—a tough shot for any shooter—and he'd be at least thirty feet away from Quinn when he pulled the trigger.

He finally decided to hide behind some black fifty-five-gallon drums. There were four drums per pallet, and three pallets stacked on top of each other. If Gino stood behind the barrels, Quinn wouldn't be able to see him as he walked down the center aisle, and when Quinn passed him, Gino would step out and shoot him in the back.

Shooting Quinn in the back didn't bother Gino. This wasn't a duel or some fast-draw gunfight in a western movie. This was a murder, plain and simple, and DeMarco wasn't going to take any chances. He'd give Quinn as much of a chance as Quinn had given Jerry Kennedy.

Now, with all the lights on in the warehouse, he needed to reevaluate his hiding place. He figured it would still be okay—that Quinn wouldn't be able to see him standing behind the barrels until he walked past him, and by then it would be too late. If he felt too exposed with all the lights on, however, then he'd just forget about killing Quinn tonight and come up with a different plan.

Gino started down the center aisle toward the office to evaluate his hiding place. He was about halfway there when he heard a noise behind him, a shoe scraping the concrete floor of the warehouse. He spun around, pulling his gun out of his holster as he did.

There was a man standing there—he must have been crouched down behind a pallet stacked with bags of coffee. Gino had smelled the coffee as he walked past the pallet. The man was dressed just like Gino—work boots, jeans, and a hard hat so he, too, would blend in with the longshoremen on the pier. With all the lights on in the warehouse, DeMarco could see the man's face. It was Quinn, the cop who had killed Jerry Kennedy.

Everything that happened next happened in just a few seconds—but it was enough time for DeMarco to think: *Carmine set me up.*

The cop had been planning to shoot him in the back, but when Gino spun around at the sound of a shoe scraping the floor, the cop's first bullet missed him. The cop's second shot didn't. The second bullet hit Gino in the chest. Gino fired back immediately and saw the cop stagger.

Gino was going to shoot the cop again—but he couldn't.. The cop's second shot had hit something vital, and Gino's vision was already blurring and his finger didn't have the strength to pull the trigger. He knew he was dying.

The cop fired two more times as Gino stood there, both bullets again hitting him in the chest. Gino felt himself falling. He never felt himself hit the floor. As he was falling, he thought: *Oh, God, Maureen, I'm sorry.*

—◆◆◆—

Quinn looked down at DeMarco. He couldn't believe how fast the son of a bitch had been.

Quinn had hidden behind the coffee bags because they were near the number-five door and they provided good concealment, but in order to hide there he had to sit in a squatting position. He'd been waiting for DeMarco for almost an hour and when he rose to shoot him, his legs had cramped up and he stumbled slightly and his shoe scraped the concrete. He should have worn soft-soled shoes.

When DeMarco heard him, he spun around so fast that Quinn's first shot passed behind DeMarco's back. What really amazed him was that DeMarco had his gun out by the time he completed the spin and he was just lucky that he was able to get off a second shot before DeMarco could fire. But he wasn't that lucky: DeMarco managed to get off one shot before Quinn could fire again, and DeMarco's bullet hit him high in the chest, near his left shoulder. Fortunately, Quinn's next two shots finished the bastard off before he could shoot again.

He was in trouble now, though. He was bleeding badly from the bullet wound and was also having trouble breathing. He wondered if DeMarco's bullet had nicked a lung. He had planned to hide DeMarco's body behind some of the crates in the warehouse to delay discovery of the body, but now he couldn't do that. He didn't have the strength to move DeMarco, nor did he have the time. He needed to get back to his car and get help before he bled to death.

He walked to the door he'd used to enter the warehouse and opened it and peered outside. No one was in the alleyway between the warehouses.

He walked slowly, pressing his hand against the wound, until he reached the pier. When he reached the pier, he forced himself to straighten up and dropped his hand to his side. Keeping his head down, he walked along the pier sticking close to the warehouse, staying out of the light as best he could. Fortunately, everyone on the pier was focused on the offloading—longshoremen knew if you didn't pay attention you could get killed by a forklift or something falling from a crane—and no one was paying any attention to him. He wasn't surprised that no one had heard the shots. He'd used a silencer and the one shot DeMarco fired wouldn't have been noticed with all the noise on the pier.

He'd been forced to park his car almost half a mile from the warehouse and had to stop a couple of times while he was walking to rest and catch his breath. Stopping wasn't good, he knew, because he was losing a lot of blood.

He finally reached his car. He unlocked the door and slipped in behind the steering wheel, then just sat there for a moment until he could find the strength to start the car. He drove slowly—and erratically. He was going all over the road and if a cop saw him, he'd get pulled over for sure.

Just when he didn't think he could drive any farther he finally spotted a pay phone. He lurched from this car and called Taliaferro. He didn't know what he'd do if Taliaferro didn't answer.

"I'm hurt," he told Taliaferro. "I got the guy but he hurt me bad." He didn't want to say DeMarco's name on the phone and he didn't want to say that he'd been shot. "I'm in a phone booth, five blocks east of the pier. I don't know the address. I need a doctor and I can't go to a hospital."

He didn't hear what Taliaferro said because he passed out.

———◆◆◆———

Quinn woke up in a bedroom—not a hospital room—but had no idea where he was. He was still wearing his pants and socks but his shirt was gone. His left shoulder was covered with white bandages and it looked like a professional had applied the bandages. He noticed a glass filled with water sitting on a nightstand next to the bed and realized he was incredibly thirsty. He reached for the glass with his right hand but the pain in his left shoulder hit him when he did, and he knocked the glass off the nightstand and it shattered on the floor.

The bedroom door opened and a man entered the room. He was in his forties, tall and skinny, and his dark hair was receding rapidly. His face was sallow and the whites of his eyes had a yellowish tinge, and Quinn's first impression was: junkie.

"Good," the man said, "you're awake."

"Where am I?" Quinn asked.

"My house in Queens. You're going to be all right. The bullet didn't hit anything important but you're going to need therapy to regain full use of your arm. Since I'm guessing you don't want to go to your regular doctor, you're going to have to come back here and see me a couple of times to make sure you're healing properly. I'm not a therapist but I know enough to help you and I'll do what I can, but don't be surprised if you lose some range of motion. I'll put your arm in a sling and you can tell people you fucked up your shoulder doing something, a fall, whatever."

Quinn wasn't worried about what he'd tell the people at work. He wouldn't take off his shirt in front of them and he could explain the sling like the doctor had said, by claiming he'd done something at home that had dislocated his shoulder. His wife was the problem. The night he killed Jerry Kennedy he'd told her he was on an undercover assignment working directly for the chief of D's, something really hush-hush that could be a big break for his career. He'd told her the same story tonight when he left the apartment to head down to Red Hook, that he was pulling a double shift because of the same undercover assignment. To explain the bandage on his shoulder, he could tell her that he had to sneak into an abandoned building to watch some criminals and he

ran into a jagged piece of rebar or sheet metal. He'd say it wasn't a serious injury and that he'd been treated by a doc at the emergency room,
but that she couldn't talk to anyone about it. Hmm. He'd give it some
more thought, but that would probably work.

"I'm going to call Carmine now," the doctor said, "and you and he
can decide how to get you home."

"Do you know who I am?" Quinn asked.

"No, and I don't want to know."

10

Joe was in bed, asleep, and the doorbell ringing woke him up. Irritated, he wondered who could be calling so early; it wasn't even seven. A moment later, he heard his mother scream.

A man in a suit and a uniformed cop were standing in the doorway. His mother was sitting on the floor, her knees up against her chest, sobbing into her hands.

"What did you do to my mother?" Joe said.

The man in the suit said, "Son, my name's Detective Lynch. I'm sorry to tell you this, but your father's dead. He was shot and killed last night."

His mother had been expecting this to happen all her life, but when it finally did, she fell apart. Joe's Aunt Connie had to take care of all the funeral arrangements because Maureen DeMarco couldn't even get out of bed. Joe was simply numb. It felt like there was a cold, empty place inside his chest and it felt like the place would remain empty the rest of his life.

The cops had no idea who'd shot his father, and Joe could tell they weren't trying all that hard to find the killer. They figured, just like everybody else figured, that Gino DeMarco's death was connected in some way to Carmine Taliaferro's criminal operations. One gangster killing another wasn't exactly at the top of the NYPD's priority list.

His mother didn't want to have a viewing or a wake for her husband. There was a simple funeral mass at the church and Joe was surprised by how many people came. Half of them were neighbors and relatives; the other half was a bunch of shifty-looking guys dressed in cheap suits. There was one large floral arrangement near the casket, an expensive wreath about three feet in diameter made from roses. None of the neighbors could have afforded the wreath. The priest made an announcement at the end of the mass saying that the family would be going alone to the cemetery—meaning his mother didn't want Taliaferro and his hoods there.

As they were taking the casket out to the hearse, Joe saw Taliaferro and a couple of his men standing at the back of the church, near the baptismal font. Taliaferro was in his early seventies and short—maybe five seven or five eight and slightly built. His gray hair was thin and he wore glasses with heavy black frames. He didn't look like a tough guy; he looked like somebody's grandfather. One of the men with Taliaferro was Enzo Marciano, Taliaferro's underboss, and the other guy was Tony Benedetto, who Joe knew was one of Taliaferro's top guys.

Joe walked up to Taliaferro and said, "Do you know who killed my father?"

"I'm sorry, Joe, but I don't. And that's the God's honest truth. I have no idea what he was doing over there in Red Hook. I swear on the heads of my wife and daughter."

Before Joe could say anything else, his mother was at his side.

"You stay the hell away from my son," she said.

"Maureen, I just wanted to say how sorry—"

Maureen DeMarco slapped him across the face. She slapped him so hard the glasses went flying off his head.

Taliaferro didn't do anything and Joe took his mother's arm and said, "Come on, Ma. Let's go."

Enzo handed Carmine his glasses, looking embarrassed for his boss, the way Gino's wife had slapped him in front of everybody. But Carmine wasn't really thinking about what Maureen DeMarco had done; the woman was understandably distraught. What he was thinking was that Gino's kid was a hard-looking young bastard, and he looked just like his old man. He'd better make damn sure that Joe DeMarco never found out what really happened with Gino.

Four months after his father's funeral, Joe passed the Virginia state bar exam. He was actually surprised he passed it on the first try. He knew people a lot smarter than him who had to take the exam more than once.

The police still had no idea who had put three bullets into his father. Joe still had an empty place in his chest.

11

Joe DeMarco soon found out that he couldn't get a job. It appeared that no city prosecutor's office—or public defender's office—or any other law office on the eastern seaboard—wanted the son of a mafia hit man on their payroll.

Hit man. That's what the papers in New York started saying after the funeral. Gino DeMarco wasn't just some ordinary hood who worked for Carmine Taliaferro; according to "sources close to the investigation," his father had been the enforcer for the Taliaferro family. One unnamed source, who supposedly worked for the FBI, speculated that Gino may have killed as many as twenty people.

Carmine Taliaferro denied this, of course, saying he was just a businessman and that he hardly knew Gino DeMarco. He only went to his funeral because he lived there in the neighborhood.

Joe talked to a professor at his law school and asked if he could sue the papers for libel, slander, whichever one applied. The professor said not a chance—and, by the way, now that he had a law degree, maybe Joe should know the difference between slander and libel.

Eight months after graduating, he still hadn't found a job and was living with two other guys in a dump in Alexandria, working as a bartender to pay his share of the rent. His Aunt Connie called one afternoon as he was getting ready to leave for work.

"I got you a job," she said.

"What?" he said.

"You remember that guy, Mahoney, I was telling you about?"

"Yeah."

"Well, you're working for him. Sort of."

"Sort of? What does that mean?"

"You'll find out."

"Why in the hell would the Speaker of the House give me a job?"

Connie laughed. "Because I've got his big balls in my hand, that's why. At eight o'clock tomorrow morning, you go to a room in the sub-basement of the Capitol and—"

"The subbasement?"

"Yeah. Your new office has a sign on the door that says COUNSEL PRO TEM FOR LIAISON AFFAIRS."

"What does that mean?"

"It doesn't mean anything. Mahoney invented the name to protect him from the man in that office. You'll find out. Anyway, there will be a guy in the office named Jake. Jake's retiring pretty soon. He just had his second heart attack and he's going to teach you the ropes before he retires or has another heart attack, whichever comes first. You'll be a GS-12."

"Really?" DeMarco said. That was a *great* starting salary. Most lawyers starting out with the government were GS-11's, which meant that he'd make about ten grand a year more than the average new hire.

"If you survive the first year, I mean if you don't end up in jail or testifying to a congressional ethics committee or appearing before a federal grand jury . . ."

"What?"

". . . I'll make Mahoney make you a GS-13. This is the best I can do for you, sweetie, and I'm not exactly doing you a favor. Maybe after some time has passed, after folks have forgotten all about your dad, you can find something else. I sure as hell hope so."

12

As DeMarco approached the Capitol, he was actually feeling pretty good about his new job in spite of what his Aunt Connie had told him. Not only was his salary better than he'd ever expected to receive just out of school, this could be the start of a bright future: working hand in hand with the Speaker of the House, getting an insider's view of politics, making connections that could help him the rest of his life. Who knows? Maybe he'd end up being a politician himself—district attorney of Arlington, congressman from some district in Virginia. Or a lobbyist. He'd heard stories about the sluglike trail of slime that lobbyists left in their wake, but they made good money and they couldn't all be bad.

His mood dimmed somewhat when he reached the subbasement and its utilitarian corridors with exposed pipes and ventilation ducts overhead. The subbasement was nothing like the grand Rotunda two floors above with its painted ceiling and all the pictures on the walls. The small, flaking gold letters on the frosted glass of a battered door— COUNSEL PRO TEM FOR LIAISON AFFAIRS—whatever the hell that meant—didn't look too impressive, either.

He knocked and a voice called out, "Come on in. It's not locked."

The man sitting behind the desk looked like he deserved the heart attacks he'd had: a jowly meat-eater's face, a big gut testing the limit of every button on his shirt, a classic, bulbous boozer's nose. A stubby, unlit cigar slick with spit was clenched between two hairy knuckles. He wasn't dressed the way DeMarco had pictured a big-time political operator, either. He wore a black and white checkered sport coat, a hunter green shirt, off-the-rack polyester slacks, and a tie with some sort of Hawaiian motif. He was the fashion equivalent of a four-car pileup.

"I'm Jake," the fat man said. "You must be the new guy. Mahoney's already pissed at you and he hasn't even met you yet."

Great. But DeMarco decided not to say anything; if Jake didn't know his Aunt Connie was blackmailing Mahoney, why tell him?

"So sit down," Jake said, pointing to the only other chair in the room. "And relax, for Christ's sake."

The office was also less than he'd imagined, a lot less. It was the size of a small tool shed and the only furniture it contained was a gray, sheet metal four-drawer file cabinet, a scarred wooden desk, and two wooden chairs all looking like leftovers from Truman's era.

"I'll take you over to meet the boss in half an hour," Jake said. "Actually, we're supposed to be there now, but since Mahoney's always late, we've got plenty of time."

DeMarco just hoped Mahoney didn't blame him if they were late. "Are you going to give me some sort of, uh, orientation before I meet Mr. Mahoney? I mean, I'm really not too clear on what I'll be doing."

"You'll be doing whatever Mahoney tells you to do," Jake said, "and he'll give you all the shitty jobs he doesn't want his staff wasting their time on. Or that he doesn't want them to have their fingerprints on. You won't be writing speeches or attending meetings with bureaucrats or researching all the bullshit buried in the bills. He's got a bunch of smart kids who all graduated from Harvard who do the day-to-day political crap. You will be doing quite a bit of what Mahoney likes to call *fund-raising*, meaning you'll be his bagman when he wants money from sources he doesn't like to list as contributors."

DeMarco didn't say anything. He didn't know what to say—but Jake must have thought he was confused.

"Come with me. I want to show you something."

DeMarco followed his broad form out of the office and about ten feet down the corridor. Jake stopped in front of a glass case containing a coiled fire hose and a red fireman's axe. He pointed at the case and said: "That's you."

"Which one?" DeMarco asked. "The hose or the axe?"

"Whichever one Mahoney needs at the time."

Well, that clarified everything.

Jake walked back to his office and dropped back into his chair. "Let me give you an example. Two years ago, Mahoney goes to a banquet in Cornhusk, Nebraska, Indiana, one of them places. He's seated next to the lieutenant governor's wife, who turns out to be a good-looking woman. The lieutenant governor's not there because he just had his prostate removed. Well, Mahoney, of course, he can't help himself.

"Last month, the wife of the lieutenant governor calls Mahoney. She says she's found Jesus. She's been saved. Halleluiah! And in order to make things right with the Lord, she feels compelled to tell the world what a sinner she's been. So my job—and this is hardly the first time Mahoney's dick has caused him problems—was to take care of the lady from Cornhusk."

"What did you do to her?" DeMarco asked.

"I didn't *do* anything to her. I just talked to her. I told her how confessing this one little transgression wasn't going to be good for anybody, the press being the cruel, heartless jackals they are. When that didn't seem to deter her, I pointed out that she had cosigned a document with her husband, something related to a development in South Cornhusk, and if people understood what was behind that document she could be talking to a U.S. attorney instead of her Lord and savior."

"You gotta be shittin' me," DeMarco said before he could stop himself. He was about to begin a job where blackmail was apparently standard operating procedure.

"The other thing is, Mahoney will sometimes loan his fire hose, meaning you, to his buddies. Or his codefendants, as I like to call them."

Jake seemed to think that was funny; DeMarco didn't. "I've got a law degree, you know. I've even passed the bar already. I think—"

"Kid, every third guy you bump into in this town has a law degree. Hell, Mahoney's even got one, if you can believe it. And if the boss needed a lawyer, why the hell would he come to you? You've been out of school for about two minutes, you didn't exactly graduate at the top of your class, and then there's your father. Uh, may he rest in peace."

Jake sucked on his unlit cigar briefly before he continued with DeMarco's orientation. DeMarco was beginning to wonder if he ever lit the damn thing or if it was just some sort of nasty pacifier.

"Look," Jake said. "There are a lot of guys like us here in this town."

Us? DeMarco didn't want to be included in *us*.

"Some of 'em work for the private sector, so-called consulting firms with names that don't make any sense. Others have government staff positions like me, and now you, that don't fit into a particular box on somebody's org chart. We're the guys the politicians turn to when they need things done that they'd just as soon not read about in the *Post*. And most of the time we stay under the radar like we're supposed to, but every once in a while somebody screws up and everybody goes crazy. The most famous example, of course, being Watergate. I mean, what do you think guys like Gordon Liddy and Charles Colson were? They were red fire axes."

"Are you saying that if Mahoney asked you to break into some politician's headquarters . . ."

"Oh, hell no. What do I look like, a cat burglar? Although there was this one time . . . Well, never mind that. Anyway, stop looking so worried. I was a Boston cop for twenty years, and this job's a piece a cake compared to that."

Jake glanced at his watch. "It's time to go meet the boss."

⚬

DeMarco thought they'd be taking the stairs up to the Speaker's office, but Jake led him out of the Capitol. They caught a cab on Independence, and five minutes later entered a small restaurant on Capitol Hill.

Mahoney was sitting at a table at the rear of the restaurant with four other men. DeMarco didn't pay much attention to politics but he recognized Mahoney: the full head of white hair, the handsome features, the mean blue eyes—or at least they looked mean to DeMarco. He was only five eleven—the same height as DeMarco—but he looked bigger than that, maybe because he was so broad across the chest and shoulders. He was also heavy in the gut but it was a hard gut, not a soft, flabby one. Mahoney glanced briefly over at DeMarco and Jake, then looked away.

"We'll just sit here at the bar until those other guys leave," Jake said. "You wanna drink? I'm buyin' to celebrate your arrival."

DeMarco said no, not bothering to add that drinking at nine in the morning didn't seem like the way to put his best foot forward his first day on the job. Jake ordered a Bloody Mary.

"Who are those guys?" DeMarco asked, figuring it was time for him to start learning the lineup.

Jake glanced over at Mahoney's table. "Three of them are union big shots. God knows what Mahoney's plotting with them. Oh, that reminds me. If you have a political opinion about anything, keep it to yourself. Nobody, including me, gives a shit about your opinion."

This was the first thing DeMarco had heard that didn't surprise him.

"Now the fourth guy at the table, the one sitting on Mahoney's right with the really bad haircut? That's Perry Wallace, Mahoney's chief of staff. Wallace is the most devious, diabolical, conniving prick you will ever meet in your life and he's also a no-shit genius. Think Machiavelli with a Boston accent. You do not ever, ever wanna get cross-wired with Perry Wallace."

Maybe he should've had the drink.

Ten minutes later, the three union men shook hands with Mahoney and left the restaurant. Wallace sat with Mahoney a couple more minutes, his lips barely moving as he talked to him, then he, too, left. As he walked by DeMarco, Wallace looked at him for only a second but DeMarco had the impression of a camera's shutter opening and closing and Wallace depositing his image in some sort of mental file cabinet.

Jake drained his Bloody Mary and said, "Let's go say hello."

DeMarco had planned to walk up and stick out his hand and say "Joe DeMarco, sir. Thank you for giving me this opportunity." But he didn't. The look in Mahoney's eyes stopped him two feet from the table.

"The first thing I want you to do is get a decent suit," Mahoney said. "The amount I'm paying you, you should be able to afford one."

DeMarco restrained himself from looking over at Jake and pointing out that dress standards for Mahoney's employees didn't seem consistent. He also didn't point out that Mahoney wasn't paying him; the taxpayers were. He found out before long that John Mahoney viewed the U.S. Treasury as a large, not-very-well-guarded cookie jar and he stuffed his paw into it whenever he pleased.

"The only other thing I wanted to tell you is you got six months before Jake retires to prove to me that you're not a total idiot. Your aunt thinks—"

"Actually, Connie's not my aunt, sir, she's my godmother."

"Do I look like I give a shit?" Mahoney said. "And don't interrupt me when I'm talking. Now like I was saying, Connie thinks she's got me by the short hairs, but I got news for you. I won't fire you because that might piss off Connie, but if you fuck up, what I will do is temporarily detail your ass to the Department of Transportation. They're trying to get a road or railroad or some goddamn thing built across a reservation in South Dakota and I'll let them borrow you and the law degree you barely got. Then you can spend the next ten years fightin' with the Indians about some treaty that was signed the day after Custer was scalped. Now, beat it."

As they were leaving the restaurant, Jake said, "I thought that went pretty good."

Five and a half months later, DeMarco walked into the office and found Jake lying on the floor, on his back, his unlit cigar stuck between his fingers. His third heart attack had arrived. DeMarco checked Jake's pulse, then pulled out the bottle of Maker's Mark that Jake kept in the file cabinet. He found out his second day on the job there wasn't anything else in the file cabinet because Jake had a saying: *They can't subpoena air.*

He sat down and drank a toast to Jake's corpse. He'd grown to like the guy.

He called the medics, told them there was no rush, then walked up to Mahoney's office to inform him of Jake's departure. He was surprised when tears welled up in Mahoney's eyes. That would not be the last time John Mahoney surprised him.

Part II

13

DeMarco was thinking that this wasn't a bad way to spend a lovely October afternoon. The guy he was supposed to meet was half an hour late and if he didn't show up at all, that would be fine with him. The temperature was in the upper sixties, there wasn't a cloud in the sky, and the turning leaves across the river looked like God's palette. The beer he was drinking was fresh and cold.

DeMarco was sitting at an outdoor table at the Washington Harbour. He didn't know what pretentious snob had stuck the *u* in *harbor*. The Harbour was in Georgetown, on the banks of the Potomac River, and consisted of a elliptical-shaped plaza surround by high-end condos and restaurants. It also offered spectacular views of the Kennedy Center, Roosevelt Island, and the Key Bridge. Included with the other spectacular views was a woman sitting at the bar, wearing a skirt that showed off long, shapely legs. She had big-framed sunglasses stuck on top of her head, nested in a mass of red hair. She saw DeMarco looking at her and she smiled at him and he smiled back. Yeah, he'd be perfectly content to spend the entire afternoon sitting right where he was, sipping beer.

Unfortunately, at that moment he spotted a guy coming toward him and he was guessing this was the guy he was supposed to meet.

He was young, in his twenties, with short dark hair. He was carrying a slim briefcase and wearing khaki pants and a polo shirt. On his feet were shiny black lace-up shoes that looked as if they might be part of an army uniform—and they were. The man was a sergeant currently assigned to the Pentagon.

"Are you Mr. DeMarco?" the young guy asked. He was so nervous he looked like he was about to come out of his skin.

"Yeah," DeMarco said. "Sit down. And relax."

DeMarco had worked for John Mahoney for a long time and he knew his boss was as corrupt as any politician on Capitol Hill. And Mahoney's corruption sometimes went beyond the typical shenanigans related to campaign financing and preferential treatment given to wealthy constituents. Only the year before, Mahoney, with DeMarco's help, had undermined three government agencies to get his daughter out from under an insider trading charge—and his daughter had been guilty.

There were, however, lines that Mahoney would not cross. The problem was that these lines were arbitrarily and inconsistently drawn, and it wasn't always easy for DeMarco to know where they were placed. One of those lines had to do with veterans. Mahoney was a Vietnam vet and when it came to the proper treatment of veterans, Mahoney would do almost anything—and the national debt be damned.

The young man sitting with DeMarco—Sergeant Gary McCormack—hailed from Boston, Mahoney's hometown, and he had sent Mahoney a letter saying that a colonel at the Pentagon was siphoning off money intended for veterans suffering from mental health issues. In terms of Defense Department spending, the amount being pilfered was meager—meaning only a few million—but Mahoney had ordered DeMarco to meet with McCormack and get the evidence he claimed to have. Mahoney wanted some facts before he started firing political artillery shells at the Pentagon.

McCormack looked around the plaza nervously before he put his briefcase on the table and took out a manila file folder. Before he could open the folder, DeMarco said, "Order a beer. And stop looking like we're two spies meeting in Red Square. Nobody has a clue you're here unless you told somebody."

It took McCormack twenty minutes to explain the contents of the manila folder as it had to do with the army's accounting system—a system that appeared to have been designed for the sole purpose of hiding from Congress where the army spent its money. After McCormack left, it took DeMarco about five seconds to decide he should treat himself to another beer. The redhead was still sitting at the bar by herself. The next time she looked over at him—she'd glanced his way half a dozen times—he was going to raise his beer glass and make a why-don't-you-join-me gesture—and that's when his cell phone rang. He looked at the caller ID at saw it was a New York area code.

"Hello," he said.

"It's Tony Benedetto," the caller said. Tony sounded odd; his voice was scratchy and he was breathing like he'd just run up the stairs to the top of the Empire State Building.

Tony Benedetto was an old-time mafia guy, now mostly retired, as far as DeMarco knew. He lived in Queens and had worked for Carmine Taliaferro; he'd been there at the funeral mass the day his father was buried. DeMarco had seen Tony less than a year ago to get some information he needed on another mobster in Philadelphia.

"I need to see you," Tony said.

"Why?" DeMarco asked.

"I know who killed your father."

14

The last time DeMarco had seen Tony Benedetto, they'd been sitting in Tony's kitchen and Tony had been checking his blood pressure, bragging about what great shape he was in for a seventy-four-year-old. He wasn't in such great shape now. He was dying.

He was wearing house slippers and a dark blue jogging suit, the clothing loose on his long frame. He had a big nose and a thin-lipped mouth and was now completely bald —a by-product, DeMarco assumed, of chemo or radiation or whatever medical procedure was being used to keep him alive. DeMarco knew the hair loss had to bother Tony: he'd always been vain about his thick head of hair. He used to have a small paunch, too. Like his hair, the paunch was gone and his face was beginning to take the shape of the skull beneath the skin.

"Lung cancer," he told DeMarco. They were sitting in Tony's living room, Tony in a brown La-Z-Boy that faced a television set too big for the room. There was a green oxygen tank next to the recliner and clear plastic tubing fed the gas to his nose. A sour smell permeated the room, a smell DeMarco couldn't identify; maybe it was the smell of a man decaying right before his eyes.

"It seems like everybody I know died from cancer," Tony said. "My wife, Carmine, Enzo Marciano. Carmine, it was his lungs, too. Enzo got skin cancer, which seems weird for a guy who lived like a vampire."

"Tell me what you know about my father," DeMarco said. He wasn't in the mood for a stroll down memory lane, nor was he in the mood for commiserating with Tony about his illness.

Mahoney had been pissed yesterday when DeMarco had told him he was flying to New York the following morning. Mahoney wanted him to pursue the veterans' scam not only because he genuinely cared about the issue but because it would generate favorable headlines, something that could matter in terms of him continuing to get reelected from his district. As a congressman with a two-year term, Mahoney was always running for reelection. So when DeMarco said it was a family thing and he had to go, Mahoney had said, "Well, can't it wait a couple of days?" A normal person would have asked: What's the problem? Can I do anything to help? Not Mahoney. He was too self-centered to care about any problems other than his own.

"No," DeMarco had said. As he was closing the door to Mahoney's office, he heard Mahoney yell, "Hey!" Whatever he had said after that was muffled by the door, and DeMarco knew he was going to get a severe ass chewing the next time he saw his boss.

"The man who killed your father is a guy named Brian Quinn," Tony said, pausing every couple of words to get air into his lungs. It was painful watching him talk. "Carmine was the guy who ordered the hit."

"What?" DeMarco said.

"Yeah. And Quinn was a cop at the time. In fact, I guess you could say he still is."

While DeMarco was still trying to get his head around the fact that his father's boss was the one who had him killed, Tony proceeded to tell DeMarco the whole story. He told him about Jerry Kennedy and why Kennedy had to be killed and how Carmine forced Quinn to kill him. He also told DeMarco how Carmine got his hooks into Quinn in the first place—about a woman seeing Quinn shoot an unarmed man and how the NYPD had covered up the shooting. Lastly, he told him how Carmine had set up Gino DeMarco so Quinn could ambush him.

It took Tony almost an hour to tell the story because DeMarco kept interrupting to make sure he understood all the details. By the time Tony finished, the old man could barely keep his eyes open, exhausted by the effort of speaking for so long.

As Tony sat there with his eyes shut, struggling to get air into his ravaged lungs, DeMarco was remembering his father's funeral and how Carmine Taliaferro had lied to him. "I swear on the heads of my wife and daughter," Carmine had said when DeMarco asked him if he knew who'd killed his father. He also remembered that Tony had been standing right next to Carmine that day.

"How long have you known about this?" DeMarco asked.

Benedetto opened his eyes. "I don't know, exactly. All the stuff about Quinn sort of came out, bit by bit, over the years. Some I learned from Enzo, some from Carmine. But I didn't learn about Carmine setting up your dad to be killed until just before Carmine died. At the end, when Carmine was in worse shape than I'm in now, he was taking lots of drugs for the pain, and I'm not even sure he knew what he was saying half the time."

Carmine Taliaferro had died eight years ago at the age of eighty-two—which meant that Tony had known about Gino DeMarco's killer all that time. DeMarco felt like ripping the oxygen tubes out of Tony's big nose and watching him slowly suffocate.

"So why'd you decide to tell me now?" DeMarco asked.

"Aw, you know. It's time to make things right before I—"

"Do you know anything else Quinn did for Taliaferro?" DeMarco asked, interrupting Tony. It didn't really matter why Tony had suddenly grown a conscience, but DeMarco was wondering if there was any way to prove that Quinn had been in collusion with Carmine on other matters. He knew it was pretty unlikely that he'd be able to prove that Quinn had killed his dad.

"No, nothing for sure," Tony said. "All I know is, after Jerry Kennedy and your dad were killed, Carmine never had a major problem with the law and he made millions, mostly off dope, and he didn't share much with anybody else. I just remember we were sitting in a bar one day and Quinn was on the TV, and Carmine laughed and said, 'I own that mick prick.'"

"What did he mean?" DeMarco asked.

"I don't know what he meant. I just know what he said."

"And why was Quinn on television?"

"He's on all the time. I thought you'd know who he was as soon as I said his name. Brian Quinn is the commissioner of the NYPD."

"You gotta be shittin' me!" DeMarco said. It had never occurred to him that Tony meant *that* Brian Quinn. It was bad enough to learn that his father's killer was a cop but now he knew he wasn't just any cop: he was the most powerful cop in New York.

"Do you have any idea if Carmine was bribing Quinn?" DeMarco asked. He was thinking that maybe some of Carmine's money could be traced to Quinn.

"Maybe, but I doubt it," Tony said. "Based on what he said about how he owned the guy, it sounded like he was probably blackmailing him or something. But I don't know for sure. I do know that Carmine didn't pay people unless he had to." Before DeMarco could respond, Tony laughed and said, "All the money Carmine had, he still lived in that same little house in Queens just a couple blocks from your mom's place and I don't think he bought a new piece of furniture after his wife died. He had a nice place down in Florida, a condo he went to in the winter, but the house in Queens . . . I guess he just didn't see the point in moving. His daughter ended up with all his money. She and her husband own a bunch a businesses—legit ones, as far as I know—and she's a big-shot politician now."

DeMarco didn't care about Taliaferro's daughter, but if she was big in politics it must be something local because he'd never heard of her.

DeMarco sat for a moment just listening to the sound of Tony breathing, and wondered what he should do next. Only one thing occurred to him. "The woman who saw Quinn shoot that guy in the alley, the paint store guy, is she still alive?" DeMarco asked.

"As far as I know," Tony said. "But if you're thinking you can get her to testify against Quinn, you're dreaming. I mean, that happened almost twenty years ago. Who's going to believe her coming forward now and especially when you look at all the things Quinn's done since then?"

"What's the woman's name?" DeMarco asked.

"All I remember is Janet something. You'd have to ask Sal Anselmo. I know he's still alive. He's just a little older than you. He's straight now, sells cars out on the island."

DeMarco rose to leave. He started to tell Tony that if he wasn't a frail old man, he'd beat the shit out of him, then figured: Why bother? He turned and headed for the door, but before he reached it, Tony said, "Kid, the only way you're going to be able to make things right is if you become who your dad was. What I mean is, you're not going to get Quinn by going after him with some bullshit legal thing. You're going to have to kill him. You think you got the stones for that?"

DeMarco didn't answer. He didn't know the answer.

15

After DeMarco left, Tony wondered if he'd done the right thing telling DeMarco that Quinn had killed his father. Maybe he shouldn't have, but if somebody had killed *his* old man, he'd want to know.

He could tell DeMarco was pissed because he hadn't told him years ago, right after Carmine died, but at that time there was no way he was going to put himself in a position where some lawyer could subpoena him to testify against Quinn. Now he didn't care about a subpoena; he'd be dead before they could drag him into a courtroom.

The other thing was, he'd never liked Quinn—Quinn was a prick—and he had liked Gino DeMarco, although he hadn't really known him all that well. Gino never had much to do with the rest of the guys on Carmine's crew; he didn't drink with them or go with them down to AC to play craps or on those fishing trips they used to take to the Bahamas. If you didn't know he was Carmine's button man, you'd think he was a civilian, like a guy punching the clock at a factory. But Tony had respected Gino, and if his kid could cause Quinn problems, that would be sweet. It was a shame that he probably wouldn't be around to see what happened. The thing was, he didn't think Joe DeMarco would be able to do anything about Quinn unless he whacked the guy and he doubted, like he'd said to Joe before he left, that he had the stones to do that. But then you never know.

The phone rang but Tony didn't reach for it immediately. Talking to DeMarco had just worn his ass out; it felt like he had gone ten rounds with fuckin' Tyson. If the phone had been across the room he wouldn't have bothered, but since it was right next to his chair and kept ringing, he reached out slowly and picked it up. He hoped it wasn't DeMarco calling to ask more questions.

"Yeah," he said.

"Pop, it's me. It's Anthony. I'm in a lot of trouble, Pop."

Aw, jeez. That's the last thing he needed right now.

Anthony Benedetto Jr. had always been a loser. Tony didn't know what he and his wife had done wrong, but Junior just didn't seem to have anything going for him. He wasn't very bright, and he did awful in school. He didn't have the size or the athletic ability to play sports. Tony had known teenage girls tougher than his son.

He'd tried his best to steer the kid into a straight job, but Junior couldn't to do anything right. For a while, Tony had let him manage an apartment building he had in Woodside—all Junior had to do was collect the rents and call the maintenance guy when something broke— but then Tony had to fire him after he stole all the rent money one month and spent it on dope.

Junior was a junkie, and had been one since he was fourteen—and he was forty-two now. He was addicted to booze and pills and anything he could snort or smoke, but especially cocaine. Tony had stuck him in treatment places three times but they didn't do any good, and after his wife died, Tony just gave up on him.

"So what's the goddamn problem this time?" Tony said.

16

DeMarco's head was spinning, his mind flooded with thoughts of his father, with things he hadn't thought about in almost twenty years.

As much as he'd loved his father, he had never made any attempt to track down his killer and avenge his death. Partly this was because at the time his father died, he was young and didn't have either the skills or the connections to do something like that. But there was also another reason. Over time, he had come to accept what the newspapers had said: that Gino DeMarco had been Carmine Taliaferro's enforcer.

Joe had called Detective Lynch one time—the detective who had informed him and his mother about his father's death—and asked Lynch who was feeding the papers this crap that his father was a hit man. Lynch, who he found out worked in Organized Crime, not Homicide, had said that even though he was never able to obtain the evidence needed for a conviction, he knew—he was positive—based on logic, circumstantial evidence, and hearsay testimony, that Gino DeMarco had been a killer. "The only good thing I can say about your old man," Lynch had told Joe, "was that as near as we can tell, he only whacked other hoods. But he whacked 'em. There's no doubt about that." Joe had called Lynch a liar and slammed down the phone—but in his heart, he knew the man hadn't been lying.

Joe never forgot one night, when he was about twelve or thirteen. He couldn't sleep and heard someone down in the basement and discovered it was his dad, wearing just a sleeveless T-shirt, washing his hands in the basement sink. It looked as if he'd cut himself and was washing away the blood from the cut, and lying on the floor was a shirt Joe had given him for Father's Day splattered with more blood. But Gino didn't have a cut on his hand.

Joe had said, "What did you do, Dad? Are you okay?" Gino whipped around, surprised to see him there, and said, "Go back to bed, Joe. Right now." That's all he'd said but he looked ashamed—like Joe had caught him doing something wrong. He'd never seen a look like that on his father's face before. For days afterward, his father barely spoke to him and his mother, and Joe never saw the shirt again although he knew it had been one of his dad's favorites and his mom could have washed out the blood.

He remembered, too, the times when his father seemed to throw himself into chores around the house, as if he was trying to drive out his demons by working himself to a state of exhaustion. One time he replaced the entire drainage system around the house, replacing all the pipes that led from the downspouts to a dry well in the backyard, and he dug the trenches by hand when he could have rented a machine. It was like he wanted to work with a pick and shovel so it would take longer to finish the job. When Joe had asked his mother why his dad was replacing all the pipes, his mom had snapped at him and said: "Don't ask. Go do your homework."

Joe had created a fantasy for himself when he was a kid. He'd convinced himself that his dad was nothing more than Carmine Taliaferro's protector and that he'd never been involved in the truly criminal things that Carmine had been accused of doing. He now knew that what he'd been trying to do was reconcile in his own mind how a person he admired so deeply could have been something less than admirable.

None of this, however, changed DeMarco's feelings for his father. He still loved and missed the man. He could still remember the way Gino's eyes used to light up when he saw Joe after they'd been apart for a while. But he'd come to accept that Gino had been the man Lynch said he was, and so although he never stopped loving him, he quit pushing the cops to find Gino's killer and moved on with his life.

Now things were different. Now he knew his father's death had been an act of treachery engineered by his own employer. And more important than Carmine's duplicity, the man who'd killed his dad wasn't some common mafia hood. Brian Quinn was a cop who had reached the pinnacle of his profession because of the way he had supposedly dedicated his life to the law. Joe couldn't accept that the man who ran the most celebrated police force in the country was as much of a criminal as his father had been.

On the other hand, he couldn't figure out what he could possibly do to make Quinn pay for his crimes. He had no intention of doing what Tony had said: there was no way he was going to kill Brian Quinn. He knew if did he'd most likely end up in jail, and he wasn't willing to sacrifice his own life to avenge his father's death.

The other thing was, Joe didn't know if he could kill Quinn. He'd killed while working for John Mahoney, but those had been acts of self-defense, not cold-blooded murder. He'd never *executed* anyone. He also knew, however, that the likelihood of Quinn being convicted for his father's murder was practically zero. It had all happened too long ago, and based on what Tony had told him, the only person who could possibly testify against Quinn was Carmine Taliaferro, who was now rotting in a grave.

So DeMarco had two choices: either do nothing or figure out a way to destroy Brian Quinn's life—and doing nothing was intolerable.

DeMarco took a cab to One Police Plaza, where the commissioner of the NYPD had his office. He didn't go into the building, however. In fact, he wasn't even sure why he went to 1PP other than a desire to see Quinn. He just wanted to put his eyeballs on the guy.

He found a coffee shop where he could see the entryway to 1PP, not having a clue if Quinn was in the building and, if he was, if he would even leave by the front entrance. While he waited, he took out his phone and went online to learn more about the man.

Being a New Yorker, DeMarco knew that NYPD commissioners ran the gamut from the despicable to the extraordinary. President Theodore Roosevelt had once been the leader of New York's finest. A number had been blatantly corrupt, the most recent example being Quinn's predecessor, who had been indicted on sixteen federal counts and sentenced to four years in prison.

Quinn, at least according to Wikipedia and the *New York Times*, had been an exceptional cop: he'd busted high-profile criminals, received multiple commendations for valor and outstanding acts of public service. He was given credit—at least by the *Times*—for reducing violent crimes in all five boroughs and was reported to be progressive, innovative, and completely intolerant of any corruption within his ranks. His greatest achievement was building an extremely competent, high-tech antiterrorism division that he claimed was better than anything the federal government had.

The final thing DeMarco learned in his Internet wanderings was that Quinn was speaking that afternoon at a symposium on counter-terrorism at Columbia University; cops from around the globe were attending the event.

DeMarco tried to get inside the auditorium to hear Quinn speak, but was informed that the event wasn't open to the general public. Maybe the organizers were worried about terrorists showing up to get some insight into how the cops would eventually catch them.

To attend the lecture, you had to be in law enforcement, politics, or journalism, and attendees had to register in advance.

DeMarco, having no better idea what to do, decided to hang around outside the building where Quinn was giving his speech; an hour later he was rewarded for his patience when he saw Quinn leave the building in the company of his security people. Quinn hopped into a black SUV illegally parked at the curb and took off, and DeMarco got lucky, caught a passing cab, and followed Quinn to the Carlyle hotel.

DeMarco took a seat at the long black granite bar in the Carlyle. He could see Quinn and another man seated in a chocolate-colored leather banquette thirty feet away. The other man was the president's chief of staff, a political warhorse who had been trampling other politicians with his big hoofs for thirty years. DeMarco had no idea why the president's chief was in New York talking to Quinn. Sitting two tables away from Quinn was his security detail, two guys in suits built like light heavyweights. They made no attempt to conceal the pistols they carried in shoulder holsters.

Quinn was tall and lean—he looked like a man who jogged every day—and although DeMarco knew Quinn was only a couple years older than him, Quinn's hair was completely gray. He had a handsome, rugged profile and his gray hair made him look distinguished and older than he was; it wasn't hard to imagine him commanding the largest, most renowned police department in the country.

But now what? How could he possibly destroy a man who had after-work drinks with the president's right-hand man?

Half an hour later, DeMarco decided that not only was he wasting his time watching Quinn, but the urge to do something stupid—like walk over and confront Quinn and maybe smash a fist into his arrogant face—was becoming overwhelming. It was time to leave.

As he was leaving he glanced over at Quinn again and this time Quinn noticed him and they briefly made eye contact. It may have been DeMarco's imagination but he thought Quinn looked startled, as if he recognized DeMarco. Or as if he were seeing a ghost.

17

DeMarco spent the night at his mother's place in Queens, sleeping in the room where he'd slept as a boy. Trophies from athletic events and framed certificates earned for minor achievements when he was a kid were no longer proudly displayed in the room; knowing his mom, those objects were carefully packed away in a box in the attic. He had no doubt she'd saved the trophies. The only thing that remained in the bedroom from when he was young was a picture of him and his dad, on the nightstand next to the bed. In the photo, he was dressed in full catcher's regalia—chest protector, shin guards, the mask tilted back on his head—and his father was standing beside him holding a baseball in the air. The day the picture had been taken, he'd just made the game-ending out, diving for a pop-up, and his dad was beaming like his son was the MVP in the World Series.

He lied to his mom about why he was in New York, just saying that Mahoney had sent him up to see a guy. His mom didn't care; she was just glad to see her son. Her hair was completely gray now and thinning a bit, and her face had wrinkles appropriate to her age. Had she been able to afford it, Maureen DeMarco still wouldn't have opted for a facelift or Botox. She thought people who did that sort of thing were silly and vain. She'd always been thin and now she seemed frail, but as far as DeMarco knew she was in perfect health. Her mom, DeMarco's maternal grandmother, had lived to ninety-two and he wouldn't be surprised if his mom lived at least that long.

Financially, she was doing okay. She'd been worried how she was going to survive after Gino was killed but found out that her husband had a half-million-dollar life insurance policy and had been paying the premiums on the policy for years. Back in those days, half a million was a lot of money. When the claims adjuster read the articles in the *New York Post* claiming that Gino DeMarco had been a hit man for the mob, he initially refused to settle the claim because he said Gino had lied about his occupation. On the insurance forms, Gino had written that he was a "property manager"—the same lie his mother used to tell when people asked what her husband did for a living. The life insurance company had a change of heart when Carmine Taliaferro's own lawyer paid the claims adjuster a visit, pointing out that numerous people would swear that Gino DeMarco had indeed been Taliaferro's property manager and that Gino had never been convicted for a crime. Carmine, the heartless prick, must have figured that he owed Maureen DeMarco that much.

After she collected from the insurance company, Maureen went to see his Aunt Connie and she steered his mother to an honest financial adviser, and between her investments and Social Security, Maureen DeMarco was doing okay. She was still living in the house that she and Gino lived in when they first got married, which she now owned outright. So his mom was doing all right. She never dated after his father died but she did charity work, helped out in a boutique during the Christmas season, and had friends at the church she still attended. She wasn't lonely, but on the other hand, she didn't seem particularly happy. But then, DeMarco could never remember her being all that happy. She was still, however, one of the best Italian cooks in Queens and DeMarco dined well that night.

DeMarco did his best not to let his mother see that something was bothering him, and tried to keep the conversation on her and what she'd been doing. There was no way he was going to tell her about his discussion with Tony Benedetto. He asked about his Aunt Connie—as old as she was, she still had a boyfriend—and his mother asked, as she always did, who he was dating. They were both starting to believe that he would never give her a grandchild, and he could tell that bothered her more deeply than she was willing to admit. He claimed he was tired and went to bed early. He didn't sleep. He spent the night thinking about how to destroy Brian Quinn.

———————

After Joe went to bed, Maureen DeMarco poured a glass of red wine—the last few years she'd started drinking a glass before she went to bed—and took a seat in the living room, in the recliner where Gino used to sit. She didn't know why she'd kept the recliner all these years; she'd even had it reupholstered once. Normally, she watched the news before she went to bed, but not tonight. Tonight she did what Gino used to do: she just sat there in the dark.

Something was bothering her son, she had no idea what, but something was weighing heavily on his mind. She didn't think it was a woman. He usually told her when he was having girlfriend problems. It could be his job, of course. She knew from talking to Connie the kind of stuff he did for that devil, Mahoney. She'd told him he should find a normal job—he had a law degree, for crying out loud, and he must have met some people down in Washington by now who could steer him toward something decent—but every time she brought the subject up, he always said work was going fine and he liked what he did. He was still such a liar.

She'd spent twenty-seven years with a man who wouldn't talk to her and kept things from her, and although her son talked to her more than Gino used to, he was basically the same way. She didn't understand it.

Was Joe trying to protect her? Was he trying to keep her from worrying? Why couldn't the DeMarco men understand that her not knowing was worse than anything they could possibly tell her.

———◆◆◆———

The next morning DeMarco rented a car and drove out to Long Island. Sal Anselmo worked at a Mazda dealership in Wantagh. DeMarco didn't know what Anselmo had looked like when he was a thug working for Tony Benedetto and Carmine Taliaferro, but now he looked like . . . Hell, he looked like a used car salesman.

Anselmo was five foot ten and packing thirty pounds too many. He had a perfect head of thick, dark hair that DeMarco was sure was a toupee, and his teeth were so white they were either false or had been dipped in bleach. He was wearing black loafers, black slacks, and a purple shirt with a matching purple tie. Imagine a Concord grape exposing its teeth as it strained to please.

When DeMarco walked into Anselmo's office, Anselmo rocked back in his chair and said, "Jesus."

Because DeMarco looked so much like his father, he was used to this reaction from people who had known his dad. He suspected Brian Quinn had noticed the resemblance when he saw DeMarco at the Carlyle.

"I'm Joe DeMarco, Gino's son," DeMarco said.

"Thank God," Anselmo said. "For a minute there . . ."

"Yeah, I get it. Tony Benedetto sent me."

DeMarco said that to simplify things. He figured telling Anselmo that he'd been sent by Benedetto was the easiest way to get Anselmo to cooperate.

"You're working for Tony? I thought he was retired."

"Not exactly. And I don't have time to explain things to you."

"Well, I don't know what you want, but let me tell you something. I'm completely legit now and no way am I going to get involved again with—"

DeMarco cut him off. "You used to go out with a teacher named Janet something. She was your mistress and she saw a cop kill an unarmed man in an alley. She told you, and you told Tony. I want to know Janet's last name and where she lives."

Anselmo didn't say anything for a minute. "I don't know. That was a long time ago and I'm not sure I feel like digging up the past."

"Sal, let me explain something to you. The mood I'm in right now, I'm about two seconds away from dragging you out from behind that desk and beating the shit out of you."

DeMarco knew what Anselmo was now thinking: he had no idea what Joe DeMarco did for a living, but he was probably figuring that the apple didn't fall far from the tree. All he knew for sure was that here was a guy who was a carbon copy of the deadliest killer he'd ever known.

"Just take it easy," Anselmo said. "I'll tell you, but I don't want this coming back at me. I'm still married and I don't want my wife hearing about Janet. I also don't want to get involved in whatever you and Tony are into."

DeMarco didn't say that the only thing Tony was into was catching his next breath of air. He didn't say anything. He just stared at Anselmo.

"Anyway," Anselmo said, "her last name is Costello. I haven't seen her in ten years but last I heard, she was still teaching at a grade school in Queens."

———◆———

Janet Costello might have been an attractive, sexy schoolteacher when Sal Anselmo was having an affair with her, but time had not been kind to her. One reason why, DeMarco suspected, was booze. He could smell the wine on her breath when she asked who he was and why he was knocking on her apartment door.

She was short and dumpy looking—broad hips and swollen ankles—and, like her ex-boyfriend, a few pounds overweight. Her hair was a mousy brown color and fixed in a frizzy, unruly perm. It appeared as if someone had painted two bright red spots on her cheeks the size of silver dollars, but the color was due to broken veins, not rouge.

DeMarco was willing to bet that she was the type of drunk who got through the school day by taking little nips from a bottle hidden in her purse and ingested breath mints continuously to disguise the odor. Once she got home at night, she probably went through a couple of bottles of cheap vino, whatever brand she could afford on a teacher's salary. He also imagined she was still employed because she had tenure and because there were probably worse teachers in the New York City school system. God help those kids.

"Ms. Costello, my name's Joe DeMarco and I need to talk to you. This has to do with something you saw when you were dating Sal Anselmo."

"What?" she said. "Who's Sal Anselmo?"

"You know who he is. He was your boyfriend and after you saw Brian Quinn shoot an unarmed man, you called him. I know this because I've talked to Sal."

"That idiot," she muttered. Then she asked, "Are you a cop?" Before DeMarco could answer, she said, "Look. I told you the last time Quinn sent people to lean on me, I wasn't going to say anything."

What the hell?

"No, I'm not a cop, Ms. Costello. I work for Congress and I'm investigating Quinn."

"Congress?"

"Yeah." DeMarco took out his ID and showed it her. "Can I come in and talk to you? Please."

The apartment was a small, cluttered, one bedroom affair. The furniture was mismatched, yard sale quality. Her TV set was an older model, a big, boxy thing, not one of the new flat screens. A few paperbacks in a low-standing bookcase were covered with a layer of dust.

The jacket she'd worn that day was draped over a chair near a small table near her kitchen, and the kitchen was the size of a galley in a not-so-big boat. There was a dish on the table that had the smeared remains of her dinner and lying on the kitchen counter was the box the dinner came in: Salisbury Steak Lean Cuisine.

She pointed him to a small couch and she took a seat at one of the two chairs near the dining room table. "I don't know what Sal told you but—"

"Ms. Costello, let me explain something to you. If you're called to testify in court or in a congressional hearing and if you lie, you'll be convicted of perjury and you'll go to jail. Perjury's a felony. I don't know what the laws are in New York for teaching positions, but I imagine if you have a conviction you'll lose your job. Now, will you tell me the truth? And maybe you'll never be asked to testify and everything could end right here, but it won't end here if you lie to me."

"Goddamnit, what do you want to know?"

"I want you to confirm that what I've been told is true: that you saw Brian Quinn shoot an unarmed man, that Quinn stuck a gun in the man's hand, and that the police brushed the whole thing under the rug."

"Yeah, it's true, but—"

"What did you mean when you said 'the last time Quinn sent people to lean on' you?"

"Would you like a glass of wine?"

"Uh, no thanks, but go ahead if you want one." He didn't think she was stalling; she just needed alcohol.

She walked over to the refrigerator, pulled out a bottle of white wine, and filled a glass almost to the brim. After she'd taken a long swallow—like she was drinking water—she said, "I used to go to bars after Sal dumped me. You know, singles bars."

DeMarco nodded.

"I'd go hoping to pick up some guy, and if the subject of New York cops came up, sometimes I'd tell people what I saw. I'd say, hey, let me tell you just how dirty the damn cops can be. I don't think most people believed me when I told them what Quinn had done, or they would just pretend to believe me, depending on if they wanted to go to bed with me or not. But one night, this was right after Quinn became the commissioner, I was in this bar and I probably had too much to drink and I told some lawyer my story.

"Two days later these two cops show up at the school and the principal calls me out of class to talk with them. They didn't tell the principal why they wanted to talk to me and later I told her some bullshit about having witnessed a robbery. I think they came to the school instead of my apartment just to show how much power they had and how they could fuck up my so-called life.

"Anyway, they took me into an empty classroom and told me they'd heard about me shooting my mouth off about Commissioner Quinn. I'd obviously talked to the wrong lawyer. I don't know how they got my name, though. I mean, when I would meet men in bars, I didn't tell them my last name until after we'd gone out on a regular date. But somehow these cops—they were big, hard-looking bastards and they scared the shit out of me—tracked me down. They told me that making unfounded accusations about the police commissioner, accusations that had no basis in fact, was a good way to get into a lot of trouble. I could be sued, for one thing. Or maybe the school would find out that I was a lush and hung out in bars and picked up married men, and some of those married men had mob connections. Or maybe, they said, the IRS would take a look at my tax returns. What they meant was, I worked as a part-time waitress in the summer sometimes, and naturally, like everybody else who worked at this place, I didn't declare my tips.

"I mean, it was apparent these guys had researched the shit out of me. By the time they left I was crying and one of them said, 'You got the picture now?' Since then, no matter how much I've had to drink, I say nothing about Brian Quinn."

"How well could you see Quinn that night?" DeMarco asked. "My source told me you were sitting on a balcony that overlooked the alley where Connors was shot."

"The balcony was on the third floor and I used to sit on it because the landlord wouldn't let me smoke in the apartment. And I didn't actually see Quinn shoot Connors—I heard the shot—but when he came running down the alley to check if the guy was dead, then I could see him. I couldn't see his face because it was pretty dark and he was wearing a cop's hat and I was looking down at the top of his hat, but I could see what he did. I saw him pull a gun out of an ankle holster and put it in the guy's hand and throw this can under a Dumpster. If he'd looked up, he would have seen me. But he didn't. When another cop came down the alley—Quinn's partner, I guess—I scooted back into my apartment."

"Then how'd you know it was Quinn?"

"Because the papers said it was him."

DeMarco didn't have any other questions he could think of and he rose to leave. "Thank you, Ms. Costello. Someone will contact you if necessary."

Costello started crying. "You goddamn people are going to ruin my life. All I've got is my shitty job and if I testify against Quinn I can guarantee you that he'll come after me and I'll get fired. I'm no lawyer, but I know damn good and well that you'll never get Quinn if it's just my word against the word of the entire police department."

DeMarco hated to admit it, but he knew she was probably right.

18

DeMarco knew from talking to Tony Benedetto and Janet Costello that Quinn had a partner the night he shot the paint store guy, Connors. He wanted to find Quinn's partner. He went to the New York Public Library and used one of their computers to search back issues of the *New York Times, New York Post,* and *New York Daily News.*

It took him two hours to learn that Quinn's partner was a man named Stanley Dombroski; Quinn got all the press coverage for shooting Connors, and his partner's name was only mentioned in one sentence, in one article, and never mentioned again after that. He checked the white pages online and discovered there were five Stanley or S. Dombroskis in the greater New York area. He figured if he called the NYPD and asked the cops to give him the home address of the Dombroski he was trying to find, they'd tell him to go shit in his hat. Frustrated, he called a man in D.C. named Neil and said, "Find this fuckin' guy for me."

Twenty minutes later he learned that the Dombroski he wanted was now retired and lived on the Jersey shore in a town with the lovely name of Brick.

After spending his evening at the library, DeMarco got a room in a Manhattan hotel—he didn't feel like staying with his mom again. His knew his mother was astute enough to realize that something was bothering him, and he didn't want to spend the evening evading her questions or causing her to worry about him. He spent a couple of hours in the hotel bar, drinking slowly, munching on peanuts, stewing over what to do about Brian Quinn.

While he stewed, he occasionally looked up at the television over the bar. It was showing game seven of the National League Championship Series and the winner would play in the World Series. The only baseball teams DeMarco cared about were the New York Mets and the Washington Nationals, and since neither team was playing, he didn't care who won. What he thought about instead were all the times he and his dad had gone to watch the Mets at the old Shea Stadium, and how that had always been a huge deal for him as a kid. He'd loved going to those games with his dad. Shea Stadium was gone now, replaced by a beautiful ballpark with the horrible name of Citi Field. DeMarco suspected his father wouldn't like it any more than he did that ballparks were now being named after banks, businesses, and insurance companies.

The next morning, DeMarco rented a car and drove to Dombroski's house in Brick, New Jersey, which was located in a neighborhood where about half the homeowners maintained their dwellings and the other half did not. Small, well-tended lawns were adjacent to weed-filled lots; houses with clean, freshly painted siding stood beside homes that hadn't seen paint in two decades. Dombroski's house was sort of in the middle in terms of appearance: no dandelions in the front lawn, but the paint on the door was peeling and DeMarco was surprised the roof had survived Hurricane Sandy.

DeMarco rang the doorbell but no one answered. He was thinking about leaving and coming back later when an old lady he hadn't noticed called out, "He's in the backyard." He hadn't seen Dombroski's next-door neighbor because, sitting down, she was so short her head was barely taller than the railing around her porch.

He walked around the house and found Dombroski in a plastic lawn chair sipping a beer. Next to his chair were two empty beer bottles and a cooler probably containing full ones. A radio on top of the cooler was tuned to a sports talk show and some guy was going on and on about the Yankees failing to make it again to the World Series.

Dombroski was in his fifties, overweight, and red-faced from booze or sun or both. He was wearing an unbuttoned blue denim shirt over a white, V-necked T-shirt and khaki shorts with cargo pockets. His big feet were shod in flip-flops. DeMarco thought it was a bit cool for shorts and flip-flops but apparently not. Dombroski looked comfortable and content sitting there enjoying the ocean view.

DeMarco figured the view had to be the main reason why Dombroski had bought the house. The house itself was maybe twelve hundred square feet, and DeMarco had seen outhouses with more architectural appeal. It was essentially a small box with a roof and had windows so narrow they looked like gun ports. The backyard, however, was an unexpected jewel. It was only fifty feet wide and thirty feet deep, enclosed by a tilting cedar fence, but the grass was a lush green carpet and the view of the Atlantic, over the rooftops of the people who lived on the next block, was outstanding. DeMarco could see the beach from where he stood and the breakers hitting the shore.

"Mr. Dombroski?" DeMarco said. DeMarco wasn't exactly sure how to approach Dombroski. He wanted him to divulge nasty information about a onetime partner and he knew that the thin blue line of the NYPD held together against outsiders. But he had to try.

Dombroski looked over at him. "Yeah. Who are you?"

"My name's DeMarco and I want to talk to you about Brian Quinn."

Dombroski turned off the radio and said, "Is that right. Are you from the Vatican? Are they thinking about canonizing the bastard now?"

Maybe the thin blue line had a few gaps in it.

"Not exactly," DeMarco said.

DeMarco decided to tell Dombroski an abbreviated version of the truth: he said he worked for Congress and was investigating Quinn.

"Why?" Dombroski asked.

"He's being considered for a federal position. I can't say which one as an official announcement hasn't been made." DeMarco had no idea when he told this lie how prophetic that statement would turn out to be. "Anyway, I've been asked to do a background check and I've learned something disturbing I need to ask you about."

"So ask," Dombroski said. "There's another chair over there by the door. And help yourself to a beer if you want one."

DeMarco placed his chair next to Dombroski's so he, too, could enjoy the view. He popped the top on a Budweiser, took a sip, and said that during the course of his investigation he'd come to believe that when Quinn was a rookie, he shot a man named Connors, lied about Connors being armed, and then the department covered up what had really occurred.

"Ya think?" Dombroski said and laughed—and DeMarco wondered how drunk Dombroski was. He was also wondering if everything he told Dombroski would get back to Quinn. Nonetheless, he told Dombroski that the night Quinn shot the so-called cat burglar a woman had seen him put a gun in the man's hand.

"You're shittin' me!" Dombroski said. "Why didn't this broad come forward when it happened?"

"She was afraid to," DeMarco said. "She figured the department would protect one of its own and maybe come after her."

Dombroski made an expression that DeMarco interpreted as *She was right about that.*

"So what are you looking for, bud?" Dombroski asked.

"I want to know if a cover-up occurred."

"You bet one did. I knew Quinn had planted a gun on that guy and so did everyone involved in the shooting investigation. But Quinn had people pulling for him even back then."

"Why didn't you say something?"

"Because, for one thing, Quinn was my partner and rattin' out your partner is usually frowned upon in police circles. The other thing was, I was dumb enough to think that helping Quinn might be good for my career. I'd been on the force for ten years before I was partnered with him and I was still driving around in a patrol car and working nights. But I knew Quinn was going places—everyone who knew him could tell he was going to rise to the top—and I knew he didn't shoot the guy on purpose. I figured if I kept my mouth shut, Quinn would give me a hand up the ladder one day. Well, he didn't. As soon as he was cleared by the shooting board, he asked for a new partner and never had anything to do with me again. I approached him a couple of times and sort of gently reminded him that he owed me, but the bastard just looked at me like I was lower than rat shit. He knew it was too late for me to change my story."

"Did you actually see him put the gun in Connors's hand?"

"No. By the time I reached Connors's body, he was already holding a gun. The thing was, the gun looked exactly like Quinn's backup piece, this little .32. I thought for a minute about asking Quinn to show me his backup gun but decided not to. I just decided to go along. So what do you want, DeMarco?"

"I want you to testify that you thought it was a bad shooting and improperly investigated." Before Dombroski could object, DeMarco added, "I realize the shooting board cleared him and that you don't have any evidence, but if I can get this other witness to testify—the woman who saw Quinn put the gun in Connors's hand—whatever you have to say will add weight to her testimony."

"Testify to who?" Dombroski asked. "If you think the department is going to reopen an investigation into a shooting that involved the current police commissioner, you're fuckin' nuts."

"I'm talking about testifying in front of a congressional committee."

DeMarco had absolutely no idea how he could get Congress to investigate a man who drank with the president's chief of staff—not when his star witnesses were people like Tony Benedetto, Sal Anselmo, Janet Costello, and Stan Dombroski. He'd worry about that small detail later.

Dombroski looked at DeMarco for a moment, then spread his arms in a gesture meant to take in his small domain. "Look around, my friend. This is as good as it's ever going to get for me. I never even made sergeant when I was on the force—I don't test too well—and that means I don't have a king-sized pension. Then there's the fact that my wife divorced me five years ago. She said I was *stifling* her, whatever the fuck that means, and she now gets half of my pension. Lucky for me, my mom died a couple years ago and . . . That came out wrong. My mom was a good woman. Anyway, when my mom died I got her house and I was able to sell it and get this place. It ain't much, but it's what I got. I sit here and I enjoy the view and I drink. I take walks on the beach; I go surf fishing when I'm in the mood. I bowl with some other fat retired guys once a week. That's my life and it sucks but I'm not going to jeopardize what I have by making an enemy out of Brian Quinn. But good luck to you, and I wish you the best."

"You can be compelled to testify, Mr. Dombroski."

"So compel me," Dombroski said.

"And if you commit perjury you'll go to jail."

"Why would I perjure myself? You never heard of the Fifth Amendment?" Lowering the pitch of his voice, pretending he was speaking from the witness chair, Dombroski said, "I decline to answer that question, Your Honor, as answering it might incriminate my fat ass."

DeMarco caught a shuttle back to D.C. that evening having no idea how he was going to deal with Quinn—short of simply killing the man.

19

DeMarco parked across from a narrow four-story building perched on the banks of the Potomac. Across the river, he could see the Pentagon. He also wasn't that far away from the Washington Harbour, where, only a short time ago, he'd sat a contented man.

He took the elevator to the fourth floor of the building—the only floor in the building where the names of the occupants weren't identified on the reader board in the lobby. The fourth floor was the domain of a man named Neil, the same Neil he'd called when he was trying to find Stan Dombroski.

Neil called himself an information broker and DeMarco had used his services many times in the past. Neil's rates were dear but if you could afford his fees—and the U.S. Treasury could—Neil would happily tell you anything you wanted to know about your fellow citizens. Most often Neil was able to get what his clients wanted by bribing people who work in places that warehouse information on American citizens: the IRS, Google, banks, telephone, and credit card companies. If necessary, however, Neil and one of his associates—a young black man named Bobby Prentiss, who rarely spoke—had the skills to slip through firewalls as if they didn't exist and pull information out of whichever computer system might contain whatever you wished to know.

Neil was sitting behind his desk, partially hidden by three computer monitors. He was dressed as he was almost every time DeMarco had seen him: a bright Hawaiian shirt, baggy shorts, and sandals. He was tapping with one hand on a keyboard while his other hand was stuffing a Reuben into his face, sauerkraut dropping unnoticed onto the surface of his desk.

"Ah, DeMarco," he said with his mouth full. "What favor does my government ask of me today?"

DeMarco didn't bother to point out that Neil didn't do *favors*— unless you called charging people an exorbitant amount of money for an illegal service a favor. He also didn't point out that the U.S. government was rarely involved in any legitimate capacity when DeMarco called upon Neil. DeMarco wasn't in the mood for banter.

"I want everything you can get me on a man named Brian Quinn. And I mean everything."

What DeMarco was hoping was that if Neil burrowed into Quinn's life he'd find something tying Quinn to Carmine Taliaferro. He particularly wanted Neil to look at Quinn's finances. As rich as Carmine Taliaferro had been, maybe some of the mobster's money could be traced to Quinn. DeMarco firmly believed that everyone has secrets—no exceptions— and Neil was the man to find Brian Quinn's.

"Okay," Neil said. "It might take me a couple of days before I can get to it as I'm in the middle of something right now, but . . ."

"Drop whatever you're doing and raise your fee accordingly." DeMarco had no idea how he was going to pay Neil's fee. He'd worry about that later.

"That sounds fair," Neil said, pretending he was a reasonable, agreeable fellow as opposed to the greedy shit he really was. "But can you give me just a little more information about Mr. Quinn. Like maybe an address or date of birth. You know, something to distinguish him from a few million other Irishmen who might bear the same name."

"Yeah," DeMarco said. "He's the commissioner of the NYPD."

"Oh," Neil said.

Neil put his half-eaten Reuben down on his desk and looked at De-Marco with a serious expression on his face. Serious wasn't normally part of Neil's smart-assed demeanor.

"I can't do it, Joe. I'm sorry."

"What do you mean, you can't?"

"Joe, there are a couple of organizations that I don't mess with. One is the NSA. It's the largest intelligence organization in this country and they employ people who are smarter than me and a few who are even smarter than Bobby. If I started messing with their computer systems they'd catch me and then they'd squash me like a bug, and they'd do so without even breaking into a sweat. Another organization I don't screw with is the New York City Police Department."

Before DeMarco could object, Neil said, "The NYPD employs some of the brightest computer people in this country and if I tried to get information on Quinn that wasn't in the public domain, there's a very good chance I would stumble over some sort of security tripwire and the smart people Quinn employs would come after me. It's like that old Jim Croce song: You don't tug on Superman's cape."

"Brian Quinn isn't Superman," DeMarco said.

Neil extended his hands, a gesture meant to include his office. The gesture reminded DeMarco of the gesture Stanley Dombroski had made the day before regarding his backyard kingdom in Brick, New Jersey. "This is how I make my living, Joe, and as you know, a lot of what I do isn't legal. I have no intention of spending any part of my life in prison, nor do I have any intention of actually working for a living." Neil, a man who rarely swore, ended his diatribe with "Joe, I am not going to fuck with the commissioner of the NYPD for you. I wouldn't even do it for Emma."

20

Emma.

Emma was a retired spy, or at least she said she was retired. She'd worked for the DIA—the Defense Intelligence Agency—for almost thirty years. DeMarco met her years ago when he saved her life, an act that had more to do with luck than valor. He just happened to be in the right place at the right time, sitting in his car at Reagan National waiting to pick up a friend, and she jumped into his car and ordered him to drive before some Iranians could kill her. And at the time, she was supposedly already retired.

She'd helped him several times on his assignments in the past. The first time she helped him, it was because she appreciated what he had done for her. After that first time, however, she helped him most often, he suspected, because she was bored being a civilian. She was not only extremely bright but also had contacts in places like the Pentagon and the CIA, which often proved useful. She also knew people in several police departments, including the NYPD, because the military personnel she worked with during her career often became cops after they mustered out.

The funny thing was, as long as he'd known her, he still didn't really know all that much about her. She took an almost perverse delight in revealing as little about herself as she possibly could. Maybe there were secrets she couldn't tell because of what she'd spent her career doing, but he knew that her need for secrecy—or privacy—went beyond the classified nature of her previous employment. In fact, he'd learned more about her from talking to other people than from her.

She was very wealthy but wouldn't reveal the source of her wealth; he knew she hadn't made millions working for the government. He knew nothing about her background—her parents or where she came from—other than when she once slipped and admitted she'd gone to private schools when she was young. She was also gay; that was the one fact about herself that she didn't hide the way she hid everything else. When they buried her, DeMarco would make sure her tombstone said: *Here lies an enigma.*

When DeMarco called and said he needed to see her, she was just leaving her house.

"I'm taking golfing lessons," she said.

Emma had always been athletic. She ran marathons. She periodically kicked DeMarco's ass on the racquetball court. She'd never played golf, however; she'd often said that a game where you barely worked up a sweat didn't really count as a sport. The thought occurred to DeMarco that she might have finally chosen a game where he could actually beat her, since he'd been playing golf for years.

"What's going on?" she asked.

"I just found out the identity of the man who killed my father," DeMarco said.

"Oh," Emma said. She knew what DeMarco's father had been. She didn't say anything else for a moment, then said, "I'm taking a lesson over at the Army Navy Country Club in Arlington; it's my last lesson this year. Meet me at the clubhouse in two hours. I mean, unless whatever you have to say can't wait two hours, in which case I'll skip the lesson."

DeMarco didn't feel like waiting—he wanted to move on this thing—he wanted to move against Quinn—but he knew he was being unreasonable. "My dad's been dead for almost two decades. Two hours isn't going to make any difference."

Emma was practicing with a pitching wedge when DeMarco arrived at the golf course—and whatever fantasy he had about beating her at golf instantly evaporated. She was shooting at a little blue flag that was about fifty yards from where she was standing, and every ball she hit landed about two feet from the flag.

Emma was almost as tall as him—about five foot ten—and she wore her blond hair short so she wouldn't have to fuss with it. She was slim because she was fanatical about exercising and eating the way you were supposed to eat. With a golf club in her hand, she reminded DeMarco of a picture he'd once seen of the legendary Babe Zaharias.

When she noticed DeMarco, she said, "I want to hit a couple more drives and then we'll go up to the clubhouse."

She teed the ball up, plucked her driver from her bag—and DeMarco noticed she'd bought a set of clubs that cost about three times what his had. She addressed the ball, pulled back the driver in an easy, fluid motion, and smacked the ball about two hundred yards—straight as an arrow. *Sheesh*.

———— ◆◆◆ ————

DeMarco and Emma had little in common. She enjoyed classical music, the ballet, and all the highbrow arts; he preferred Springsteen, baseball, and HBO. They did, however, share one pleasure: they both liked a good, dry, vodka martini—so that's what they ordered.

"You've got nothing," she said when DeMarco told her everything that Tony Benedetto had told him. One thing about Emma was that she was a good listener; she paid attention to the details, and never forgot anything.

"Brian Quinn," Emma said, "is one of the most respected law enforcement people in this country. Maybe the most respected. The only witness to him killing Jerry Kennedy was your father, and he's dead. The only witness to Quinn shooting the paint store guy in the alley is a schoolteacher who drinks and who's been sitting on her story for years—a story, by the way, that conflicts with an official NYPD investigation into the shooting.

"As for Quinn's partner, based on what you've told me, he didn't actually see Quinn do anything wrong. He just suspects that a cover-up occurred and then didn't have the integrity to do anything about it. Lastly, you have a dying mobster who told you about Quinn killing your dad, a man who has zero credibility and not one bit of evidence to support his story."

"I realize all that," DeMarco said, becoming irritated. She wasn't telling him anything he didn't already know.

As if he hadn't spoken, Emma said, "I don't have any idea who would have jurisdiction over all this. Kennedy was killed near Poughkeepsie, the paint store guy in Queens, and your father in Brooklyn. I imagine the Queens and Brooklyn DAs would laugh you out of their offices if you brought this mess to them."

"I know that," DeMarco said again. "So what should I do? I'm looking for some ideas here."

"I don't have a clue what you should do, Joe. The chance of Quinn being convicted for murder is less than zero. I also think, although I don't know for sure, that even if you could get Neil to dig through Quinn's life to find some dirty secret, he wouldn't find one."

"Sure he would. Everybody has secrets."

Especially you.

Emma shook her head. "Quinn didn't rise to the top of the pyramid without making enemies—people in his position always make enemies—and if his enemies had any old information that could hurt him, it would have come out before he was appointed to the commissioner's office."

DeMarco felt like lashing out at her for doing nothing more than telling him all the reasons why he'd never be able to get Brian Quinn. Instead of saying something he'd probably regret, he took a sip of his martini and watched a distinguished-looking white-haired guy try to pitch a shot up onto the green closest to the clubhouse. The guy missed the shot badly, his ball ended up in a sand trap, and he responded by smashing his club into the ground.

Emma laughed. "You know who that guy is?" she asked.

"No," DeMarco said.

"He's a retired four-star general and former member of the Joint Chiefs of Staff. He was known for never losing his cool in the tensest of situations."

Normally, DeMarco would have found that funny. Not today. "If I wanted an unregistered weapon," he asked, "where could I get one?"

Emma looked away from the retired general and stopped smiling. "Are you insane?" she said. "Please tell me that you're not thinking about trying to kill Quinn."

"I don't know. All I know is that I can't let him get away with what he did."

"Joe, your father may have been a killer, but you're not one. I *know* you; you don't have it in you to execute someone."

DeMarco didn't respond. He didn't bother to say that he'd had the same thought about himself when he first learned that Quinn had murdered his dad—but now he was beginning to believe that if killing Quinn was the only option he had, then he'd somehow find the courage or the coldness or whatever it took. If necessary, he would become the man his father had been.

"And if you did try to kill Quinn," Emma continued, "most likely he or his security people would kill you. They all have guns and, unlike you, they actually know how to use them. And if by some fluke you succeeded, you'd get caught and spend the rest of your life in jail. The NYPD would never stop looking for the man who killed its commissioner, particularly a man as popular as Quinn, and I can guarantee that they'd catch you."

Emma, who wasn't normally the sympathetic sort, put a hand on his forearm and said, "Joe, I know you loved your father, but you need to stop thinking about getting a gun or killing Quinn or anything foolish like that. If there's no way to get him legally, and I don't think there is based on what you've told me, then you're just going to have to . . . to trust to karma, as sappy as that sounds."

"Karma?" That had to be the dumbest thing Emma had ever said to him.

"Yes," Emma said. "One day, Brian Quinn will get what he deserves. You have to believe that. If you try to kill him, you'll destroy your own life."

DeMarco nodded his head slowly, as if he was reluctantly agreeing with her, but he was thinking: *Karma, my ass.*

***

Emma watched DeMarco walk toward his car.

She had never seen him like this before. He was one of the most laid-back, easygoing people she'd ever met. In fact, he was *too* easygoing, as far as she was concerned, and she probably would have fired him if he'd ever worked for her. He didn't really care about his job—he cared only that he got a paycheck—and although he didn't particularly like working for an unethical bastard like Mahoney, he continued to work for him anyway.

He just wasn't invested in what he did. It wasn't personal for him the way it had been personal for her when she'd worked for the DIA. She'd had a job that mattered and was vital to national security; DeMarco had a job that he did his best to avoid and tolerated when he couldn't. He was basically a man marking time until he could retire and spend his days playing golf.

But this thing with his father was as personal as it could get and DeMarco's attitude was completely different. It appeared as if he might be willing to do whatever it took to avenge his father's death, even if that meant doing something as self-destructive as trying to kill Quinn. Emma had never been close to her father—or her mother, for that matter—so she wasn't able to fully appreciate the way Joe felt. All she knew for sure was that he wasn't going to stop going after Quinn. And in spite of what she'd said about karma—she wished she hadn't said that—she knew it was more likely that karma was on Quinn's side.

DeMarco was the one who was going to suffer, not Brian Quinn.

21

The next morning, after another bad night's sleep, DeMarco was sitting at his kitchen table pondering his next move. Two cups of coffee later, he decided he didn't have a next move.

He did conclude that one thing he needed to do was go talk to Mahoney. He didn't think Mahoney would help him; in fact, he was almost certain Mahoney wouldn't. Mahoney acted almost totally out of his own self-interest, and he would immediately realize that siding with DeMarco against the commissioner of the NYPD would most likely not be to his advantage. Nonetheless, DeMarco needed to let his boss know that he was planning to devote his life, at least for a while, to the destruction of Brian Quinn. He didn't know how things would eventually work out with Quinn—not well, he suspected—but if he was still alive and not in jail, he'd like to be employed when it was all over.

He called Mahoney's secretary and said he needed to speak to the man.

"He's not happy with you," Mavis said.

"Yeah, I know."

"Anyway, his schedule's completely full but if you show up here at eleven forty-five maybe you can get in to see him for a couple of minutes before he heads off to lunch. He's eating over at the White House today but I know he's coming back here to change his shirt before he goes. He spilled something on it."

When DeMarco walked into Mahoney's office, Mahoney was standing there in a sleeveless T-shirt, maroon suspenders dangling down beside his legs, ripping the dry-cleaner's plastic off a crisp blue shirt. His first words to DeMarco were "You gonna tell me what the fuck's going on with you?"

Mahoney was pissed, of course, but not quite as pissed as DeMarco had thought he would be. One reason why was today's *Washington Post,* which had a nice front-page story about the Pentagon veterans' scam and prominently discussed Mahoney's role in exposing the culprits.

"You know about my father?" DeMarco said. "I mean, what he used to do for a living and how he was killed?"

"Yeah," Mahoney said, giving him a puzzled glance, not sure where DeMarco was going with this, then turned his attention to buttoning up his shirt.

"The reason I had to go to New York the other day was I just found out who shot my dad. It was Brian Quinn."

"Brian Quinn?" Mahoney said. "Wait a minute. You don't mean the NYPD guy, do you?"

"Yeah."

"Jesus!" Mahoney said. "How did you find this out?"

Before DeMarco could answer the question, Mahoney said, "Look, I have to get to the White House. Come on over to the house tonight . . ."

Mahoney meant his condo in the Watergate.

". . . and you can tell me what the hell's going on. But in the meantime, I don't want you to do a damn thing about Quinn and I don't want you talking to anybody about him, either. You understand?"

DeMarco was about to tell him, as diplomatically as he could, that he was going to do whatever the hell he felt like doing when it came to Quinn. Before he could say anything, however, Mahoney said, "I mean, do you have any idea what's going on with Quinn right now?"

"No. What are you talking about?" DeMarco said.

Mahoney ignored him as he tucked in his shirt, then muttered, "Where the hell did I put my tie?" He found the tie slung over the back of his chair and started tying it.

"The president's about to make Quinn the director of the FBI," Mahoney said. "I guess he's tired of all the shit he's been catching for Simpson, and Quinn's probably looking for a job with national exposure to move into politics."

DeMarco knew that Simpson, the current FBI director, had been in a lot of hot water in recent months for a couple of boneheaded things the Bureau had done.

"The president hasn't told Simpson he's fired yet but he will tomorrow and then he'll hold a press conference praising Simpson for all his fine work but saying it's time for a change. The next day, because the president likes to keep his face in front of the cameras, he'll hold another press conference to introduce his nominee, Brian Quinn. Because the White House is so good at keeping secrets, there're probably fifty people up here on the Hill that know what's going on, but for some strange reason no one's leaked the story yet.

"Anyway," Mahoney said as he finished tying his tie with a large, clumsy, off-center knot, "it's a done deal except for the Senate confirmation hearing and neither party is going to fight Quinn's nomination. He's a popular guy. So things are complicated and I don't want you screwing around with Quinn until I have a chance to think about all this."

Mahoney pulled up the suspenders and shrugged into his suit jacket. On the way out of his office, he said, "Come by around nine tonight. I oughta be home by then."

"Okay," DeMarco said, but he was thinking: *Karma*.

———————◆◆◆———————

DeMarco had known, even before he talked to Emma, that he'd never be able to go after Quinn in a court of law for killing his father. As Emma had said, the only witness to Gino DeMarco's murder was Brian Quinn himself. All the other people who could help him damage Quinn's reputation—Janet Costello, Stan Dombroski, and Tony Benedetto—were flawed witnesses and none of those witnesses wanted to testify.

A Senate confirmation hearing, however, was a whole different animal than a court of law. There was no judge to stop the senators from calling whomever they wanted to testify; no defense lawyer would be able to object to the inadmissibility of hearsay evidence proffered by witnesses with less than sterling characters. If DeMarco could persuade one of the senators on the committee to go after Quinn, and if he could persuade that senator to call Tony Benedetto and the others and force them to testify, that would definitely get the media interested.

The media didn't care about evidence anymore than the senators did; it seemed the media, these days, was more about entertainment than uncovering the truth. Ratings trumped serious journalism and a story about the top municipal cop in the country being a killer in cahoots with the mob—particularly if the story was delivered by a dying mobster like Tony Benedetto—would certainly be entertaining. Moreover, if the right senator was pushing for an in-depth investigation into Quinn's past *before* he was confirmed, maybe some independent agency with clout—an agency like the FBI—might actually find something that could be used against Quinn in a courtroom.

DeMarco decided to overlook the fact that if Quinn was confirmed by the Senate, the FBI would soon be working for him.

So DeMarco didn't know what might happen. All he knew was that a televised Senate confirmation hearing was a gift from God insofar as going after Quinn and shining a public spotlight on everything he had done.

Karma.

———◆◆◆———

Eighteen United States senators sit on the Senate Judiciary Committee. DeMarco needed to know if one of those eighteen had an axe to grind against Brian Quinn, and the man who would know this was Perry Wallace, Mahoney's chief of staff. Perry knew everything when it came to the body politic.

Perry was on the phone when DeMarco entered his office; he spent 90 percent of his waking hours on the phone. As he listened to Perry scheme with whomever he was speaking to—it sounded like he was trying to convince someone in the supposedly independent Congressional Budget Office to doctor the numbers on an upcoming bill—DeMarco wondered who cut Perry's hair. Whoever it was should have been drummed out of the profession because it appeared as if Edward Scissorhands—a movie character with gardening shears for appendages—had attacked Perry's hair while wearing a blindfold. Perry Wallace was not a good-looking man to begin with—triple-chinned; small, cunning eyes; a porcine snout—but a decent barber could have improved the situation.

"I thought Mahoney fired you," Perry said after he hung up, and the way he said this, it was apparent he had not lost any sleep pondering the consequences of DeMarco being unemployed.

"Not yet." Before Perry could say anything else, he asked, "Do you know about Brian Quinn being nominated to be the next FBI director?"

"Of course," Perry said—but then Perry was the kind of guy who would say "of course" even if he hadn't known about Quinn. Perry didn't like to be thought of as not being completely in the loop.

"Who's the most likely person on the Senate Judiciary Committee to oppose his nomination?" DeMarco asked.

"Why are you asking?" Perry asked.

"I can't tell you," DeMarco said.

"Then fuck you," Perry said.

"Perry, the boss doesn't want me to tell you why I'm asking, at least not yet. Okay? So who on the committee hates Brian Quinn?"

"Nobody. Everybody loves him. He's Mr. Law and Order."

"Come on. Somebody must have some reason for opposing him. I mean, the Republicans hate the president so much, half of them wouldn't confirm Lincoln if he came back from the dead."

"Sure they would. Lincoln was a Republican."

"Perry . . ."

"Beecham," Perry said.

"Ah," DeMarco said. That made sense. Hiram Beecham was the senior senator from Georgia and the last time he ran for office, the president had helicoptered into Atlanta and stumped for Beecham's opponent. He accused Beecham of being misguided, out of touch, an enemy of the common man—and, most important, implied that Beecham was too damn old to be in the job. Hiram Beecham was eighty-four and sensitive about his age.

Yes, if Beecham could humiliate the president via Quinn, he'd delight in doing so. And DeMarco couldn't imagine a more embarrassing nominee for the job of top law enforcement official in the country than a man who'd committed three murders.

"Thanks, Perry. By the way, who cuts your hair?"

"My sister. Why?"

DeMarco left Perry's office and walked over to a place on Pennsylvania Avenue for lunch. When he opened the menu, he saw they offered a Philly cheesesteak with caramelized onions and green peppers, which brought back another memory of his father.

There'd been a place on Queens Boulevard operated by two brothers who said they were from Philly but sounded like they were from someplace farther to the south—like Puerto Rico. At any rate, his dad always raved about their cheesesteaks, claiming they made the best ones in New York—and when DeMarco was a kid, he'd agreed. He'd been back in Queens visiting his mother one time, long after his father was dead, and he drove out of his way to stop by the place. It was still there and so were the brothers, now old men, but the cheesesteaks hadn't been as good as he remembered them—and the guy now doing the cooking was Korean.

As he waited for his sandwich, he tried to figure out if he should go see Beecham next or wait until after he'd talked to Mahoney. He was afraid that after he talked to Mahoney, Mahoney would order him to stop pursuing his vendetta against Quinn. Another possibility was that Mahoney might fire him if he refused to stop going after Quinn, which meant that he'd not only be out of a job, but his access to folks on Capitol Hill would be limited. So should he obey Mahoney or not?

For DeMarco it was simple: he was going to do his best to destroy Brian Quinn, and nothing else much mattered. And while Mahoney might sympathize with his desire to avenge his father's death, Mahoney was going to be more concerned about the political ramifications of DeMarco going after a man the president was appointing to run the nation's police force. All this meant that since DeMarco planned do whatever he felt was necessary in regard to Quinn, and regardless of what Mahoney said, unemployment was a distinct possibility.

The thought of being fired scared the hell out of DeMarco. The economy was supposedly recovering, but people were still having a hard time finding work—and he would have a harder time than most: he was a lawyer who'd never practiced law and who had had only one employer since he graduated from college. And although he'd worked on Capitol Hill for almost two decades, he'd never been involved—in a legitimate way—on a reelection campaign or doing the legwork needed to pass legislation. In other words, he'd never done the sort of work that would make him attractive to an honest politician. Instead, he'd been stuck down in a subbasement office doing the things Mahoney *didn't* want his legitimate staff doing, and he couldn't talk about half the things he'd done, not unless he wanted to be indicted or appear as a witness to testify against Mahoney. There were, however, as his first boss, Jake, had said, other guys like him in Washington, guys employed by lobbyists and special interest groups and politicians like Mahoney—guys who operated in the shadows of the political process. But the people who hired guys like that didn't post ads on the help-wanted pages.

The other thing that occurred to him at that moment was that in some ways, he wasn't much different than his father: His father had been—or so Joe had always thought—a basically decent man who worked for a criminal and did things he couldn't have been proud of. But somehow Gino had been able to rationalize what he did; if he hadn't been able to, he would have quit. Joe now realized the same thing could be said about him: he'd always considered himself a good guy, yet he wasn't always proud of the things he'd done for Mahoney and had never really made the effort to find a different job. It seemed the apple really didn't fall far from the tree.

By the time he finished his cheesesteak—which also wasn't as good as the ones he'd eaten as a kid with his dad in Queens—he decided to talk to Mahoney before he talked to Senator Beecham. He'd give Mahoney a chance to do the right thing—knowing that Mahoney and the "right thing" didn't necessarily go hand in hand. He hoped he wasn't making a mistake.

———◆◆◆———

DeMarco arrived at Mahoney's condo at exactly 9 P.M. and was surprised that Mahoney was there. Mahoney rarely let an appointment with DeMarco affect his schedule and he didn't mind keeping DeMarco waiting for hours.

Mahoney had been at some black-tie affair, the sort he attended once or twice a week. He was dressed in tuxedo pants; a clip-on bow tie that looked like a mangled black butterfly lay on the dining room table. Mahoney's jacket was on the floor near one of the dining room chairs as if he had tried to drape it over the back of the chair and it had fallen, and he'd been too lazy to stoop down and pick it up. Also, as might be expected of a man who laced his morning coffee with bourbon, at 9 P.M. Mahoney was drunk. Being drunk, however, didn't mean he was ready to stop drinking; a tumbler filled with bourbon and crushed ice was clenched in his big right fist.

"Is Mary Pat here?" DeMarco asked. Mary Pat was Mahoney's wife and DeMarco preferred not to talk about Quinn in front of her.

"Nah. She flew up to Boston yesterday to see her mom. Some shit going on at the nursing home."

Mahoney flopped down on a couch, and DeMarco was betting that since Mary Pat wasn't home, he'd eventually pass out on the couch. "So what's going with Quinn?" Mahoney asked. He didn't bother to ask DeMarco if he wanted a drink.

DeMarco took a seat and told him the whole story. Unlike when he'd told Emma, Mahoney interrupted him frequently during the telling, saying "Jesus Christ" and "You gotta be shittin' me" more than once. When DeMarco finished, however, Mahoney came to the same conclusion Emma had: "So all you got is an old mafia hood who says Quinn killed your dad and some other hood, but you have no evidence. And this schoolteacher who claimed Quinn got off for killing the paint store guy . . . Shit, who's gonna believe her?"

"Yeah, but they're telling the truth," DeMarco said.

"How do you know that this mob boss . . . What's his name again?"

"Tony Benedetto."

"Yeah, Benedetto. How do you know he's telling the truth? How do you know he's not making the whole thing up?"

"Why would he?" DeMarco said. "He has nothing to gain by telling me what Quinn did."

"Maybe he heard Quinn was going to become the FBI director and wants to fuck him over just for the fun of it."

"Come on, boss. You said maybe fifty people on the Hill knew about Quinn getting the nomination. How would some retired gangster in Queens know? He told me about Quinn and my dad because he's dying and thought I should know."

Mahoney didn't say anything for a moment and DeMarco knew he was trying to work his way through the political consequences of Quinn being exposed. The other thought that suddenly occurred to him was that maybe Mahoney didn't want Quinn exposed, so he could later use the information DeMarco had provided to blackmail Quinn. Considering the sort of things Mahoney had pulled over the years, having something on the director of the FBI could be a real ace in the hole.

Finally Mahoney said, "I think I better talk to the president about this. He needs to know that if any of this stuff about Quinn gets out, even if it can't be proven, it could result in a shit storm."

"So what you're saying is, you're not concerned about a murderer becoming the next FBI director but you are concerned about the president getting embarrassed by his appointment."

"Don't you go all holier-than-thou on me," Mahoney snapped. "You know as well as I do that Quinn isn't going to go to jail for what he did, and that's assuming he even did what you said. The best you can do is sling mud at the guy. Now, I personally don't give a shit about Quinn but—"

"Well, I do," DeMarco said. "He killed my father."

As if DeMarco hadn't spoken, Mahoney continued. "What I do care about is him becoming a problem for the president and wasting a lot of time dealing with the media about a bunch of wild-eyed accusations that can't be proven. The president needs to know about this so he can make a decision and maybe change his mind about nominating Quinn."

"I don't want that to happen," DeMarco said. "I want the Senate confirmation hearing to take place as scheduled."

"What?" Mahoney said. Then his brain caught up with where DeMarco was going. "You mean you intend to get somebody to spring this shit on Quinn during the hearing?"

"That's right," DeMarco said.

"Well, that ain't gonna happen," Mahoney said.

DeMarco didn't say anything for a moment because he was once again considering the question: How far was he willing to go to get Brian Quinn? Maybe he wasn't willing to murder the man, but was he willing to lose his job? Yeah, he was.

"If you tell the president about Quinn, and if the president withdraws his nomination or if the hearing gets postponed, I'm going to talk to the press and the Justice Department about you. You've pulled a lot of crap over the years and I know that because I've helped you. What you did last year for your daughter is enough all by itself to get you bounced out of Congress. So don't cross me on this, boss."

"Why you son of a bitch," Mahoney said, standing up, sloshing bourbon on the couch.

DeMarco stood up, too. "I'm not screwing around here. I'm going to get Quinn for what he did to my dad. If you get in my way, I'll do whatever I have to do."

"You actually got the balls to stand there and try to blackmail me?"

"Yeah, I guess so."

Mahoney's face turned so red that DeMarco thought for a minute he might have a stroke.

"You're fired," Mahoney said. "Now get the fuck out of here before I throw you through a goddamn window."

DeMarco left Mahoney's building in a state of shock. He was stunned by what had just happened and by what the consequences were likely to be. For the first time since graduating from law school, he didn't have a job.

Instead of returning to his car and going home, he walked down to the Potomac and took a seat on a bench. He could see the dark shape of Roosevelt Island from where he was sitting.

DeMarco didn't have a lot of debt, just the mortgage on his house and what he still owed on his car. On the other hand, he hadn't saved much at all in the time he'd been working. The only real savings he had was the money he'd invested in his civil service pension fund, and if he spent that money, what would he retire on?

DeMarco's dream, as modest as it was, had been to retire before he was sixty-five—which was still a long way off—sell his house in Georgetown, and buy a cheaper place in a community on some golf course in North or South Carolina or maybe Florida. But if he started spending the money in his pension fund to live on, he could kiss that dream good-bye, and if he sold his house now, there would be very little left over after he paid off the mortgage.

Once again he was also confronted with the fact that he'd spent almost two decades in a career that he wouldn't be able to parlay into a better job or even another job that paid as well. The smart thing to do would be to march right back to Mahoney's place, apologize, and beg for his job back.

He thought about that for all of two seconds and thought: *Fuck the smart thing to do.* He wasn't going to beg for anything and he was going to keep going after Quinn.

22

DeMarco showed his congressional ID as he passed through security at the Dirksen Senate Office Building. He knew he wouldn't have the ID for much longer but figured that Mahoney hadn't had time yet to get the word out that DeMarco was no longer employed by the legislative branch of the government. By the end of the day, however, he was willing to bet that somebody would track him down and take his credentials away from him.

DeMarco needed to talk to Senator Hiram Beecham but knew that if he called Beecham's office he wouldn't get an appointment unless he wanted to tell whoever answered Beecham's phone all about Brian Quinn. DeMarco wasn't going to talk to some low-level aide about Quinn. He would, however, talk to Beecham's chief of staff.

Beecham's chief was a tall, shapely brunette who was closing in on fifty but looked better than most thirty-year-olds. She was a former Miss Georgia, a former GU cheerleader, and a mostly absent mother of two. Like many educated southern women that DeMarco had met, her manners were flawless and she was always soft-spoken—the type who could rip you to shreds with her tongue without swearing or ever raising her voice. Her name was Amelia Sherman and according to Perry Wallace, Sherman was devious and tricky and you could trust her about as far as you could throw a Volkswagen. Since Perry Wallace was the same sort of person, DeMarco figured Perry would know.

Also, according to Perry, at the age of eighty-four, Senator Beecham spent more time napping than working. (One of the things the president had done to embarrass Beecham when he was stumping for Beecham's opponent in Georgia was mention a video that had gotten heavy play on the political talk shows. In the video, the old senator had been caught sleeping in the Senate chamber and someone had to wake him up to cast his vote.) While Beecham napped, Amelia Sherman stayed awake and did his work, and his political agenda was pretty much steered by her. DeMarco knew that Sherman was the one he had to convince.

He had gained entrance to Sherman's office by telling her assistant that he was a lawyer who worked in the House and knew something negative about Brian Quinn that was not known to the general public. "I'm intrigued, Mr. DeMarco," Sherman said as soon as he took a seat in her office. "Tell me what you think you know about Commissioner Quinn."

One difference DeMarco noted between Amelia Sherman and Perry Wallace was that not only did Sherman have a better haircut than Wallace, but her office was also neat and orderly. Wallace was some sort of legislative hoarder and his office contained every bill proposed in the last decade; it looked like a landfill. The furniture in Sherman's office was dust-free and smelled of Pledge, and her desk was bare except for an outbox holding a few slim manila file folders. You could actually sit on the chairs in her office since they weren't covered with reams of paper.

"I have information related to Brian Quinn that Senator Beecham could possibly use to embarrass the president," DeMarco said, leading with his best foot forward.

Sherman frowned as if DeMarco had just said something crude and uncouth. "What makes you think the senator wishes to embarrass the president?" she said.

DeMarco just smiled at her.

"Okay. What do you have?" she said, smiling back.

"I have a witness who can testify that Quinn murdered two people and was being controlled by the New York mob for years. I have another witness who will testify that Quinn shot an unarmed man when he was a patrolman, and he and the NYPD covered up the killing."

Except for a brief widening of her eyes, Sherman didn't react. No *oh-my-God* expression crossed her face. She was probably an excellent Texas hold 'em player.

"Why are you doing this?" she finally asked.

"Because one of the people Quinn killed was my father."

She punched a button on her phone and said, "Brad, cancel my next appointment."

Sherman grilled him for almost an hour. By the time she was finished, she'd come to the same conclusion DeMarco had: dragging Quinn through the mud in the confirmation hearing might not be enough to convict Quinn of any crimes, but it could possibly spoil his chances of being confirmed and would be phenomenal in terms of embarrassing the president.

One thing Sherman decided she wanted was a videotaped statement from Tony. She desired this for two reasons: First, she wanted to be able to assess before the hearing what sort of witness Tony would make. Second, she wanted Tony on record before he died. The confirmation hearing didn't start for a couple of weeks and Sherman didn't want to take the chance that Tony's health might further deteriorate, so she told DeMarco to head back to New York immediately and get the video made. Amelia Sherman seemed quite comfortable giving DeMarco orders.

Before he left her office, DeMarco told Sherman he was no longer employed so the next time he needed to see her, he wouldn't be able to show a badge and waltz into the Dirksen Building. For years, DeMarco had denied working directly for John Mahoney and no organizational chart connected him to Mahoney. Mahoney liked things this way just in case DeMarco ever did something that could come back and bite him on the ass. Now, however, since Mahoney had fired him, he told Sherman the truth: that although he was listed as an independent lawyer employed by the House, his real boss had always been Mahoney. He also told her that when he'd told Mahoney about Brian Quinn, Mahoney's initial reaction had been to run to the president and advise him to consider dropping Quinn—and when he threatened to blackmail Mahoney, Mahoney fired him.

"John Mahoney is not a man I'd want for an enemy," Sherman said.

"Me either," DeMarco admitted. "But that's the way it goes."

Sherman picked up her phone. "Brad, when Mr. DeMarco leaves my office I want you to get him a temporary ID so he can get into this building and the Capitol for a week."

"Yes, ma'am," Brad said.

Tony looked a little better than the last time DeMarco had seen him. There was more color in his face and he wasn't struggling quite so hard to breathe. He still looked like a dying man. When DeMarco said he wanted to videotape Tony's statement, Tony initial response was "There's a bottle of scotch in that cabinet over there. Actually, there're a couple bottles. The Dewar's is what I used to drink. The one with the long name that says it's been aged for eighteen years is what I drink now. I figure at this point, why not indulge myself."

DeMarco poured him the drink and said, "So. You gonna let me make the video or you want to stall some more?"

"I haven't decided yet. Maybe. Tell me what's going on."

DeMarco did. He told him that he'd never be able to get Quinn for killing his father and Jerry Kennedy, but what he could do was derail the sweet, upward trajectory of Brian Quinn's life. He explained to Tony about the upcoming Senate confirmation hearing and that if Tony would testify, and if the Senate could force Janet Costello to testify, then what Quinn had done would be out in the open. Tony's testimony might not be enough to put Quinn in jail, but it would be enough to get the media interested and demanding some answers, and might even prevent him from being confirmed as the FBI director.

"So will you make the video?" DeMarco asked again.

Tony took a while to mull this over, sipping his scotch slowly, and DeMarco grew impatient.

"Tony, what the hell's the problem? It's not like anyone's going to throw you in jail if you testify. I mean, and I'm sorry to say this, but no one's going to bother with you because you're going to be dead pretty soon."

"Okay," Tony finally said.

An hour later, using a video camera he'd borrowed from Neil, DeMarco had what he wanted: Tony Benedetto telling everything he knew about Brian Quinn, his relationship to Carmine Taliaferro, and the deaths of Connors, Jerry Kennedy, and Gino DeMarco. Tony, just like the last time DeMarco had spoken to him, was exhausted by the time he finished giving his statement.

DeMarco turned off the camera and said, "I want you to say a couple more things. I want you to say that you're dying of cancer and you have no reason to lie. And I want you to say that you're willing to take a lie detector test."

"Yeah, okay," Tony gasped. "Let's just get this over with."

23

The day after returning from New York, the first thing DeMarco did was call Neil, but Neil wasn't at home or at his office or answering his cell phone. DeMarco couldn't help but wonder if Neil was ducking him.

DeMarco had never been a camera guy, much less a video guy. He'd never seen the point in taking a million pictures of relatives and vacation scenes and then throwing all the pictures into a box and never looking at them again. Or these days, instead of throwing them into a box, you downloaded them to your computer and never looked at them again. DeMarco owned a cheap digital camera he'd used a few times on assignments Mahoney had given him but had never owned a video camera and didn't know anything about the camera other than what Neil had shown him. Which meant, he basically knew how to turn it on and off.

The camera Neil had given him fit easily into the palm of his hand and had a little screen that flipped out, and while DeMarco was taping Tony's statement, he'd watched Tony on the screen. Neil had told him that inside the video camera was a little chip or smart card or whatever the hell it was called, and the video of Tony actually resided on that card and DeMarco could later transfer it to a CD or a flash drive or a computer. The problem was, DeMarco was afraid to mess with the video camera because he might screw up the video; the last thing he wanted to do was accidently delete it. Which was why he'd called Neil, because he wanted Neil to help him make copies of the video—but Neil was avoiding him.

He called Amelia Sherman next to tell her he'd completed the assignment he'd been given, but was informed that Sherman and her boss were in Atlanta, and wouldn't be back until tomorrow. Since he couldn't reach Neil or Sherman, DeMarco puttered around the house doing the sort of chores that required just enough mental activity to keep him from thinking about Brian Quinn. He washed a load of clothes, vacuumed a couple of rooms in his house—he didn't see the point of vacuuming the rooms he rarely used—and emptied things out of his refrigerator that were starting to look like science experiments.

The last job he tackled was the back door, which wasn't shutting quite right. He took the door down and planed the edge a bit and adjusted the lock plate so the dead bolt would go in without him having to yank back on the door so hard. He remembered helping his dad one time do a similar job on their house in Queens, his dad saying doors got used so much you had to fuss with them periodically. Just one of the joys of owning a home, his dad would say.

Unlike his son, Gino DeMarco had genuinely enjoyed working on his house and there wasn't any job he was afraid to tackle. He reroofed the place himself and did all the plumbing work. He totally remodeled the kitchen once, putting in new cabinets and countertops. His mom wasn't happy it took him so long—almost three months—but his father couldn't have been happier. Gino DeMarco would have liked being a carpenter and Joe and his mom always tried to buy him some kind of tool for his birthday. It didn't matter what kind of tool; his dad just liked tools. DeMarco never would have guessed at the time that the tool his father used best was a gun.

That evening, he called Neil again, and again Neil didn't answer. Neil was starting to piss him off.

It was time for dinner, but he didn't feel like cooking and then having to clean up the mess after he cooked, so he strolled down to George-town, to a Vietnamese place on M Street. The restaurant was the only one he'd ever eaten at that made trout—normally a tasteless fish—taste good. After dinner, he stopped in a bookstore, thinking maybe a good book would get his mind, at least for a while, off Quinn and his father. He left the bookstore twenty minutes later with a couple of paperback mysteries, and was thinking when he got home he'd crack open a bottle of wine and read until he drifted off to sleep.

When DeMarco unlocked his front door, he didn't immediately notice that the alarm system wasn't making the little beeping sound it makes until you punch in the code. He didn't notice the absence of the beeps because it looked like a tornado had cut a path directly through his living room.

His home had been thoroughly and completely searched. The con-tents of every drawer in the house had been dumped onto the floor and seat cushions had been cut open to see if there was anything hidden inside them. The contents of cereal, rice, and pasta boxes had been emptied onto his kitchen counters and every item in his freezer had been removed and tossed into the sink.

He didn't bother going to his bedroom. He expected that the bed-room would be in the same condition as his living room and kitchen: clothes on the floor, drawers removed and emptied, the mattresses slashed. Instead, he immediately headed for the basement. The base-ment contained his furnace, a washer and dryer, a worktable, and a bunch of tools. It also contained a fireproof lockbox. In the lockbox he kept important papers: his will, the deed to the house, his birth cer-tificate, passport, and five grand in cash for the day all the ATMs failed to work. Yesterday he'd put the video camera in the lockbox as well.

He hid the lockbox by placing it on the basement floor behind a pile of obvious junk—pieces of scrap wood, old paint cans, and rusted gardening tools—then chained the box to a cast iron drainpipe. He figured that if anybody robbed his house, they'd recognize the junk pile for what it was—junk—and leave it alone and if by some chance they found the lockbox, they couldn't just walk away with it unless they had something to cut the chain.

Whoever had searched his house wasn't fooled, however, and they brought the tools they needed: the chain had been cut and the lockbox was sitting open on the worktable. All his important documents were still in the box, but his five grand in cash and the video camera were missing.

DeMarco went to his den next. He used to own a desktop computer but when it died, as all computers eventually do, he'd replaced the desktop with a laptop. The laptop was gone. The contents of everything that had been in his desk were on the floor and he noticed that all his CDs were missing. The CDs were mostly backup programs for his computer and copies of old tax returns.

DeMarco figured it had taken a team to search his house in the two hours he'd been gone—three, maybe four guys. They must have been watching him and they waited until he went to the restaurant before they broke into the house. They pried open the back door using a simple crowbar but they must have had some sort of high-tech gadget that could figure out his security code before the alarm sounded. He bet they also had someone watching him while he was eating dinner, and that person was ready to call whoever was in the house to tell them when he was on his way back home.

Whatever the case, this was a well-planned operation, not simple burglary—and DeMarco had no doubt whatsoever as to who was responsible: it was Brian Quinn. He'd sent a team to look for the Tony Benedetto video and any copies of it, which was why they'd taken his laptop and all of DeMarco's compact discs. He figured they'd taken the cash in the lockbox to make the break-in look like a robbery—or maybe they took the cash because they were greedy bastards. He had no idea what Quinn told his men regarding the video or who DeMarco was.

At Quinn's rank, you didn't have to explain a whole lot to the people who worked for you.

DeMarco also knew who had told Quinn about the video.

Only three people knew he was going to video Tony Benedetto's statement—himself, Amelia Sherman, and Tony. He knew he hadn't told anybody, and he was about a hundred percent certain that Sherman hadn't, either—which left only Tony Benedetto.

Tony had betrayed him.

———— ❖ ————

DeMarco called the cops not because he figured they could do anything useful but because calling them was a necessary step for filing an insurance claim. When the cops got there he told them the thieves had taken cash, a laptop, and a video camera. He didn't tell them anything regarding who he suspected had sent the thieves or why they had stolen the camera.

"Mostly, what they did was just trash the place and they only took small stuff they could carry easily or put in their pockets," DeMarco said. "I guess that's why they didn't take the TVs."

"Didn't you have your alarm set?" one cop asked.

"I must have forgot," DeMarco said. He wanted the cop to think that those responsible were just ordinary thieves and not the type of people who would have access to high-tech gadgets that could disable alarms.

"It was probably junkies," the cop said.

"Yeah, probably," DeMarco said.

"Well, we'll talk to your neighbors to see if they saw anything." The cop's tone of voice said: *Don't get your hopes up.*

———— ❖ ————

DeMarco spent the next two hours restoring some sort of order to his home, documenting all the stuff that was going to have to be replaced, like his laptop, two couches, his back door, and the mattresses on two beds. Tomorrow morning, he'd call his insurance agent and somebody to replace his back door—the same door he'd just spent hours working on earlier in the day. While he cleaned things up, he tried to figure out why Tony had betrayed him. When he couldn't figure it out, he finally just called the old bastard and asked him. He didn't care that it was after midnight.

"Why did you tell Quinn about the video?" he asked as soon as Tony answered the phone.

DeMarco could see Tony there in his living room, in the dim light, gasping for his next breath, the oxygen line running to his big nose. But instead of the image of a frail old man on the verge of death, DeMarco envisioned an ancient cobra coiled in the dark, smiling.

"Sorry, Joe, I had to do it."

"But why?"

"My kid."

"Your kid? What the fuck does your kid have to do with this?"

"He got himself arrested. He ain't the brightest kid in the world, and he ain't the toughest, either, and this was his third bust for dope-related shit. Him and a couple other morons got hooked up with some doctor selling OxyContin to junkies and the DA told him he wouldn't make any kind of deal with him. My boy was going to go away for at least five years.

"Anyway, when you told me how you were planning to go after Quinn in that Senate hearing, and made me make that video—"

"*Made* you?"

"Yeah. I'm a sick old man. You took advantage of me. You scared me. Anyway, I called Quinn but I didn't give him your name right away. I said you were a heavy hitter down there in D.C. and you'd been involved in some heavy shit in the past. I told him you were digging stuff up to use against him at his hearing and you knew about his connection to Carmine."

"Then you cut a deal with him."

"Yeah. I had to. For my kid. I told Quinn if he got the charges dismissed against Anthony, I'd give him your name and he could take it from there. I also said I wouldn't testify at his hearing—that I'd go into a hospital so you couldn't drag me down there—and I wouldn't be starring in any more videos."

"And Quinn agreed to this?"

"Sure. Why wouldn't he? My kid's small potatoes. Nobody gives a shit about him, and Quinn knows it. He knew if the charges against my boy were dismissed, that wouldn't even cause a ripple in the legal system. I also told Quinn if he didn't do what I wanted then I was going to testify at the hearing. That is, I'd testify unless Quinn killed me, in which case the video you made would have to do."

"So you were actually planning to do this when you made the video."

"That's right, and Quinn took the deal. I gave him your name and he squeezed whoever he had to squeeze in the DA's office, and they dropped the charges in return for Anthony testifying against the other idiots he was arrested with. My kid's lawyer says there's no way they can come back at him and he's free until he fucks up again, which, knowing him, he probably will."

DeMarco didn't say anything for a long time. Finally, he said, "You old son of a bitch. I feel like—"

"Yeah, fuck what you feel like. You're not gonna do shit. If you really wanted to get back at Quinn for your dad, you'd have killed the guy instead of coming up with some bullshit political thing to screw him over. You take care, Joe. Tell your mom hi for me next time you see her."

There was no point throwing the handset of the phone across his living room but he did anyway, knocking a picture off the wall.

Now what? His entire half-assed plan for destroying Brian Quinn had just evaporated.

24

The next morning didn't start off too well, either.

DeMarco's doorbell rang at 7 A.M., waking him up. Dressed in boxer shorts and a wash-faded Nationals T-shirt, he opened his front door to find two U.S. Capitol cops standing on his porch. He recognized one of them, a potbellied old timer named Leary, who could usually be found leaning against a wall on the side of the Capitol that faced the Library of Congress. Leary was holding a cardboard box in his hand. The other guy, DeMarco had never seen before. His nametag said P. Martin, and he was at least twenty years younger than Leary and looked about twenty times harder.

"What's going on?" DeMarco said. He doubted they were there because his house had been broken into last night. There was no reason for the Capitol Police to be involved in that.

"We're here to collect your security badge," Martin said.

Mahoney hadn't wasted any time.

The first response that occurred to DeMarco was *Couldn't this have waited until nine or ten?* But he didn't say that. "Hang on, I'll go get it," he said. He came back a moment later and handed Martin his badge.

Leary, who looked a bit sheepish, held out the cardboard box to him. "What's this?" DeMarco said.

"The shit from your office," Martin said. "Oh, I forgot. I need the key to your office, too."

DeMarco got his keys, pulled his office key off the key ring, and handed it to Martin. "Inside that box," Martin said, "is an envelope with instructions telling you what you have to do when you separate from government service. There's a phone number in there of a lady to call in personnel if you got any questions, and you're supposed to be in her office at ten this morning to sign the stuff you have to sign. Have a good day."

Martin turned and walked away but before Leary left, he muttered, "Sorry, Joe."

DeMarco shut the door and headed back to bed. He had no intention of meeting with the lady from personnel today. He'd get to her when he had time—or when he was in the mood. What were they going to do if he missed the appointment? Fire him?

DeMarco got out of bed again at nine and called his insurance company to start the process for replacing the things that had been damaged and stolen. He called Home Depot next and told a clerk he needed a new door and the frame that went around the door. Home Depot informed him a guy would be there in a couple of hours to take some measurements. Next he called Amelia Sherman and told her he needed to see her as soon as possible.

"Did Benedetto let you video his testimony?" she asked.

"Yeah, but I no longer have the video."

"What?"

"I don't want to talk about this on the phone."

After a brief pause, she said, "Be here at two."

Two was good. That would give him time to deal with the insurance guy and the door guy. He made one other phone call. This time Neil answered his phone.

"Neil, I need Bobby to come over to my house and make sure my phones aren't tapped?"

"Who do you think tapped them?"

"What difference does it make? Just send him over. Okay? Please?"

"All right," Neil said, not sounding enthused.

Amelia Sherman was wearing a navy blue suit, a simple white blouse, small pearl earrings, and a matching pearl necklace. Simple, elegant, and stunning. The skirt hugged her form and stopped a modest one inch above her knees, but when she sat down and crossed her legs it was a show worth watching. DeMarco told her about his house being ransacked, and how the video he'd made of Tony had been stolen. He also told her about the conversation he'd had with Tony last night, and how Tony had admitted that he'd sold DeMarco out to Quinn to keep his son from going to jail.

"Tony, that sly old bastard, knew while he was making the video that he was going to use it to get his son off the hook," DeMarco said.

"Why on earth didn't you make a copy of the video?" Sherman asked him.

"I didn't know how. I tried to get a hold of the guy who lent me the camera but—"

"Oh, for God's sake," Sherman said. "Couldn't you have asked somebody else to help you make a copy?"

"Yeah, of course, but I didn't think making a copy was urgent. It never occurred to me that Tony would do what he did."

"And you think it was Quinn's people who broke into your house?"

"Yeah. Who else could it have been?" DeMarco said.

"Benedetto," Sherman said. "After he made the deal with Quinn, he needed to get rid of the video, so he sent some of his people to get it."

"No, it was Quinn," DeMarco said. "They stole the video less than twenty-four hours after I talked to Tony. Tony couldn't have gotten a team together that fast. He's basically retired and he's sick. Quinn, on the other hand, controls his own army."

"Ordering people to break into your home seems like a rather risky thing for Quinn to do."

"Hey, the stakes are high for Quinn," DeMarco said. "We're talking about information that could destroy his life. And who knows what he told the guys who did the job. At his rank, you don't have to tell people much when you give them an order."

Neither of them said anything for a moment, and when Sherman shook her head—obviously disgusted by DeMarco's incompetence—DeMarco rose to leave. "I really appreciate that you were willing to help me and I'm sorry, but without Tony, I don't think there's anything else that can be done."

"Sit down, DeMarco. I'm not ready to give up quite yet. I'm going to subpoena the teacher, her old boyfriend, and Quinn's old partner. I want them all telling what they know about the cover-up that took place when Quinn killed Connors."

"They won't testify," DeMarco said. "Quinn's old partner said he'd take the Fifth."

"It's one thing for them to tell *you* they won't testify. It's a whole different story when they're sitting in a hearing room, eighteen senators staring down at them, knowing they'll go to jail for perjury if they lie."

"I don't know," DeMarco said. He was thinking that Dombroski wouldn't have any problem at all telling eighteen senators to go shit in their hats.

Sherman ignored DeMarco's skepticism. "And one other thing. See if Quinn's old partner knows who investigated the Connors shooting. We'll subpoena those guys, too, and see if they're willing to lie for Quinn." Before DeMarco could say anything, she added, "I realize the teacher and these other people won't have the same impact as the gangster saying that Quinn murdered two people, but if they testify, it's going to raise a stink and cast some doubt on Quinn's character. More important, I'm willing to bet that Quinn's made a lot of enemies over the years. You don't usually make it to the top unless you walk on a few people to get there. So maybe some of his enemies will come forward when they see us banging on Quinn."

"That's kind of a long shot," DeMarco said.

"Long shots are all we have. And we do have one other thing working to our advantage. As you may know, Senator Beecham is a very wealthy and influential man, and . . ."

"What? You want me to tell people he'll pay them to testify?"

"You know, when you say stupid things like that, DeMarco, it makes me nervous. What you say is that there are some people in Washington who don't want to see Quinn appointed and these people could be quite grateful, in an indirect way. You can just never tell what good fortune might befall folks who are cooperative. Are we clear?"

"Yes, ma'am."

"Good. I want you to go back to New York again and get me more names, as many people as you can find that were involved in the cover-up of that poor man's death . . ."

Sheesh. Connors had become "that poor man."

. . . and anyone you can find that can link Quinn to these mobsters, Taliaferro and Benedetto. I want a whole parade of people marching through that hearing room, telling stories about Brian Quinn."

DeMarco caught a late-afternoon shuttle to New York, rented a car, and by 7 P.M. was knocking on Janet Costello's door. He was going to let Janet know it was in her best interest to cooperate at the confirmation hearing and tell the truth. He was also going to do what Sherman had said and get any names Janet could give him regarding who else in Taliaferro's outfit, besides Sal Anselmo, might know about Quinn shooting Connors. It didn't appear that Janet was home, however.

He knocked again, and as he was doing so, a woman came out of the apartment across the hall, dressed in a bathrobe. She had some variety of long-haired canine on a leash, the dog smaller than most New York rats.

"Janet's gone," she said when she saw DeMarco. "She's on some sort of sabbatical. She left yesterday."

"A sabbatical?" He wasn't aware fifth-grade school teachers could take sabbaticals.

"That's what she said. She looked really happy."

"Did she tell you where she was going?"

"No. When I asked her she acted rather coy and just said it was someplace lovely this time of year. I was glad for her; she's always struck me as such an unhappy person."

DeMarco knew what Quinn had done: After he learned from Tony that DeMarco was trying to derail his confirmation hearing, Quinn convinced somebody in the New York school system to reward Janet Costello for her many years of service educating the city's children—and then got her out of town.

DeMarco thanked Costello's neighbor and left the apartment building. Standing out on the street, he looked at his watch. It was an hour-and-a-half drive from New York to Brick and it was the tail end of the rush hour. He'd get a room for the night and see Dombroski tomorrow.

Normally, when DeMarco was in Manhattan, he enjoyed himself. He liked New York and he liked New Yorkers. He liked the restaurants and bars, where all the young waitresses and bartenders seemed better looking than normal, probably because they were all wannabe actors waiting for their big break. He liked looking at the fashionably dressed, exotic women on Fifth Avenue and eating the tamales and falafel and hot dogs you could get from street vendors. He just liked the atmosphere of the place.

He didn't like the atmosphere now, however; he felt like he was behind enemy lines. This was Brian Quinn's town. He had an army at his disposal and he had DeMarco outmanned and outgunned—outgunned not just literally but in the sense that he had a lot more power than DeMarco had.

DeMarco also wondered if he was being followed. That would be a logical thing for Quinn to do, put a tail on him and keep tabs on what he was doing. He didn't have a sense that anyone was following him, and he hadn't noticed anyone, but he figured that if Quinn had people tailing him they'd be too good for him to spot. He checked into a hotel in Manhattan that had a decent restaurant and a good bar, but he was thinking that as he no longer had a steady income, he'd better start looking for cheaper places to sleep in New York. He wasn't going to stay with his mom, however, while he was going after Quinn; there was no way he was going to allow her to get caught up in what he was doing. To somewhat offset the cost of his room, he passed on the hotel's gourmet restaurant and bought two slices of pizza from a place a block away.

Like the last time DeMarco had seen him, Stan Dombroski was sitting in his backyard, drinking beer, enjoying his low-rent view. The fact that it was only 10 A.M. didn't appear to matter to Dombroski when it came to ocean-watching and beer drinking. The *New York Times* was in a pile next to his lawn chair; Dombroski was reading the sports pages.

When he saw DeMarco, he said, "Get the fuck out of here. I don't need any more trouble."

"What are you talking about?" DeMarco asked.

"Yesterday a couple guys showed up here. New York cops. They told me if I talked to you anymore, I was going to have a problem with my pension."

"Can they actually do that, mess with your pension?"

"Yes and no. If they try to screw up my benefits, I'll get the union involved and they'll go to bat for me, and eventually I'll win. But what they can do is stop my retirement check for a while and screw with me for about six months, making me and the union jump through every fuckin' hoop they can find. I can't last six months without a paycheck. I can't last six weeks."

"I'm sorry," DeMarco said.

"You may be sorry, but you're not the one pissing blood."

"What?"

"Yesterday when these guys started leaning on me, I got mad and started yelling, and one of them hit me in the kidney so hard I couldn't even move for about ten minutes. He said I'd tried to assault his partner and I was lucky they weren't arresting me. I don't know who they were. They showed me badges but I didn't pay any attention to the names. All I know is, they were two hardnosed motherfuckers and I don't ever want to see them again. And I don't want to see you again, either."

DeMarco was about to tell him that Amelia Sherman was going to subpoena him when Dombroski said, "Do me a favor before you go. Go into the house and bring out the six-pack in the fridge. It just hurts too much when I try to get up."

"You want me to take you to a doctor?" DeMarco said.

"No. Just get the beer."

DeMarco did as Dombroski asked and put a six-pack of Budweiser in the cooler next to Dombroski's chair.

"Stan, I'm sorry you got dragged into this but there's a good chance you're going to be subpoenaed to testify at Quinn's confirmation hearing."

"Goddamnit, I'm not going to do it. I'll take the Fifth."

"Well, you can try. And maybe you should get a lawyer, too."

"I can't afford a fuckin' lawyer, DeMarco! Why in the hell are you doing this to me?"

"I'll tell you what, Stan. If you can give me someone bigger than you to testify against Quinn, then maybe we can leave you out of this."

"Like who?

"I don't know. How 'bout the names of the people who investigated Quinn when he shot Connors? Maybe some of those guys got some rank after they helped cover up what Quinn did, and they'd be more impressive witnesses than you."

"I don't remember who investigated the shooting. That was a long time ago. But there's probably a file somewhere unless Quinn made it disappear."

DeMarco figured Sherman would have to subpoena the file. There was no way DeMarco would ever be allowed to see it.

"What about Quinn's enemies? There must be people in the department who don't like him." DeMarco told him what Sherman had said, about how people who made it to the top usually stepped on a few folks to get there.

"DeMarco, you gotta remember I spent twenty-five years in uniform. I was a grunt. I wasn't involved in all the political shit that Quinn pulled. If he made enemies, they would be people who were ten pay grades above me."

"Come on, Stan," DeMarco said. "He sent two of his thugs over here to rough you up. Give me something."

When Dombroski just sat there scowling, DeMarco said, "Okay, Stan, have it your way. But if you do get called to testify, I'd suggest you cooperate."

DeMarco turned to leave.

"Wait a minute," Dombroski said. "There's one thing but I don't know if it will help you. Quinn's got a girlfriend."

"A girlfriend? How do you know this?"

"From a buddy of mine who's still working. His patrol area is the East Village, Alphabet City, and one night he sees Quinn get out of a cab, all by himself, and he goes into this old brownstone. What struck my buddy was that Quinn was alone and his security guys weren't with him. You never see Quinn when he doesn't have security and Quinn doesn't usually take cabs; he has someone drive him."

"A couple weeks later, my buddy sees him again. He takes his breaks at a Greek place right across from the brownstone that he saw Quinn go into; he's got a thing for a waitress that works at the restaurant. Anyway, Quinn shows up in a cab again and without his bodyguards. This time my buddy hangs around for a while, and pretty soon a kid shows up with food from a takeout place. My friend catches the delivery kid when he comes back down and asks who he delivered the food to, and he said it was a woman named Pamela Weinman. Weinman is a nice-looking lady in her thirties, who also happens to be an assistant DA in Manhattan."

"How many people know about this?" DeMarco asked.

Dombroski laughed. "Knowing my pal, Bill, I'd say about half the fuckin' department. He's not the type who can keep a secret. I know he told guys who patrol the same area, and they kind of make a game out of it, seeing if they can spot Quinn visiting his girlfriend."

"How do you know she's his girlfriend?"

"Come on, DeMarco. Quinn sneaks out without his security, shows up at a lady's apartment at night, and orders out so they're not seen in a restaurant. What else could she be?"

DeMarco knew from the research he'd done on Quinn that Quinn's wife was the daughter of a federal judge and that from her mother's side of the family she'd inherited a ton of money. A ton being like maybe a hundred million. He knew Quinn lived in a co-op near Central Park and the place was probably worth ten million bucks, just based on the address. He didn't know how Quinn would feel about his extraordinarily rich wife divorcing him. He also didn't know if Quinn's infidelity could be used against him at the confirmation hearing. All he knew was that this was potentially good news.

He left Dombroski's place and drove around for a while to see if he could spot anyone tailing him. When he couldn't, he decided to have fish and chips at a place called the Cove Bar and Grill, which overlooked some body of water that he assumed was a cove. He took a seat on an outdoor patio at a table covered by a white and blue umbrella, and while he was waiting for his food to arrive, he called Amelia Sherman and told her what he'd learned: that Quinn had disappeared Janet Costello and it would probably be impossible to find her before the hearing; that two of Quinn's goons had threatened Stan Dombroski and roughed him up a little; and finally that Quinn had a girlfriend who worked in the Manhattan DA's office.

"Well, poop, DeMarco," Sherman said after he gave his report. "It looks like Brian Quinn is going to become the next director of the Federal Bureau of Investigation. There's no point calling Dombroski to testify without the teacher. She was the one who actually saw Quinn do something."

"Maybe we can track her down," DeMarco said. "Check with TSA and see if she caught a flight to somewhere. I don't have the clout to do that, but you do. Check cruise ships leaving New York, too."

"I'll do that," Amelia said, "but I doubt her name will be on a passenger list. Quinn's too smart for that."

"What about Quinn's girlfriend?"

"I don't see that helping much. For one thing, a rumor of marital infidelity without any proof isn't going to be enough to keep him from getting confirmed. The other thing is, my boss isn't in any position to raise the issue. He's too old to run around on his wife anymore, but I'm afraid that Senator Beecham has a long, very well documented history of straying from the marital bed."

"Shit," DeMarco said.

"Indeed," Sherman said.

They waited until he passed through the Holland Tunnel and was in New York City before they pulled him over.

DeMarco had no idea how they knew where he was. Cameras in the tunnel? He didn't think they'd followed him to Brick and he hadn't see any sign of them while he was in Brick or driving back from New Jersey to Manhattan. He wondered if they'd used a helicopter to monitor him. Whatever the case, a few blocks after he emerged from the tunnel, a black SUV appeared behind him, blue and red lights flashing in the windshield.

He pulled over and two guys in suits, one guy black, one white, exited the SUV. It was the same guys DeMarco had seen with Quinn at the Carlyle hotel. He wondered if it was the same guys who had Dombroski pissing blood. He rolled down the window and the white guy showed him a badge and said, "NYPD. Get out of the car. You're coming with us."

"Fuck you," DeMarco said.

"Fuck me?" the guy said, and he looked over at his partner and smiled. "Sir, you can either get out of the car and come with us peacefully or me and my partner will drag you out, beat the shit out of you for resisting arrest, and you'll come with us in handcuffs. Which would you prefer?"

The mood he was in, DeMarco was thinking he would actually enjoy trading punches with these two cops, even though he knew he'd lose. But what he didn't want was to waste his time sitting in a jail cell. He stepped out of the car and the white cop frisked him. "I'm not armed," DeMarco said as the cop patted him down.

"Well, I gotta make sure. We'd look like dumb shits if you ended up shooting our boss." As they were leading him back to their SUV, DeMarco said, "What about my car? It's a rental. I can't just leave it sitting there."

"Not my problem," the cop said. "But I imagine before long someone will come by and steal it or it'll get towed." He seemed to think this was funny.

Inside the SUV, the black guy sat in the back with DeMarco while the white guy drove.

DeMarco didn't ask where they were taking him because they'd already given him the answer to that question: they were taking him to see Quinn. And other than the fact that he was going to have a major hassle getting his car back, what was happening was actually fine with him. He was going to come face-to-face with his father's killer.

They drove silently for twenty minutes, using lights and the siren periodically to move traffic out of the way. DeMarco thought they would take him to 1PP, where Quinn's office was, but they didn't. Maybe Quinn didn't want anybody to see DeMarco near his office. They took him instead to Battery Park, where Quinn was waiting at an outdoor table, talking on his cell phone. Two men, who looked like Quinn's security detail, stood near him, scanning the crowd.

When they reached the table where Quinn was sitting, he nodded at the two cops who had brought DeMarco to him and they walked over to join the other two security guys.

"Sit down, DeMarco," Quinn said.

The night he'd seen Quinn at the Carlyle, DeMarco had been sitting some distance away. All he'd noticed was Quinn's prematurely gray hair, his patrician looks, his lean build, and how Quinn had struck him as being confident and in command even when talking to the president's chief of staff. Up close, he noticed that Quinn was at least three inches taller than him, had gray eyes, and was carrying a weapon in a shoulder holster, a black automatic. His arrogance was palpable—which infuriated DeMarco.

DeMarco sat there with his jaw clenched, his hands formed into fists, and it was taking all the willpower he possessed to keep from attacking Quinn. He may not have had it in him, as Emma had said, to shoot Quinn in cold blood, but he wouldn't have any problem at all with beating the man to a bloody pulp. He figured the best he'd be able to do, however, was throw one punch—and then four good-sized guys would wrestle him to the ground and handcuff him.

"This has to stop," Quinn said. "Whatever you think you know, whatever you've been told, you have no proof. You can't hurt me, DeMarco. Thanks to me, the rate of violent crime in New York has never been lower and I've been given awards by almost every civic organization in the city. And the media loves me. Did you see the profile they did on me last month in the *New Yorker*? I'm a personal friend to the mayor, the governor, and both of New York's senators, and the president practically begged me to take over the Bureau. He said there's no one else in the country that can match me in terms of my experience and accomplishments. So you can't hurt me, DeMarco, and you can't stop me. All you can do is annoy me. The question is: What should I do about you?"

"You killed my father," DeMarco said.

As if DeMarco hadn't spoken, Quinn said, "For the last twenty-four hours I've had an NYPD intelligence team pulling your life apart. I know about your connection to John Mahoney and I know you and Mahoney have pulled a lot of crap over the years. As director of the FBI, if I decide to do so, I'll find something I can use to put you in a federal prison. Given your history with Mahoney, that shouldn't be hard, but if I have to, I'll frame you. I will also do everything I can to make sure you never hold a decent job for the rest of your life, and by the time I'm finished with you, you'll either be in jail or living out of the back of your car. So you have a choice to make, DeMarco: you can either crawl back into your hole and hope that you never come to my attention again or you can continue to pursue a pointless vendetta against me, in which case I will destroy you."

Quinn gave DeMarco the full force of his eyes one last time, then put on sunglasses and walked over to join his security detail. With Quinn leading the way, he and his four men left Battery Park, reminding DeMarco of a pack of wolves, Quinn, of course, being the alpha male.

And that was the moment that everything changed. That was the moment when DeMarco decided he was going to kill Brian Quinn.

25

After Quinn left, DeMarco continued to sit at the table in Battery Park, gazing out at the Statue of Liberty, thinking about his decision to kill Brian Quinn and trying to figure out exactly how he was going to do it.

The way Quinn had spoken to him—acting as if killing Gino DeMarco had never really happened—was one reason why he'd decided to kill the man. Another was Quinn's insufferable arrogance, bragging about his accomplishments, so confident that with his power and connections, someone like DeMarco wouldn't stand a chance against him. But the final reason was that DeMarco knew that if he didn't find the courage to kill Quinn, Quinn would not only get away with what'd he done, but with his record and his abilities, he could very well end up in the Senate or even the White House.

DeMarco was still afraid that if he attempted—or succeeded—in killing Quinn, he would end up either dead or in jail. But now he didn't care. He was not going to allow Quinn to get away with what he'd done and become even more powerful than he already was.

The only question now was, How was he going to do it? Fifteen minutes later he had a plan.

DeMarco caught a cab back to the last place he'd seen his rental car. To his surprise and delight, the car was still there.

The first thing DeMarco needed to do was shake any cops who were tailing him. He had no doubt they were following him even if he couldn't see them, and he suspected they would continue to follow him until Quinn was confirmed. Or maybe they weren't physically following him. He could be tracked via his cell phone and his rental car almost certainly had some sort of anti-theft GPS device.

He dropped off the rental car back at LaGuardia, then found a cash machine and took the maximum he could get from his checking account: five hundred bucks. Money was going to be a problem. Every time he used a credit card or hit a cash machine, Quinn's people would be able to get a fix on the location where he used the cards. While he was waiting for a cab, he dismantled his cell phone and dropped the pieces into two separate trash cans. That decision not only cost him two hundred bucks, but like most people he'd become used to the convenience of a cell phone and knew that life without one was going to be painful. Pay phones were going the way of the dodo.

The next item on his agenda was acquiring a gun, one that was untraceable. He didn't want to fill out whatever paperwork it was that allowed nuts to buy weapons and shoot school kids and theaters full of people; he didn't want there to be any record of him purchasing a firearm. He could probably wander around flea markets and yard sales and gun shows, but that was all too slow and required too much work. The easiest way for him to obtain a gun was to get one from a man who used to work for Tony Benedetto: his cousin, the asshole.

———————◆◆◆———————

DeMarco had married Marie the year he went to work for Mahoney, about eight months after his father's funeral. He was making a decent salary; in fact, he was making a salary that was even better than he'd been expecting to make at that phase of his life. The wedding wasn't exactly a joyous occasion, however. His mother had never liked Marie—she thought Marie was a self-centered airhead—and thought her son was mistaking lust for love. Marie's parents weren't happy that their precious daughter was marrying the son of a mafia hit man, didn't like that Marie would be living in D.C., and considered DeMarco's employer—a politician—not much better than the mobster who'd employed DeMarco's father. The only ones who had a good time at their wedding were Marie's bridesmaids, who all got roaring drunk.

He didn't tell Marie a lot about what he did for Mahoney—and Marie didn't seem to care—nor did he tell her what his Aunt Connie had told him about the possibility of being indicted if he continued to work for Mahoney. No, he didn't tell her those things. He chose to be optimistic and they bought a house in Georgetown on P Street; it was a narrow, boxy, two-story structure made of white painted brick. Although it wasn't a big house, because it was located in Georgetown it was horrendously expensive. Marie thought of the place as her "starter" house. DeMarco soon found out that his wife excelled at spending more money than he made, and it wasn't long before the house was well furnished.

Looking back on what happened, DeMarco figured the root cause of the problem with his marriage was most likely boredom. Marie didn't have anything to do all day because she made no effort to get a job and she didn't have any hobbies—other than shopping and adultery. At some point, she started making trips up to New York. To see her mom, she said. To see her old girlfriends, she said. He found out later the trips were to see his cousin, Danny DeMarco, the handsomest guy in Queens.

When she divorced him to marry Danny, DeMarco managed to keep his house and his federal pension—assuming he'd be in the job long enough to collect a pension. Marie took everything else—their savings (which didn't amount to much), his car, and all the furniture in the house. It was really the furniture she wanted most, since she was planning to use all the expensive things she'd bought in D.C. to decorate her new place in New York. DeMarco ended up with no car, no cash, the bills for all the furniture she'd bought, and the exorbitant mortgage on a barren house. At the time his marriage ended, he wasn't sure whom he hated more: his ex-wife or his cousin.

Oddly enough, Marie had called him a few years ago when his cousin landed in jail, accused of murdering a man he actually hadn't murdered. Danny was a small-time thief, a fence, a con man, and as crooked as a mountain road, but he wasn't a killer. When Marie asked for his help getting Danny out of jail, he'd laughed and said a) he couldn't help him and b) he wouldn't help him. He told Marie that her husband could rot in prison for all he cared—and then it turned out he needed his cousin's help on a case he was working on at the time, so DeMarco made an under-the-table deal with the Queens DA to get Danny out of jail. He hadn't seen Danny since then and he hadn't seen Marie since she divorced him.

───◆◆◆───

DeMarco had a cab drop him off in Manhattan, then he spent two hours ducking in and out of buildings, taking short subway rides, ducking in and out of more buildings, trying to spot a tail. If they were tailing him, he couldn't tell. Finally, he ended up at his cousin's place of business, a mob-affiliated pawnshop in Queens.

The pawnshop was a shabby, dusty, dingy place with sheet metal screens that could be rolled down over the door and the windows at night. It was overflowing with an unimaginable collection of crap: musical instruments, tools, knives, fake antiques, rings, bicycles, and baby carriages—and one cigar-store wooden Indian that looked like it might actually be worth something. DeMarco knew the pawnshop was just a front for merchandise hijacked from trucks and pilfered from warehouses, then sold to shoppers who never questioned how it was that a pawnshop could beat the prices at Target.

Danny had been working in the pawnshop when he married DeMarco's ex-wife—and he still worked there, although he now ran the place. He wondered if Marie was disappointed that her husband hadn't climbed farther up the corporate ladder. DeMarco was, in fact, surprised that Marie was still married to Danny. One reason why, he supposed, was that his cousin was still a handsome man. He looked like DeMarco—nobody would be surprised to hear they were cousins—and they had the same thick, dark hair and almost identical noses and chins. That is, *almost* identical but not identical. For whatever reason, all Danny's facial features seemed to be organized in a more appealing way than DeMarco's and the end result was that where Joe was a good-looking man, Danny looked like a leading man.

The other reason that Marie might still be married to him was that Danny DeMarco was actually a lot of fun to be around—that is, he was a lot of fun when he wasn't turning you into a cuckold. He was a charming, likable guy and DeMarco suspected Marie had fallen for him in the first place because she was bored in D.C. being Joe's wife, and Danny was simply more entertaining.

There was a third possibility, DeMarco realized: maybe Danny was making a lot more money than DeMarco thought. All DeMarco knew was that his cousin had always been a small-time crook, but maybe over time he'd gotten into things that were more lucrative than fencing stolen goods. He could be connected to money laundering or drugs or God knows what. All DeMarco knew for sure was that his cousin couldn't be involved in anything legitimate and that he most likely had to be making a decent income to keep Marie happy.

The one possibility DeMarco refused to consider was that his ex-wife just plain loved the damn guy regardless of what he did or how much money he made.

———◆◆◆———

When DeMarco walked into the pawnshop, Danny was sitting behind the counter on a high stool, his feet up on the countertop, drinking a Pepsi, and watching a *Sopranos* rerun on a television set mounted high on one wall. DeMarco had the fleeting thought that maybe guys like Danny watched *The Sopranos* hoping to learn something—like the HBO series was some sort of mob training film. Danny was laughing at something one of Tony Soprano's hoods had said, when he saw DeMarco. His eyes widened in surprise and delight, and he used the remote to turn off the television.

"Jesus, Joe. I can't believe it." He said this with a big smile on his face—and had the counter not been in the way, he probably would have tried to hug DeMarco. Oddly enough, his cousin wanted to be friends. He was grateful that DeMarco had gotten him free of the murder charge and he figured that by now DeMarco would have gotten over his wife's unfaithfulness and his own treachery. DeMarco hadn't.

"I need a loaded gun with a silencer," DeMarco said without any preamble. "The gun can't be a piece of shit and the silencer has to be good."

"You're kidding," Danny said.

"Does it fuckin' look like I'm kidding?"

"Hey, okay. Take it easy. You going to tell me what's going on?"

"No." Then he paused and tried to lighten his tone. "I need you to do this for me, Danny. It's important. But I can't tell you why. So can you get me a gun?"

"Yeah, sure. It'll take me a couple of hours, but I can get one."

"How much will it cost?"

"Don't worry about that. I owe you."

DeMarco didn't argue with him; he needed all the cash he had on him. In fact, he needed a lot more than he had on him. He didn't know how long he'd be in New York and the cheapest hotel he'd been able to find in the area where he needed to be was two hundred bucks a night—tax not included. He thought about asking Danny for money but decided not to. He didn't want to be any more beholden to the guy.

"When you get the gun," DeMarco said, "stick it in a box and wrap up the box. Then I want you to drop it off before four P.M. tomorrow at the front desk of the St. Marks Hotel in the East Village. I haven't checked in yet and won't until tomorrow, but tell the guy at the front desk it's for me and I'll pick it up when I check in later."

"I can get you the gun today, Joe."

"No. Deliver it to the hotel before four tomorrow." He didn't bother to tell Danny why.

"Okay," Danny said. "You want to give me a phone number so I can reach you if I have to?"

"No. After you drop off the gun, you forget I was ever here. I'm serious, Danny. You don't want to be involved in what I'm doing and you have to make sure the gun can't be traced back to you."

"The gun will be clean. But I'm telling you, Joe, you don't want to get caught with an unregistered weapon with a silencer on it. Not in this town."

"Is there a back way out of here?" He knew his cousin had to have some kind of bolt hole, through an adjacent building or the one that butted up against the back of his shop. Rats like Danny always had an escape hatch.

"Sure," he said. "Come around behind the counter."

As DeMarco was leaving, Danny said, "It's really good to see you again, Joe."

And the damn guy was actually being sincere.

DeMarco left Danny's shop, and as he walked, he looked back frequently, checking for a tail. He didn't think anyone was following him. He slipped into a Chinese restaurant that had a pay phone and called Neil.

"I need you to send me five grand in cash. I can't use my credit cards or my debit card."

"Jesus, Joe, what the hell are you doing? Does this involve Quinn?"

"Will you send me the money? I'll repay you when I get back to D.C."

He didn't bother to add: *If I get back to D.C.*

Neil hesitated. DeMarco didn't know if the money bothered Neil—he was a tightwad—or if Neil just didn't want to be involved in any way with what DeMarco was doing. "Neil," DeMarco said, "I've sent a lot of business your way over the years. Don't be an asshole."

"Yeah, all right," Neil said. "Where do you want me to send the money?"

DeMarco told him the same thing he'd told Danny: FedEx the money to the St. Marks Hotel and make sure it gets there before 4 P.M. tomorrow. Then something occurred to DeMarco. "Also send me a cell phone, a smartphone, one that's not traceable to you." DeMarco didn't have time to go phone shopping and didn't want to spend his cash on a phone.

"Okay," Neil said. Then he added, "Joe, I'm telling you, you don't want to screw around with Quinn. Whatever you have in mind, whatever you're doing, you need to drop it."

DeMarco hung up.

He didn't want to check into a hotel, mainly because a hotel would want a credit card. So for the next twenty-four hours—the time it would take Neil to FedEx the cash—he was just going to move around New York, maybe catch a couple of movies so he could get some sleep. He also needed to buy some clothes: a few changes of underwear, a couple of shirts, a pair of pants, and a duffle bag to put everything in. Also a few items that could be considered a disguise: a couple of hats, a sweatshirt with a hood, sunglasses.

He hadn't thought about it before, but there were a lot of details involved in killing a man and he didn't have his father's experience. He wondered what he was overlooking.

26

Quinn's cell phone vibrated on the nightstand next to the bed.

"Damn it," Pam muttered. "I hope you don't have to go tearing out of here."

Quinn reached for his phone and checked the caller ID. "Sorry, I need to take this." He answered the phone, saying, "Quinn."

"It's Hanley, boss. I'm sorry to bother you, but we lost DeMarco."

"How the hell could you lose him?" Before Hanley could answer he said, "Hang on a minute." He turned to Pam and said, "I need to talk to this guy," and he left the bed and walked naked into the living room of Pam's apartment. Pamela didn't know about the DeMarco problem and he was hoping he wouldn't have to discuss the issue with her.

He took a seat in the living room and said to Hanley, "What happened?"

"He took his rental car back to LaGuardia and we figured he was catching the shuttle back to D.C. But he didn't. After he dumped the rental car, he caught a cab into the city and then he shook Grimes. I mean, he deliberately shook him. He started ducking into buildings, going in one entrance and out the other, taking subway rides, hopping on and off the trains, and he eventually shook him."

"So use his cell phone to find him."

"He dumped the phone in a trash can at the airport."

"Goddamnit," Quinn muttered. "So what are you doing now?"

"He's got relatives here. His mother, a couple of cousins, uncles. I've pulled together a list of all the ones I could identify and I've got guys watching their houses and apartment buildings in case he shows up at one of them."

"What did you tell the people you have looking for him?"

"Nothing. I just gave them his DMV photo and told them you wanted him located."

"Good. You got somebody looking to see if he's using his credit cards?"

"Yeah."

"Let me think a minute," Quinn said.

What the hell could DeMarco be doing? Quinn couldn't imagine him being able to come up with something else to use against him at the confirmation hearing. The only thing he could have used that might have been effective was Tony Benedetto's testimony or his videotaped statement. But the video was gone—Quinn had personally destroyed it—and Benedetto wasn't going to cooperate with DeMarco, not if he wanted to keep his son out of jail. In fact, Benedetto had already gotten himself admitted to a hospital so if he was called to testify, he could claim he was too ill to travel. The schoolteacher was at an upscale resort in the Adirondacks under a phony name; a female cop drove her there in an unmarked car so there wouldn't be any transportation records. Quinn doubted anyone would be able to find the teacher before the confirmation hearing, and without Benedetto and the teacher, DeMarco had nothing.

So what could DeMarco be doing? Was he in New York to see if he could squeeze Benedetto and force him to testify? If he was, that would be a waste of time. Tony, the old bastard, even as sick as he was, wouldn't cave in. He'd also been to see Dombroski, but Quinn figured there was no way they'd subpoena Dombroski to testify at the hearing, not without the teacher backing up Dombroski's statement. At least he didn't think so—but maybe he should get Dombroski out of town, too. Whatever the case, he wanted to find DeMarco. He didn't want the damn guy running around town without knowing what he was up to.

It occurred to him that DeMarco might be planning to kill him. That seemed pretty unlikely, however. DeMarco, as near as he'd been able to tell from the research his people had done, was a lawyer who'd never practiced law and did John Mahoney's dirty work. The guy was basically Mahoney's bagman; he wasn't a gunslinger. On the other hand, since DeMarco thought that he had killed his father and because vengeance was a hell of a motivator, he shouldn't underestimate the potential danger DeMarco posed.

"I want you to assign somebody to watch my place," Quinn said.

"You think he might try to do something to you, boss?"

"I doubt it, but you can never tell with a nut like him. I'm also going to get his picture out to the guys in patrol and transit. I want the whole department looking for him. So I want you to email DeMarco's DMV photo to John Braddock, then I'll talk to Braddock. Don't give Braddock DeMarco's name, just his picture."

"Okay, but what if somebody finds him? What do you want them to do?"

"I want them to call me. I need to make sure everybody understands that, Hanley. I don't want anyone approaching him. I just want them to call me when he's been located and then I'll call you. You understand?"

"Yeah, boss."

Quinn hung up and sat there, thinking. So far he'd limited knowledge of the DeMarco problem to Hanley and Grimes because he knew he could trust them completely, and he essentially told them the truth without giving them any details. He said he'd made a dumb rookie mistake and DeMarco was trying to exploit the situation and derail his chance of being confirmed as director of the FBI. He said he needed their help to get DeMarco off his back, knowing that Grimes and Hanley would do anything for him. He'd also told them that when he went to Washington, and if they wanted to go with him and continue to be his personal security guys, he'd get them temporarily detailed to D.C., where they'd not only collect their current salaries but also collect per diem the whole time they were down there.

He then told Hanley and Grimes that DeMarco had in his possession a video of an old mafia guy named Tony Benedetto and Quinn needed to get the video. Benedetto was a sick old man and DeMarco had forced him to tell a pack of lies that DeMarco could use to build a trumped-up case against him. And that's all it took. Hanley and Grimes got three other guys, two of them retired cops and one of them a technical guy who could deal with alarm systems and computers, and they broke into DeMarco's house and recovered the video. Hanley didn't tell the people who accompanied him to D.C. anything other than that he was looking for a video of an old guy talking. When they found the video camera in DeMarco's basement lockbox, the only one who looked at it was Hanley and he told Quinn he only looked at it long enough to confirm that Benedetto was on it—and Quinn believed Hanley. Fortunately, it didn't appear as if DeMarco had copied the video; at least Quinn hoped so. They hadn't found any evidence on DeMarco's computer that a copy had been made or emailed, nor had they found Benedetto's statement on any CDs or flash drives in DeMarco's house.

The teacher had been easy. Quinn and his wife were big supporters of the New York public school system, donating money and helping out on a variety of projects with at-risk kids. Quinn called up the school superintendent and told her he needed to get Janet Costello out of town for her own safety but he didn't want Janet to know she was in danger. The superintendent told Janet that a big donor—a man who wished to remain anonymous—wanted to reward Janet in a small way for her years of service. The donor claimed that she had made a lifelong impression on him, and because he was now a rich man in a position to pay her back, he was treating her to two weeks at a resort in the Adirondacks. The school system was giving her the time off without making her use her vacation time. Janet obviously didn't have a clue who this person could be; she wasn't aware she'd ever made an impression on any of the idiots she'd taught, but she gladly accepted her reward.

Quinn didn't have to tell Hanley and Grimes much of anything regarding Dombroski. He just told them that Dombroski was co-operating with DeMarco and he wanted Hanley and Grimes to let Dombroski know that he'd better stop cooperating.

Quinn had a problem, however. Hanley and Grimes may have been willing to do anything for him, but it wasn't going to be so simple to get the entire police department looking for DeMarco. Quinn knew that if he ordered a full-scale manhunt, his cops would find the damn guy in a couple of days, maybe in a couple of hours, but a manhunt meant getting people looking at both public and private surveillance camera feeds, checking to see if he was registered in hotels, and plastering his picture in the papers and on television. The problem with doing that was that at some point he'd have to tell the media *why* he was looking for DeMarco, and he didn't want to go down that path. He finally decided to search for DeMarco in a more low-key way, knowing in advance that the chances of finding the bastard were smaller.

He called John Braddock. Braddock was the deputy commissioner in charge of NYPD's antiterrorism division. He told Braddock that Hanley was emailing him a picture of a man and he wanted every beat cop and transit cop in the city to get a copy of the picture. He also told Braddock he wanted him to employ the so-called Ring of Steel.

The Ring of Steel, named after a similar surveillance system in London, uses more than three thousand surveillance cameras to watch for terrorists and common criminals. In New York most of the cameras are located in midtown and lower Manhattan, and the majority of those were focused on high-value terrorists targets: the New York

Stock Exchange, the World Trade Center memorial, federal buildings, bridges, and tunnels. The system uses artificial intelligence software in addition to human eyeballs, and the software contains algorithms that direct the cameras to search for specific shapes and sizes—like suspicious packages that might contain bombs—and specific human faces. The cameras would now be hunting DeMarco.

Quinn told Braddock the same thing he'd told Hanley: that when DeMarco was found no one was to approach him; they were to call Quinn. When Braddock asked why Quinn was hunting for this unnamed man, Quinn said, "I can't tell you, John. It's just something the guys in D.C. asked me to do."

Although a man of Braddock's rank was normally in the loop, he wasn't totally surprised that Quinn didn't tell him more about the person they were hunting for. This sort of thing had happened before, and almost always for something related to terrorism. The CIA or FBI or NSA—or one of the dozen other alphabet agencies in D.C. involved in counterterrorism—would get a whisper about some Muslim fanatic being in the United States. They might not have a name, only a grainy picture taken by a satellite or a predator drone, and they'd ask police departments around the country to be on the lookout for the person of interest. Because the information was classified or came from classified sources, the feds didn't share a lot of details with the local cops. And that's basically what Quinn was telling John Braddock, and because Braddock owed his job to Quinn and was hoping that Quinn might endorse him to be the next police commissioner, he would do as Quinn asked.

After Quinn finished talking to Braddock he rejoined Pamela in bed.

"Is everything okay?" she asked. She was sitting up, the sheets down around her waist.

"Yeah. I just needed to talk to a couple of people to get something moving."

"I'll be so glad when you're out of that job. The stress you're under is unimaginable." They both thought that being in charge of the Bureau was going to be less stressful than being the New York City police commissioner.

Pamela Weinman looked good sitting there, the sheets down around her waist. She had long dark hair, but the only time she let it down was when they were in bed together. When she was working, she always wore it tied in some kind of bun or piled on top of her head in a fancy braid. She thought she looked more professional if she wore her hair that way. He loved to watch her pull the pins from her hair and let it fall to her shoulders as they undressed for bed.

She had a narrow face and luminous dark eyes, eyes he thought of as Gypsy eyes, although as far as he knew her family didn't have any Romani blood in them. She was slim like him because she jogged almost every day like he did. Her breasts were works of art. As far as he was concerned—although he'd never said it out loud—she could have posed for the *Venus de Milo*.

But it wasn't just her looks and it wasn't all about sex. He loved being with her. He loved the way her mind worked. He loved her quiet, sophisticated sense of humor. He loved that she understood the politics of the city and what it took to get things done in New York, New York. She was a realist, not an idealist.

He'd met her on a case she was trying two years ago and they both swore that the moment they saw each other was one of those events that happens only once in your life: an instant connection that was lust but more than lust. His marriage had been over years ago, not so much sexually but intellectually. He'd found Barbara interesting at first, mostly because she came from a higher social class than him. She knew the people who made things happen in New York—people in politics and business and the media. Just listening to her talk about those people had impressed him then. Barbara had also traveled all over the world, and at that time he met her, he'd never left the United States, not even a trip to Canada.

Later, after they'd been married not all that long, he realized that his wife may have been sophisticated and cultured, but she wasn't really all that bright. In fact, she was extraordinarily shallow. Her primary interest in life was looking good and making her homes look good. Their apartment was perpetually being remodeled.

But he had needed her in the beginning. He had needed her family's influence. And when her mother died and left Barbara all her money, he had to admit that he liked that, too. Now he didn't need her connections and he didn't really need her money, either. These days she simply bored him to tears. After he started seeing Pam he couldn't stand to be around Barbara.

He would miss the money after they divorced, although his highest priority had never been money. It had always been his career. He also now had money of his own from books he'd written and investments he'd made, and when he finished his term as director of the FBI, he could write his own ticket with a dozen different companies. But he wasn't thinking that far ahead yet. He'd spend the next two years running the Bureau, make his mark on the job, and when the president left office, he'd decide what he wanted to do. Most likely, it would be something in politics, as opposed to a lucrative private sector job. Governor of New York, senator from New York, and then, maybe, who knows, a run at the Oval Office. And Pam understood all this. She, too, believed that public service and the challenges that came with it were more important than money. They were the ideal couple.

He was going to divorce Barbara within the year. Thank God, they'd never had children. He and Pam had talked the plan over and she agreed it would be best to wait until after he was confirmed and had been in the job for a couple of months. That way, they decided, the divorce wouldn't generate much of a political ripple. He didn't think Barbara would fight the divorce unless he went after her money and he didn't have any intention of doing that. Then he and Pam would get married and . . . Once again, he didn't see the point in looking farther ahead, but he knew she would be the last wife he would ever have.

Right now the only thorn in his side was this fool, DeMarco. Quinn had made only one big mistake when he was young—accidentally shooting Connors—but after he'd killed Jerry Kennedy and Gino DeMarco, he'd been able to put that mistake behind him. He felt bad about what Carmine had forced him to do but it was water under the bridge, and since that time he'd done a lot of good, more than enough good to compensate for the deaths of a couple of mafia hoodlums. There was no one who would disagree that he had been a champion of law and order and he'd done as much as anyone to keep terrorists from attacking his great city again. He also believed, sincerely, all false modesty aside, that the country would be safer if he was in charge of the FBI.

Yes, the good he had done and would do in the future far outweighed a youthful mistake and his inability to get out from under that bastard Taliaferro. Carmine Taliaferro had been the devil, and even from the grave he exerted an unwelcome influence on Quinn's life, but it was now an influence that was tolerable.

He was not going to let Gino DeMarco's son ruin his life.

———————————◆◆◆———————————

Hanley emailed DeMarco's photo to John Braddock, assigned a couple of men to park outside the building where Quinn and his wife lived, and then checked in by phone with the cops he had watching DeMarco's relatives. Nobody had seen the damn guy.

Hanley didn't know exactly what was going on with DeMarco. He believed Quinn's story, that Quinn had made some sort of rookie mistake and that DeMarco was trying to use it to ruin Quinn. Quinn's story rang true. He suspected, however, that Quinn hadn't told him and Grimes everything—that there was a whole lot more going on with DeMarco—but it didn't really matter, not to him or Grimes.

Hanley didn't know what Quinn had done for Grimes. He and Grimes had been partners for four years and spent ten or twelve hours a day together, but they weren't friends. In fact, Hanley wasn't sure Grimes had any friends. He was one of those people who stayed totally inside himself. At any rate, he knew Quinn had done something for Grimes, something huge, because Grimes was just as loyal to the man as he was—and Hanley would do anything for Brian Quinn.

When Hanley got back from Iraq, he was kind of fucked-up. No, that wasn't right. He was *totally* fucked-up. He'd been a New York cop for five years before he went overseas with the Army Reserve, and he'd seen all the violence and mayhem the Big Apple had to offer. He'd been in gunfights, he'd seen a score of dead bodies, he'd ended up in the emergency room twice as a result of tussling with assholes so high on drugs they thought they were supermen. But Iraq was different. For one thing, you could never relax; it wasn't like being a cop where you could go home after the end of your shift. You just never knew when the crazies were going to blow you up or when some guy you thought was an ally might decide to shoot you.

The other thing was he'd never seen people blown up before. He'd seen rotting corpses, dead babies in plastic bags lying in Dumpsters, guys' heads turned to red mush by shotguns—but he'd never seen detached arms and legs and scorched body parts splattered all over the inside of a personnel carrier. The worst thing he saw was one of his buddies, a guy he'd been close to, walking ahead of him one day when an IED went off. His buddy was literally blown in half. The top half of him looked normal—his face oddly enough actually looked peaceful, wearing the expression he'd been wearing right before the blast—but below his waist there was nothing left but a slimy trail of blood and entrails. That had really messed up Hanley; it messed him up for months.

He didn't know how he got assigned as Quinn's driver and bodyguard, but he was really glad that he was given the job. He just hadn't been ready to go back out on patrol when he got back from that insane, pointless war. He was afraid he just might lose it and start shooting people. Fortunately, when he was interviewed by the department's psychiatrists after he returned from Iraq, he didn't say anything about the PTSD and he tested normal. He knew a bad psych eval could have messed up his career and he might have been put behind a desk, which was the last thing he wanted. Luckily, somebody in personnel made the decision to assign him to the commissioner's security detail, and they probably chose him because he looked good on paper: an Iraq War vet with a bunch of medals, an experienced cop with commendations, a guy who could shoot and who was strong and would most likely throw his own body in front of Quinn if it ever came to that.

At first, and just like he'd expected, Quinn didn't have much to say to him. He was aloof and curt, and got pissed if he had to repeat an order. He ignored Hanley most of the time as he sat in the back of the car talking on his phone or reading something as he went from meeting to meeting. Basically, it was just like the army: Quinn was an officer and Hanley was a grunt. After a while, though, he loosened up and they'd talk, particularly in the evening, when Quinn was pretty much finished for the day and on his way home.

One night, after Quinn had had a couple of drinks at some party, he asked Hanley about his family and Hanley told him he had a wife, a girl he'd know since grade school, and two kids, a boy and a girl. Then for some reason, probably because it was weighing so heavily on his mind, he told Quinn his son had just been diagnosed with a rare cancer. He said they didn't know what kind of treatment his boy was going to need or how curable the disease was, but he and his wife had an appointment in two weeks where they'd learn more. He concluded with: "I mean, two fuckin' weeks? You'd think they'd move faster than that." He wished immediately that he hadn't said *fuck* and knew he was saying a whole lot of shit that Quinn wasn't interested in hearing.

"Who's his doctor?" Quinn asked.

"Some Indian guy at Beth Israel. Or maybe he's Pakistani. I don't know. He has a long name I can't pronounce. But he seems like a smart guy."

"Hmm," Quinn said, and Hanley figured that meant Quinn had probably heard enough about Hanley's problems, and when Quinn pulled out his cell phone, he was certain he had. Quinn dialed a number. "Bill, it's Brian Quinn. I'm fine, how are you? Look, I'd like you to do me a favor. One of my guys has a sick kid, cancer, and I'd like you to take a look at him for me. Thanks, Bill, I really appreciate it. I don't know. Hang on. Hanley, what number can your wife be reached at?"

Hanley rattled off the number, unable to believe what Quinn was doing, and Quinn repeated it to Bill, whoever the hell Bill was.

After he and Bill chatted a bit more, Quinn hung up and said, "That was Dr. William Layman, who's possibly the best oncologist in this city. He was my mother-in-law's oncologist and thanks to him, she lived until she was eighty-seven. Someone from Bill's office will call your wife tomorrow and make an appointment for your son."

"Jeez, boss, I . . . I don't know what to say." Hanley realized he was crying and hoped Quinn didn't notice.

"You don't have to say anything. Just get your kid in to see him tomorrow."

In the end, his boy ended up down in Houston and they hooked him up with some super cancer doctor down there doing cutting-edge stuff and his son was now cancer-free. And Hanley never saw a bill. His insurance handled the medical stuff but he never even saw a bill from when his wife and daughter had to stay in Houston for six weeks while they were treating his son.

Hanley would do anything for Brian Quinn.

27

DeMarco entered the St. Marks Hotel carrying a small duffle bag. He was wearing a blue baseball cap decorated with a Nike swoosh, a lightweight dark jacket, blue jeans, and a dark blue T-shirt. His Ninja outfit—he'd be one with the night. He'd also stopped shaving the day he made up his mind to kill Brian Quinn.

DeMarco had a heavy beard and normally shaved every day. If he didn't, he didn't look sexy like those actors and male models who had a perpetual three-day beard—he just looked like a guy who needed a shave. In four days, he'd look like a bum. A beard, a hat, and sunglasses, however, were the best he could do for a disguise.

He started toward the front desk to see if the clerk had two packages for him when he heard, "Joe."

He turned to the speaker. He'd recognized the voice. It was Marie. Goddamnit, what was she doing here?

She looked incredible. It had been years since he'd last seen her, and he'd expected that she would have put on some weight because her mother had put on weight as she'd aged. But Marie hadn't. If anything, she'd lost a few pounds and her cheekbones were like knife blades. Her hair was shorter than she'd worn it when she was married to him and it perfectly framed her face. Her body was as flawless as it had always been, and she was wearing a dress that clung to every curve she had.

One of DeMarco's recurring fantasies was running into Marie and Danny on the street one day. In his fantasy, Danny was fat and bald. Marie was fat, too, and she'd have a slight mustache and wobbly skin under her chin. His fantasy was not to be. Marie and his cousin were still two of the best-looking people DeMarco knew. Even though she was almost forty, she just took his breath away.

The thing about Marie was that she was the sexiest woman he'd ever known. There are some women, for whatever reason, who just ooze sex appeal and it wasn't just a matter of their appearance. Like Amelia Sherman. Most people would probably consider her better-looking than DeMarco's ex-wife—DeMarco doubted that Marie would have been voted Miss Georgia—yet Marie was more desirable than Amelia Sherman. Marie had an air of wantonness about her, a sexual energy, an animal heat. Whatever the hell it was, you knew, just looking at her, that she'd be incredible in bed—and she was. DeMarco had known almost from the day he met her that she was vain and self-centered—but none of that mattered. He just wanted her. He wanted her even after he knew she'd cheated on him. Hell, he wanted her now.

He walked over to her and whispered, "What are you doing here?"

"You're looking kind of rough, Joe," she said, then reached up and ran a soft hand over his unshaven face. "Rough, but sexy."

"Why are you here?"

"I bought you the . . . you know. We didn't think it would be smart for Danny to bring it, not with his record. Anyway, I gave it to the guy at the desk but decided to hang around for a while to see you."

So his idiot cousin had told his idiot ex-wife everything. Goddamnit.

"Marie, you have to get out of here. You and Danny have no idea what I'm involved in, and you're putting your lives in danger by helping me. Now you need to leave and just hope than nobody tailed you here. And if anybody asks you about me, you have to say you haven't seen me."

"I thought maybe we could just have one drink. You know, catch up a bit."

"Marie, you're not listening to me. You can't be seen with me. It's too dangerous." Then he took her hands—and when he touched her it was as if an electric current ran through his body. "I really appreciate you and Danny helping me but you have to go. Now."

"Okay, Joe," she said, giving him a look that said, *I've missed you so.* He knew the look was just part of her act, something designed to get his heart racing—or to be accurate, to get his heart to pump all the blood in his body to his dick. Then she stood on her tiptoes and gave him a soft kiss on the lips and turned and walked away and he followed her with his eyes. And she knew he was looking.

———◆◆◆———

He retrieved his two packages from the clerk at the front desk. One package—the one Marie had brought—was the size of a shoe box, wrapped in brown paper, and contained the gun and silencer that Danny was supposed to get for him. The five thousand dollars in cash and the cell phone Neil had sent were in a padded FedEx envelope. He put the box containing the gun into his new duffle bag, then opened the FedEx envelope and removed a thousand dollars in cash. He put the thousand in the front pocket of his jeans and then put the envelope containing the cell phone and the rest of the cash in his duffle bag and left the hotel. He'd never intended to stay at the St. Marks, mainly because Danny and Marie thought he was staying there. He didn't trust Danny and Marie.

He walked a mile to a Comfort Inn in the East Village, continually checking to see if he was being followed, and entered the hotel.

"I called just a while ago," he said to the woman at the front desk, "and was told you had some vacancies." He actually had called the hotel's central booking number and knew this to be true.

"Yes, sir, we do have some rooms available."

"What's the rate for your cheapest room? I don't need anything fancy."

She told him and DeMarco pretended to be surprised. "Well, that seems kind of steep," he said, "but okay. I need a room for at least three days, maybe longer, but I don't know yet. But I have a problem."

"Oh?" the woman said—and she took stock of DeMarco's somewhat grubby appearance.

"My kid brother's apartment building caught on fire last night and he's in the hospital. Smoke inhalation." DeMarco knew, thanks to the *Times*, that there actually had been two apartment building fires in Manhattan the previous night. He was also hoping the tragedy he'd invented would make the clerk feel sympathetic. "Anyway, I just found out about it this morning and caught the first flight I could get out of Vermont. I barely made the plane, and I didn't have time to book a room in advance." He figured an unshaven guy dressed in jeans and a baseball cap would be how most New Yorkers would picture folks from Vermont. "The thing is, right after I saw my brother at the hospital, I got robbed. This asshole—excuse my language—came up behind me when I get off the subway, right in broad daylight, and stuck a gun in my back."

"I'm very sorry to hear that," the clerk said, but looked more skeptical than sympathetic. Fuckin' New Yorkers were skeptical of everything.

"The thing is," DeMarco said, "he got my wallet and everything in it: cash, my ID, my Visa card, and my ATM card. So I don't have any credit cards or an ID. But fortunately, he didn't take my bag and I always carry extra cash when I travel."

DeMarco pulled a wad out of his pocket and said, "That's a thousand bucks. Enough to pay for a room for three days with money left over to use for a deposit on any room charges. I already called Visa to cancel my old card and they're sending me a new one and my wife's going to FedEx my passport to me so I'll have ID to get back on the plane, but I won't get either one of those things for a couple of days. So can I get a room here? I want to be someplace close to the hospital, and I can't afford to spend an arm and a leg."

"I'll need to check with my manager, sir."

DeMarco wondered when cash had become a bad thing.

She walked away from the desk and through a small door located behind her. Two minutes later she came back and pushed a registration form toward him. "I'm so sorry about what happened to you, sir. And really, the crime rate in New York is much smaller than in most large cities. I hope the rest of your stay here will be better and that your brother recovers, of course."

"Thanks," DeMarco said and filled out the registration form using the first name that popped into his head—Jack Williams. Now he had a room in the East Village—in other words, a base from which to operate—and the hotel didn't have his real name.

DeMarco went up to his room, plugged the charger into the phone Neil had sent him, and then looked at the gun. It was a matte black Heckler & Koch P30, 9mm semiautomatic. He screwed the silencer into the barrel—it fit but he had no idea how well it would suppress the noise of a gunshot. Included with the gun were two full magazines, each containing fifteen stubby bullets. All DeMarco needed was one bullet, maybe two—if he ended up needing thirty that would mean that something had gone terribly wrong.

He dry-fired the weapon a couple of times, then ejected all the bullets from the magazines. Putting on a pair of latex gloves, he wiped each bullet and the entire gun to remove fingerprints, including any that might have been left by his cousin. His intent was to wear gloves every time he touched the pistol from this moment forward.

He looked at his watch. It was 5 P.M. He slipped off his shoes and set the bedside alarm clock for six. He'd nap for an hour before the hunt began.

28

DeMarco's plan for killing Brian Quinn was simple.

He knew from Stan Dombroski that Quinn had a mistress named Pamela Weinman, and Quinn visited Weinman at her apartment in the East Village, which was directly across from a Greek restaurant. He'd called Dombroski the day before to get the name of the restaurant. DeMarco figured that Quinn would see Weinman at least once a week, and probably more often than that. He also knew from Dombroski that when Quinn met with his mistress, his security guys wouldn't be with him. So his plan was to hang around Weinman's apartment building every evening and wait for Quinn to show up, and when Quinn left the building, he was going to kill him.

He knew that there would almost certainly be people on the street when he shot Quinn—in New York there were always people on the street—so he was going to shoot Quinn through his jacket with the silenced Heckler & Koch pistol. After he fired a shot—maybe two—he'd simply walk away, hoping passersby would focus on Quinn lying on the ground and not on him. If someone pointed at him or yelled that he was the shooter, then he'd run. As he was running he'd drop the gun and head for the nearest subway entrance or catch a passing cab, then he'd ride to New Jersey and catch a train back to D.C. Before he caught the train, if he had time, he'd buy a new set of clothes and throw away the ones he was wearing, which would most likely have gunshot residue on them.

He also knew that after he killed Quinn he would be a suspect and the cops would come after him—and he decided that there wasn't anything he could do about that. He wouldn't have an alibi for the time when Quinn was killed and Quinn's people—his security guys—would know that DeMarco had been in New York before the shooting. But if nobody saw his face clearly when he shot Quinn, and since he was staying in New York under a phony name and not using his credit cards, they might not be able to prove that he'd been in New York when Quinn was killed. So if nobody was able to ID him—and he'd be wearing a ball cap and his face would be unshaved and it would be after dark—and if the cops didn't have any physical evidence that he'd killed Quinn—then maybe he'd be able to keep from getting convicted. Maybe.

It was, he realized, a really shitty plan for getting away with murder, but he couldn't think of a better one.

He also would have preferred to look Quinn in the eye before he shot him. It wasn't just that shooting a man in the back seemed cowardly; it was also because he would have liked the opportunity to tell Quinn why he was killing him. He would have said that it wasn't just because Quinn had killed his father. This was about more than revenge. He couldn't allow a man like Quinn, a man without a conscience, a man willing to kill if necessary to advance, to become even more powerful than he already was. But DeMarco knew that he wasn't going to have the satisfaction of making a speech before he killed Quinn; as distasteful as it was, he was going to have to simply shoot the man in the back and run.

——— ◆ ———

DeMarco didn't go into the Greek restaurant across from Weinman's apartment building because Dombroski had said that it was a place where cops sometimes took their breaks. Instead he entered a Thai place that was just a couple of doors down from the Greek restaurant. He could see the entrance to Weinman's building from there. He ordered a meal—one that he intended to linger over for as long as he could.

As he was waiting for his meal, he studied the apartment building. It was an old four-story brownstone. There was no doorman; it wasn't a ritzy place because Weinman couldn't afford a ritzy place in Manhattan on an assistant DA's salary. There were a few steps leading up from the street to the building's entrance, and when you passed through the door, you were in a small foyer where the mailboxes were located. A few feet from the mailboxes was a set of stairs.

When Quinn left the building after spending time with his mistress, he would walk down the steps and then probably walk immediately over to the curb to catch a cab. That is, DeMarco assumed that since he'd arrived by cab, he'd catch one when he was ready to leave and not call somebody to pick him up. It wouldn't take Quinn more than a couple of seconds to reach the curb and then he'd be standing—with his back to the building—only long enough to flag down a taxi. And that's when DeMarco would kill him.

The problem DeMarco had was that there was no place for him to hide before he shot Quinn. After Quinn entered the building, DeMarco would have to stand a few feet away from the entrance and simply wait until Quinn came out. He was guessing that when Quinn came to see Weinman, he would be inside her place for at least an hour but more likely two or three hours, which meant that DeMarco was going to have to linger outside the building for all that time. DeMarco also figured that Quinn would show up sometime after 6 P.M. if he showed up at all. The police commissioner of New York would most likely work until at least six every day and probably longer.

DeMarco stayed inside the Thai restaurant until seven thirty—he couldn't stretch out his dinner any longer—and by the time he left the restaurant, the sun had gone down. This didn't mean, however, that he would be invisible standing outside Weinman's building—the street was too well lit—but he was hoping that in the dimmer light, his face would be less recognizable.

After leaving the restaurant, he stood in a couple of different places on the street—places where he could see the entrance to Weinman's building—and the whole time he waited, he felt totally exposed. At 11 P.M., he decided that Quinn wasn't going to visit his mistress that night and returned to his hotel.

The following day he stayed inside his room watching TV and reading the *Times*. He left his room only once, making a quick trip to a nearby deli to get a couple of sandwiches. He thought it possible that Quinn could have people looking for him and he wanted to minimize the risk of some cop seeing him on the street during the daylight hours. It was hard to do, but he forced himself not to think about what lay ahead. He didn't want to think about how he'd feel after he killed Quinn and he didn't want to think about the manhunt that would follow after he murdered the man.

———————◆◆◆———————

At 6 P.M., he was back in the Thai restaurant where he'd eaten the night before. It wasn't ideal to eat in the same restaurant two nights in a row, but he wanted to be off the street as long as possible while waiting for Quinn. He couldn't go to the Greek restaurant for fear of running into cops and the other restaurants on the street—a by-the-slice pizza place and a falafel joint—were on the same side of the street as Weinman's building, which meant he couldn't see the entrance to the building.

He ordered a large meal and ate it slowly, and just as he was finishing his dinner, about 7 P.M., he saw a cab stop in front of Weinman's building and watched Quinn exit the cab. DeMarco finished his dinner, left cash on the table to cover the check, and went into the restroom. The gun was stuck in the back of his pants and every time he'd touched it, he'd worn gloves. He put on the gloves now, almost clear, transparent latex gloves; he was hoping the gloves wouldn't be too noticeable. He screwed the silencer into the barrel of the gun.

He shoved the gun into the right-hand pocket of his jacket. The jacket had deep pockets and he'd torn a hole into the right-hand pocket so the silencer would fit through the hole. When it was time to shoot Quinn, he'd aim the gun through the jacket. It would be awkward shooting that way but it could be done and he wasn't worried about not being able to aim well as he planned on being very close to Quinn when he pulled the trigger.

Just before he left the restroom, he looked into the mirror—at the hard, unshaven face staring back at him, the face that looked just like his father's face. *Are you sure you can do this?* he silently asked the man in the mirror.

He didn't have any moral qualms about killing Quinn. His conscience wouldn't bother him at all. But he was about to do something that was going to jeopardize his own life and freedom and, ironically, unless he was caught, no one would even know why he'd killed Quinn. People would think that Quinn had been assassinated because of who he was—a cop who had put criminals in jail and who had prevented acts of terrorism—and DeMarco could already hear the grand eulogies lamenting the great man's death. But the real question, the question he was asking the man in the mirror, was would he have the courage to pull the trigger when the time came?

Yes, he would. He wasn't going to back down now.

He left the restaurant, crossed the street, and took up his position, leaning against the wall of Weinman's apartment building about five feet from the door. He was wearing his Nike baseball cap pulled down low on his forehead. He would like to have worn sunglasses but it was now dark outside, and he figured the baseball cap combined with the sunglasses and his unshaven face might make him look like a mugger. In case anybody was watching him, every few minutes he looked at his watch to give the impression he was impatiently waiting for someone. He wondered how long he was going to have to wait for Quinn.

He couldn't help but notice that there were a lot of people on the street even though it was now 8 P.M. Single folks walking rapidly to get to a bus or subway stop; couples strolling holding hands; people walking their dogs, little plastic poop bags in their hands. DeMarco had no doubt that when it was time to shoot Quinn, somebody would be passing within a few feet of him. To occupy his mind, and to keep from thinking about what he was about to do, he focused on the good-looking women he saw—but then he couldn't help but think that if he went to prison for killing Quinn, he might not see a good-looking woman again for the rest of his life.

Stop it, he told himself. If he started thinking about prison, he'd never be able to go through with this. Working for Mahoney, he'd been tossed into a cell a couple of times, but never for more than a few hours. He didn't know if he'd be able to stand spending the rest of his life in a cage surrounded by people who really belonged in cages. Suicide had to be preferable to that. *Stop it*, he again told himself.

John Martinez held his wife's hand, and she held the hand of their five-year-old daughter. He looked at his watch: 8:10 P.M. He'd just wasted two hours of his life. As they walked toward the subway, Martinez was wondering if there was any way he could stop these weekly dinners with his mother-in-law. She was a miserable, dour, unhappy bitch of an old woman and the weekly dinners were worse than a visit to a proctologist. But his wife—who wouldn't admit it, but who didn't really like her mother, either—felt obligated, since her father died, to visit the old bat so she wouldn't be so lonely. As near as Martinez could tell, his mother-in-law wasn't lonely at all and he could also tell that she hated having her granddaughter inside her apartment. The whole time they were with her, the old lady watched Sara like a hawk, terrified the little girl was going to knock over one of her stupid Hummel figurines, which she claimed were worth a fortune.

Martinez's wife and daughter were jabbering about something, and he wasn't even paying attention to what they were saying, still thinking that he'd just wasted two hours of his life that he'd never get back, when they passed a guy in a ball cap leaning against a brownstone. Martinez walked about three more paces when he thought: *Whoa! That was the guy.*

Martinez had been on the force only two years and being an NYPD cop was a dream come true. He'd always wanted to be a cop. He was currently working the day shift, and twelve hours ago, at the start of his shift, he'd been handed a photograph of a man that looked like it had come from a driver's license. The sergeant said that finding the man in the photo was currently NYPD's highest priority—although no one said who the man was or what he was wanted for. All Martinez was told was that if they spotted the guy they weren't to approach him but were to immediately call their supervisor.

The first thing Martinez needed to do was make sure the man leaning against the brownstone was really the one they were looking for. He'd just gotten a glance at him. He also needed to get his family out of the area. He walked half a block, forcing himself not to look back, then stopped and told his wife, "Honey, I want you and Sara to take a cab home. There's something I have to do."

"What? What are you talking about?" his wife said.

"Look, I don't have a lot of time here, but this is a big fuckin' deal. I mean for my career."

"Jesus, John, watch your language," she said, looking down at their daughter, and Sara looked back up at him, big brown eyes like you'd expect Bambi to have. God, he loved those eyes.

"Yeah, sorry," he muttered. "Look. I don't have time to explain, but you and Sara need to get out of here right away."

"Are you going to be safe?" his wife asked.

"Yeah, sure, it's nothing dangerous. I just want you out of here before I call this in."

Before she could argue with him, he stepped into the street and waved down a passing cab. After his wife and daughter were inside the cab, he said to his wife, "I'll call you as soon as I can."

"John, I don't know what's going on here," his wife said, "but I don't like this."

"Yeah, yeah, me either. Look, I'll be home as quick as I can, and if I get stuck here, I'll let you know."-

The cab took off and he looked back up the street. The man was still leaning against the brownstone. He didn't know if he'd noticed Martinez go by with his family, but he doubted that he had paid any attention to their faces. Martinez pulled out his cell phone and walked back up the street and pretended to have a conversation with somebody. He was hoping that by holding the phone to his mouth the man wouldn't get a good look at his face as he passed him. As he walked by the brownstone he said, "Yeah, Bob, that sounds good. I should be there in about twenty minutes. Yeah, yeah, I know."

Martinez didn't stare as he passed; he just glanced over at him again and kept on walking and talking. Yeah, it was the guy. He was sure—or at least 90 percent sure. The man in the photo had been clean-shaven and this man had two or three days' worth of beard, but the cleft in his chin was what made Martinez sure it was the hard-looking son of a bitch in the picture. He walked to the corner, still holding his cell phone to his ear, then crossed the street.

There was a boutique on the corner, on the other side of the street from the brownstone, and it was still open. He'd be able to see the guy from the boutique's windows. He entered the boutique, pulled out his ID, and approached the clerk, a pudgy girl in her twenties with big, ugly eyeglasses. She was reading one of those movie star gossip magazines. "NYPD," Martinez said. "I'm undercover and I need to stay here in this store for a few minutes. Okay?"

"Yeah, sure, I guess," the girl said, then started reading the magazine again. She seemed so unconcerned that Martinez wondered if she was stoned.

Martinez punched a number into his cell phone. "Sarge, it's John Martinez. I'm watching that guy in the picture you handed out at roll call today."

29

Quinn's phone rang just as he was handing Pam a glass of wine.

"Quinn," he said.

"Commissioner, this is Captain Dick Heller, Fifth Precinct. I was told you were to be contacted directly if a certain man was spotted, the man in the photograph that was passed out this morning."

"Yes, Captain, that's correct."

"Well, sir, he's standing outside an apartment building," and Heller gave him the address.

Quinn didn't say anything. He recognized the address, of course. DeMarco was right in front of Pam's building. The bastard was obviously waiting for him.

"Sir," Captain Heller said, "what would you like me to do?"

"I don't want you to do anything, Captain. Is somebody watching the man right now?"

"Yes, sir. A rookie named Martinez. He's the one who saw him."

"Captain, call Martinez and tell him he's to leave the area immediately. He's to make no contact with that man or do anything that might scare him off. Do you understand?"

"Yes, sir."

"And tell Martinez his vigilance in this matter will be recognized, as will your promptness in reporting this situation to me."

"Uh, yes, sir," Heller said, and Quinn disconnected the call.

"Honey," Quinn said to Pam, "I'm going to have to leave soon. It's, well . . ."

"I understand," Pam said. He knew she was disappointed but he also knew she understood that with his job emergencies happened, and she wouldn't whine about him having to leave abruptly. This was another difference between her and Barbara, and another reason why he loved her.

"Excuse me for a moment," Quinn said, "I need to make a call." He walked into Pam's bedroom and shut the door, grateful that Pam also understood there were some things that he couldn't discuss even with her.

———◆◆◆———

Hanley was sitting on the floor playing cars with his son. The game was pretty simple: Hanley and his son each had a little toy car and they'd "drive" the cars at each other and smash them together, and then Hanley's son would shriek and laugh like that was the funniest thing in the world. To Hanley, the game could become tiresome after a short while, but his boy could play it forever. Hanley looked at his laughing little boy, now flat on his back, tennis shoes up in the air, and couldn't help but smile; not that long ago, he thought he'd lost his son. He'd play the game with him as long as the little guy wanted to play.

Hanley's cell phone rang. He pulled it off his belt and looked at the caller ID. He stood up and his son said, "Daddy, where are you going?"

"I'm sorry, buddy," Hanley said, "but I have to talk to this man." Answering the phone, Hanley said, "Yes, sir."

"I'm in the East Village," Quinn said, and gave Hanley the address.

Hanley didn't need to write down the address; he knew where Quinn was. He was visiting his girlfriend, his mistress, whatever the hell she was. Half the damn force knew he was sleeping with a Manhattan ADA, but Quinn, as smart as he was, thought his affair was a secret. Hanley, of course, had never let on to Quinn that he knew Quinn was seeing the woman. That wasn't the sort of thing a guy his rank could talk to his boss about.

"DeMarco's standing in front of the building," Quinn said. "He's waiting for me to leave and when I do, he's going to try to kill me."

"What do you want me to do, boss?" Hanley said. Hanley knew Quinn wanted him to do something. If Quinn had just wanted DeMarco taken off the street, he could have had a couple of squad cars pick the guy up. Hell, he could have had a whole damn SWAT team there in five minutes if that's what he wanted. There was no reason for him to call Hanley if Quinn just wanted DeMarco arrested or detained.

"I want you to get down here," Quinn said. "How long will it take you?"

"About thirty minutes," Hanley said.

"Okay," Quinn said. "Now DeMarco's seen you, so you can't stand near him or approach him immediately. When you get here, wait down at the corner, where he can't see you, then call me. I figure it will take you thirty seconds, walking quickly, to reach the front of the building where he's standing. When you call me and tell me you're on the corner, I'll go downstairs and wait by the front door of the apartment building. Then I'll call you back, and exactly thirty seconds after I call you, I'm going to step outside, and when I do, and if DeMarco approaches me, I want you to kill him. Do you understand?"

Hanley didn't respond. He didn't know what to say.

"Hanley, I need to make something clear. DeMarco obviously followed me to this building. There's no other way he could have known I'd be here. This means that if all he wanted to do was talk to me, he could have stopped me before I went inside the building. But he doesn't want to talk. The reason he's waiting outside is that he plans to assassinate me. Do you understand?"

"Yeah, boss, but—"

"Hanley, I don't want this guy arrested. If he goes to jail for attempting to kill me or for carrying a weapon, he'll be out in a few years and he'll come after me again. He isn't going to go away. He's obsessed with killing me; he said as much the other day in Battery Park. I don't want to spend the rest of my life looking over my shoulder for him."

"I understand, boss," Hanley said, and he did.

The best-case scenario, Hanley was thinking, was if DeMarco actually pulled a gun, then Hanley, as one of the commissioner's security people, would be perfectly justified in killing him. Or if not exactly *justified*, no one would really blame Hanley for killing the man. If DeMarco didn't pull a gun—or worse yet, if DeMarco didn't even have a gun on him—and Hanley killed him . . . well, that could be a problem, but he knew Quinn would protect him. Hanley would say: *I thought he was going for a gun and I shot him*—and Quinn would make the whole thing go away. He hoped. Whatever the case, he wasn't going to let Quinn down. He owed Quinn too much.

Quinn left the bedroom and walked back to the living room, where Pam was sitting. He took a seat on the couch next to her and picked up his wineglass.

"I have half an hour or so before I have to go. So tell me again what the judge said."

Before he'd been called and told that DeMarco was lurking outside, Pam had been telling him about her day and a bizarre ruling a judge had made. The judge's ruling was in fact so bizarre that Pam seriously believed the judge might have been bribed, as the case involved an enormously rich Wall Street crook. This was the sort of corruption that Quinn couldn't tolerate and wanted to obliterate, but he really didn't want to talk about the judge or the case.

Quinn wanted to take Pam to the bedroom and make love to her before he left, but he knew she wouldn't appreciate him having a quickie, then departing five minutes later. Plus, they weren't a couple of teenagers and neither one of them liked to have sex that way. They liked to take their time. So Quinn suppressed the urge but he really wanted her. Maybe it was knowing that DeMarco was waiting outside to kill him that was making his desire for her so strong.

Hanley called thirty-five minutes later, and once again Quinn walked into the bedroom to talk to him. Hanley said he was waiting at the corner and he could see DeMarco standing outside the building; DeMarco would be on Quinn's right-hand side as Quinn came down the steps.

"Hanley," Quinn said, "I'm not going to look at him when I leave the building. Do you understand? I'm counting totally on you not to let him kill me. I'm putting my life in your hands."

"He's not going to kill you, boss," Hanley said.

Quinn left the bedroom and walked over to Pam and kissed her softly on the lips. "I'm sorry, but I have to leave now."

"Okay," she said, "but if you have a chance, call me later."

"I will," he said.

He left the apartment and immediately stopped thinking about Pam as he walked toward the stairwell. He needed to figure out how he was going to handle the media after DeMarco was killed; an attempt on his life would be a very big deal, and there were going to be a lot of questions from the press. To complicate matters, he'd asked Braddock to use the Ring of Steel surveillance cameras, as well as beat cops to look for DeMarco. That would probably be leaked to the media, who could then very well ask him why he was hunting for DeMarco before the man was killed. The other problem was that DeMarco had most likely talked to other people about his insane idea that Quinn had killed his father, and whomever he'd talked to might leak that information. So what would he tell the media?

It looked as if he was going to have to tell them the truth: that De-Marco, who was certainly mentally unstable, had gotten into his head that Quinn was somehow responsible for the death of his mobster father, Gino DeMarco. Joe DeMarco had, in fact, accosted him in Battery Park a few days ago and had accused him directly of murdering his father, even though Quinn had never met Gino DeMarco. Then a confidential source in D.C. had told Quinn that DeMarco appeared to have gone over the edge, was headed to New York, and might be intending to assassinate him—and that's when he'd told his cops to see if they could locate the nut. It was tragic that they'd been unable to capture DeMarco, and that one of his security people had been forced to kill him.

Hmm. He'd have to give that some more thought, but he figured that would work. The good news was that after Hanley had dealt with DeMarco, he'd have the rest of the night to come up with an approach for dealing with the media. He wouldn't hold a press conference until the following day, saying that he delayed until his people could gather the necessary facts. Then something else occurred to him: an assassination attempt could be a real bonus in terms of his confirmation hearing. Politicians' approval ratings always rose after an assassination attempt.

Quinn walked down the stairs but didn't step into the foyer. He called Hanley from the stairwell. "I'll be stepping outside in exactly thirty seconds. Don't fail me, Hanley."

Hanley knelt down and pretended to tie his shoe. As he did so, he took out the backup piece he carried in an ankle holster. The little .32

automatic could hardly be seen when he held it in his big right hand, a hand big enough to palm a basketball. He stood up, the gun held down at the side of his right leg, and began walking toward DeMarco.

DeMarco was looking to his left, toward the entrance to the apartment building. He'd been looking in that direction the whole time Hanley had been watching him, so he didn't see Hanley coming toward him. Hanley was an excellent shot with the .40-caliber Glock he carried in his shoulder holster but not so good with the stubby-barreled .32. He wanted to be no more than ten feet from DeMarco when he fired.

30

DeMarco was surprised when the front door opened and Quinn stepped outside the apartment building. DeMarco had not expected him to leave for at least another hour. His heart began to hammer in his chest as he thought about what he was about to do. He took in a deep breath to calm himself, then reached inside his jacket pocket and placed his finger on the trigger of the P30.

Quinn came down the steps without looking in DeMarco's direction, and as DeMarco had expected, walked over to the curb and looked up the street as if he was searching for a cab.

DeMarco glanced up and down the street quickly. There was an old lady walking toward him on his left-hand side and behind her, a young couple. Coming from the other direction, from his right, were two single women, a single man, followed by another single woman. DeMarco figured that when he fired at Quinn, most of these people, with the exception of the old lady, were going to be very close to him. Some might be standing right next to him; some might even hear the shot being fired even though the gun was silenced. And if any of them happened to be looking in the right direction, they would see his face clearly—but there was nothing he could do about any of those things.

DeMarco took a stride toward Quinn—he wanted to be just a couple of feet away when he fired—and aimed the gun in his pocket at Quinn's back. Then he stopped, unable to move. He froze. Was he really going to do this? Was he really going to kill a man and probably ruin his own life in the process?

"Joe! Stop!"

At the same time he heard the woman's voice, he heard something metallic clatter on the ground behind him. He turned and saw Emma. A black man was lying on the ground near her, and a few feet from the man's hand, there was a small gun on the sidewalk. Emma was holding something in her hand, but DeMarco couldn't see what it was. What the hell was she doing here?

An instant later, Emma was standing next to him, tugging on his arm, hissing, "Come with me, you idiot." Quinn had turned to face him when Emma yelled. Emma tugged again on DeMarco's arm, then stopped and pointed at Quinn. "Gun!" she yelled. "That man has a gun." And DeMarco could see Quinn pulling his weapon from his shoulder holster. Emma threw something at Quinn—whatever it was that she'd been holding in her hand—and it bounced off Quinn's chest, making him stagger backward. "Gun!" Emma yelled again, and a woman started running, another began screaming, and a man yelled something DeMarco didn't understand.

Emma tugged hard on his arm again, but DeMarco didn't move, and for just an instant DeMarco and Quinn looked directly into each other's eyes—Quinn's gun was now in his hand but he wasn't pointing it at DeMarco—and then DeMarco broke eye contact, cursed, and turned in Emma's direction and they both started running. As they ran, they stepped over the man lying on the sidewalk and DeMarco realized he was one of Quinn's security people, one of the guys who had taken him to see Quinn in Battery Park.

He and Emma were running hard now, weaving their way through pedestrians on the sidewalk and the whole time DeMarco was expecting

Quinn to shoot him in the back. He glanced back once and saw Quinn holding his left hand up in the air—his right hand, the one holding the gun, was down at his side. DeMarco realized later that Quinn was probably holding up his badge to calm the people on the street.

They reached the corner at the end of the block when Emma suddenly darted out into the street and raised her hand to stop a passing cab. The driver had to slam on his brakes to keep from hitting her. She yanked open the back door of the cab and turned to DeMarco and said, "Get in!"

DeMarco got into the cab and Emma slid in after him. To the cabbie, she said, "Move it!"

The cabbie started driving. He was a tiny Asian man barely tall enough to see over the steering wheel. He looked frightened. "Where are we going?" he asked.

"Just drive," Emma said.

DeMarco looked behind him and could see Quinn's bodyguard, the man Emma had hit, standing in the middle of the street, looking at the cab. He was holding a gun in his hand, but he wasn't aiming at the cab. He was probably trying to get the license plate number. DeMarco also wondered why Quinn hadn't shot him and figured the reason was because DeMarco hadn't shown a weapon and Quinn was afraid to shoot an unarmed man with witnesses nearby. He'd already made that mistake once before with Connors.

Emma and DeMarco were both breathing heavily—more from the surge of adrenaline than from the distance they'd run. A few blocks later, Emma told the cabbie to pull over. Emma quickly paid the fare, they got out of the cab, and Emma immediately flagged down another cab. "Take us to Brooklyn," she told the driver.

A few minutes after they crossed the Brooklyn Bridge, Emma told the cabbie to pull over. She and DeMarco exited the cab, and as soon as the cab pulled away and they were alone, DeMarco said, "Goddamnit! What the hell are you doing here?"

"Give me the gun," Emma said.

"What gun?" DeMarco said.

"The gun in your jacket. Give it to me. Now."

"No."

"Joe, I just hit a man on the head and assaulted the commissioner of the New York Police Department. I can be arrested for what I did. I could also be considered an accomplice to the stupid thing you were about to do. And if you get caught with that gun, that's going to make things worse for both of us."

"I didn't ask you to help me."

"Give me the damn gun."

DeMarco looked around to make sure no one was watching, and pulled out the gun.

"Christ! A silencer!" Emma said. She jacked the shell out of the chamber, ejected the magazine from the gun, and unscrewed the silencer. She walked a few paces over to a gutter drain, tossed the gun down the drain, then dropped the magazine and silencer into a waste container.

DeMarco started to say something, but she held up her hand, silencing him, and pulled her cell phone off her belt.

"Susan," she said, "it's Emma. I need a favor."

DeMarco had no idea who Susan was, but whoever she was, she had a small beach house near the town of Islip on Long Island. It took him and Emma more than two hours to get there from Brooklyn because they changed cabs two more times on the way.

DeMarco followed Emma around to the beach side of the house—he could hear the surf but couldn't see the ocean in the dark—and waited as she groped into a planter box for a key. Once inside, she shrugged off her jacket and walked directly to a cabinet in the small living room—she'd obviously been to the place before—and pulled out a bottle of vodka.

"Martini?" she said.

As Emma made the martinis, DeMarco paced the living room. His emotions were in turmoil. He was angry at Emma for stopping him from killing Quinn, and at the same time, if he was honest with himself, he was relieved that he hadn't actually killed the man—and yet he still wanted to kill him. He also thought that because of what Emma had done, he'd never get another shot at Quinn.

Emma handed him his drink, flipped a switch near the fireplace, and a gas fire came to life. She took a seat in a rocking chair near the fireplace and took a sip of her drink. "Um, that's good," she said. "Sit down," she ordered DeMarco, and he sat on a small couch across from her, still agitated.

"How did you find me?" DeMarco said.

"Neil," Emma said. "He called me this afternoon and told me about everything you asked him to do. I don't know why he didn't call earlier. Anyway, he said he was worried about you, so I caught a shuttle up here and had Neil track you down using the phone he sent you.

"When I saw you standing outside that apartment building, I didn't approach you right away because I wanted to see if you were being watched. I was also trying to figure out what you were doing in that part of town, because I was pretty sure that Quinn didn't live in the East Village. And that's when I spotted the man I hit. I saw him watching you and then I saw him take a gun out of an ankle holster and start walking toward you, and I crossed the street and fell in behind him. He was so focused on you, he didn't notice me. I hit him when he raised his hand to shoot you." She paused then said, "Joe, if I hadn't been there he would have killed you."

"What did you hit him with?"

Emma laughed. "A sugar container; you know, one of those heavy ones made out of glass. I picked it up off an outdoor table at that coffee shop just up the street from where you were standing. And that's what I threw at Quinn when he reached for his gun. Did you recognize the man I hit?"

"Yeah. He's one of Quinn's goons. One of his security guys."

"Well, he wasn't planning to arrest you. He didn't bother to identify himself as a cop before he raised his gun. Somehow Quinn knew you were waiting for him outside the building and he told that man to kill you. And because you were dumb enough to be carrying a weapon— one with a silencer, no less—it would have been a free killing. Quinn would have claimed you were trying to assassinate him—and he would have been right—and you would have been dead. What in God's name did you think you were doing, Joe?"

"He killed my father."

"So what?"

"What do you mean, *so what*?"

"Just because he killed your father—and keep in mind it was some mafia lowlife who told you he did—that doesn't give you the right to assassinate the man."

"There was no other way to get him. I tried to screw up his confirmation hearing but I couldn't pull it off."

"What are you talking about?" Emma said.

DeMarco told her how he'd gone to Senator Beecham's chief of staff and how he'd videotaped Tony Benedetto telling all the things that Quinn had done—and then how Tony had betrayed him.

"Beecham was going to have Tony testify at Quinn's nomination hearing. He was going to get him to talk about Quinn killing my father and Jerry Kennedy and covering up the shooting of Connors. The video I made of Tony's testimony was in case Tony croaked before the hearing. But then Tony sold me out to Quinn to keep his son from going to jail, and Quinn disappeared the teacher. The only thing I could think to do was kill Quinn."

"Yeah, except if I hadn't been there," Emma said, "Quinn's guy would have killed you. And if you had killed Quinn, you would have almost certainly been caught and spent the rest of your life in prison. Now I have a problem because I assaulted a cop and the police commissioner."

"Hey, the guy you hit pulled a gun and you didn't know he was a cop."

"I'll be sure to mention that to my lawyer. Fortunately, you never showed the gun you were carrying and there were a lot of people around who saw the cop's gun. I don't know if any of those witnesses will come forward, but there were witnesses."

Before DeMarco could say anything, she said, "I'm going to have another drink. Do you want one?"

"Yeah," DeMarco said. "I might as well get hammered since I can't think of anything else to do."

Emma went into the kitchen, made two more martinis, and when she returned to the rocking chair near the fireplace, she said, "Quinn could have us arrested, but I don't think he'll do that. I don't think he wants us—particularly you—blabbing to the press right before his confirmation hearing. On the other hand, I don't think Brian Quinn is going to spend the rest of his life looking over his shoulder for you or waiting for you to come up with something that could screw up his life."

"So what do you think he'll do?" DeMarco said.

"I don't know. But if Benedetto's telling the truth, Quinn killed two people in cold blood to save his career when he was a young man. And now he's a different person than he was back then—meaning he has a lot more power—so maybe he'll decide he doesn't have to kill you. Maybe he'll frame you for a crime and get you tossed in jail. Or maybe, considering some of things you've done for John Mahoney, he won't have to frame you. When Quinn is in charge of the Bureau, he just might give his agents a new prime directive: Get DeMarco. At that point, you can say all you want about him killing your dad but since you have no evidence, you'll sound like a maniac. Quinn on the other hand will have evidence.

So I don't know, Joe. Maybe Quinn will try to kill you or maybe he'll try to put you in a cage—but he's going to do something."

DeMarco just shook his head. He wasn't denying what Emma was saying—she'd just said almost the exactly the same thing Quinn had said to him in Battery Park, about what he might do if DeMarco continued to "annoy" him. He shook his head because he couldn't believe that his life had come to this.

"By the way," Emma said, "I noticed you haven't thanked me yet for saving your life."

"I'm still trying to decide if I'm grateful," he said, which made Emma laugh—and him smile. Slightly.

31

The next morning, DeMarco could hear Emma showering in the only bathroom in the small beach house, so he made a pot of coffee and walked out onto a rocky beach. He noticed a battered-looking rowboat with flaking blue paint lying on the beach and a long rope attaching the boat to the house so the boat wouldn't be swept away by a high tide. He didn't think the boat looked particularly seaworthy, not that he had any intention of using it. He'd always thought: Rowboat versus the Atlantic Ocean—bet on the ocean. He walked up the beach about half a mile, and the whole time he was walking, seagulls flew over his head, screeching at him, as if they thought he was going to steal their eggs.

He had to figure out what he was going to do next. He thought Emma was probably right that Quinn wouldn't have him arrested for trying to kill him yesterday and that he'd wait until after the confirmation hearing before he did anything. In the meantime, he'd beef up his security so DeMarco wouldn't have a chance of getting near him again.

Emma was also right about Quinn having the power and the ability to ruin him. As she and Quinn had both said, Quinn might frame him for a crime but he wouldn't even have to go to that extreme to destroy DeMarco. He was already unemployed, with few prospects for finding another job anytime soon, and by the time Quinn was finished with him, no one would hire him. He could just see Quinn keeping tabs on him—and as most job applications these days were submitted via the Internet, that wouldn't be hard. Then he could imagine FBI agents visiting potential employers, asking questions about DeMarco without ever saying why they were asking the questions while at the same time revealing DeMarco's past: his hit-man father, his connections to mobsters like Tony Benedetto, and how he'd been fired from his congressional job for reasons they couldn't disclose, but which were serious issues related to integrity and politically skullduggery. So he was going to lose his house and blow through what little savings he had in a matter of months as he futilely searched for work. He could just see himself moving back in with his mother and becoming the night shift cook at a Mickey D's in Queens.

If he was going to prevent all this from happening he needed some sort of plan to neutralize Quinn. And half an hour later, when both his shoes were filled with sand—he had one. Well, that wasn't exactly true. He didn't have a plan—but he had a question and the answer to the question might lead to a plan.

He returned to the beach house and found Emma sitting on the steps, drinking a cup of coffee and looking out at the surf.

"What a lovely morning," she said. "I wouldn't mind spending a couple more days here, but I think we should head back to Washington. There's no point staying in Quinn's backyard."

"Yeah, maybe," DeMarco said. "Let me get a cup of coffee. I want to bounce something off you."

———◆◆◆———

DeMarco took a seat on the steps next to Emma. He could see a guy with a black Labrador down the beach a ways, flinging a stick into the surf, and the dog would plunge into the waves and dutifully retrieve it.

DeMarco thought the dog's willingness to fetch a stick from freezing water was sufficient proof that it wasn't a particularly intelligent critter.

"When Quinn was young," DeMarco said, "he killed an unarmed man and got the department to cover it up, but Carmine Taliaferro found out and got his hooks into Quinn. To get out from under Carmine, Quinn killed Jerry Kennedy and my dad. And I can buy all that because at the time Quinn was young, didn't have a power base, and he was worried that Carmine might kill his career. The cover-up was also bad because high-ranking guys in the NYPD had to have been involved and they could have been hurt, too, which would have made things even worse for Quinn.

"But time passes, years go by, and Carmine can't use the killings against Quinn. There's no evidence that Quinn killed Jerry Kennedy or my dad, and Carmine can't say that he knows Quinn killed them without admitting that he ordered the killings. Carmine wasn't going to admit that he was an accomplice to murder."

"What about the teacher knowing about the cover-up?" Emma said. "And Quinn's old partner?"

"The teacher was a problem at first because I imagine Quinn didn't have her name. But he learned her name, years ago. She told me Quinn sent some guys over to lean on her when she started talking in bars about Quinn. And when Quinn learned that I knew who the teacher was and was going to use her to testify against him at the confirmation hearing, he disappeared her. Once he knew her name, Quinn could have dealt with her at any time, but he didn't think she was a significant threat."

"I don't see where you're going with this," Emma said.

"Carmine told Tony before he died—and this was a long time after Quinn killed my dad—that Carmine owned Quinn. Those were Carmine's exact words. He said, 'I own that mick prick.' How could that be, Emma? How could Carmine own Quinn when he couldn't say that he ordered Quinn to do the killings, and after Quinn already had the teacher's name? What I'm saying is, I think Carmine had something else on Quinn.

"Which brings me to Carmine's daughter. Tony told me she's a big-time politician—who I've never heard of, by the way. But how does the daughter of a mob boss become a big-time politician?"

"I don't know but . . ."

"I think it's possible that whatever Carmine was holding over Quinn, he passed it on to his daughter."

"Huh," Emma said. *Huh* meant she didn't totally disagree with DeMarco's logic. She sat there a moment, watching the waves hit the beach, then took her phone from a pocket and made a call. "Neil, I want you to get me everything you can find on the daughter of an old-time mafia guy named Carmine Taliaferro. Taliaferro is dead and his daughter is some sort of politician."

DeMarco had noted several times in the past that whenever Emma gave Neil an order he instantly complied—like a good Labrador fetching a stick from the water—and he didn't give her a ration of shit as he usually did when DeMarco asked him to do something. However, since Emma was Emma, he had no idea what hold she had over Neil.

Neil must have asked a question because Emma said, "No. For now just get me whatever's available in public records. If I need you to go deeper than that, I'll let you know." She paused. "Yeah, he's okay. I'm sitting right next to the fool."

She put the phone back in her pocket and said, "There's a café a couple of miles from here. Let's walk down there and get some breakfast."

"Two miles?" DeMarco said.

———————◆◆◆———————

They were back at the beach house—DeMarco admittedly feeling better after the walk and a good breakfast—when Neil called back. Emma put her phone in speaker mode so DeMarco could hear.

"Carmine Taliaferro has one daughter named, Stephanie. She's married to a guy named Roger Hernandez, and they have one daughter, Katherine, who's a sophomore at Barnard. Stephanie met her husband when they both attended NYU. Stephanie and Roger now own a bunch of property in Queens, apartments and commercial buildings, a partnership in an auto body place, a partnership in a copy place, a partnership in a house painting outfit, a . . . Anyway, they've got money and are involved in a lot of small businesses. Roger, as near as I can tell from the Internet and public records, was as poor as a church mouse before he married Stephanie. He went to college on a scholarship, his dad was a bus driver, and his mother cleaned houses. He's apparently a smart guy and manages all their businesses."

"What about Stephanie?" DeMarco asked.

"I'm getting to her. She started to get involved in local politics in a big way after her father died and is currently the borough president of Queens. She's made a couple of speeches recently about running for Congress against Chris Barlow, the current Democrat representing the Seventh District up there."

"Is she a Democrat or a Republican?" DeMarco asked.

"Democrat. She's very big into women's issues and at the same time she's liked by the business community. And although she's not Hispanic, being married to a Hispanic, and having a Hispanic last name, helps her. The thing that's impressive about her is the people who have endorsed her. Almost from the get-go she's had the backing of a lot of big New York names, including the mayor and a couple of governors. The Democrats up there love her for some reason, although I can't tell how they feel about her going after the incumbent in her district."

"What about her father?" Emma asked. "How does she explain that her old man was a big-time mafia guy?"

"The only thing I saw online about her relationship to her father, is her talking about him being a successful businessman. She said he started out with nothing, bought into some businesses, and invested wisely. The American Dream, and all that crap. She admitted in one speech that when her father was a young man he spent time in prison for a youthful mistake, not mentioning that the youthful mistake was almost beating a guy to death. Carmine did two years for assault but that was the only time he was convicted for anything, and he was nineteen years old when it happened. His daughter says he turned himself around and became a pillar of his community, gave to local charities, sponsored Little League teams, et cetera, et cetera, and when he died, she and Roger inherited everything he owned."

"And nobody mentioned that he was *the* mobster in Queens for most of his life?" DeMarco said.

"I never saw the words *mob* or *mafia* once in the stuff I found online, but keep in mind I was looking at articles talking about Stephanie Hernandez and not her old man."

"It's like Jack Kennedy," DeMarco said to Emma. "All the rumors about Joe Kennedy being a bootlegger and having ties to the mob and getting rich on insider trading never really hurt Jack. It sounds like the same thing with Stephanie. By the time she jumped onto the political stage, her old man was dead, his money had been laundered clean, she had nothing to do with his past life."

"Yes, but don't you find the endorsements intriguing?" Emma said. "Why would a bunch of big-shot New Yorkers support her? She was just a girl from Queens, had no political connections of her own, and certainly these people would have known who her father was."

"Quinn," DeMarco said. "Or maybe not him directly, but his very wealthy, well-connected wife was probably the one who introduced Stephanie to the folks who later endorsed her. And Quinn could have endorsed her behind the scenes. He just never came out for her publicly."

"I think I'm going to hang up," Neil said. "It doesn't sound like you need anything else from me." Which meant Neil didn't want to know what Emma and DeMarco were plotting with regard to Quinn.

"Thanks, Neil," Emma said. "So, what do you want to do next?" she asked DeMarco.

"Find out what Stephanie Taliaferro Hernandez has on Quinn."

"And how do you propose to do that?"

"I have no idea."

32

Quinn strolled through Central Park, walking slowly, enjoying the brisk autumn air and the colors of the dying leaves. Hanley and Grimes were trailing a few paces behind him. Whenever he had a major decision to make, he usually went for a walk, and if he was in New York, he walked in the park. Central Park was a gift to every New Yorker and Quinn had done everything he could as a cop and as commissioner to make it safe.

After Hanley failed to kill DeMarco, he'd thought about getting a warrant for DeMarco's arrest. He'd say that DeMarco had tried to assassinate him. He'd claim, and Hanley would back him up, that DeMarco had a gun even though Quinn hadn't actually seen one. He'd get every cop in the tri-state area looking for DeMarco, plaster his picture on the news, and also let the FBI and the cops in D.C. know that DeMarco was wanted. He figured that unless DeMarco left the country, he'd find him in a couple of days.

He also didn't know who the woman was who'd helped DeMarco. Unfortunately, there weren't any surveillance cameras near Pam's apartment and neither he nor Hanley had gotten a good look at her. He might have been able to identify her by her fingerprints—she'd thrown something at him—a jar or bottle, something made of glass—but in all the confusion following DeMarco's escape, and while trying to disburse the crowd that had gathered, he'd forgotten to pick it up, and when he sent a cop back to retrieve it, it was gone.

But what would happen after he arrested DeMarco? He doubted DeMarco would be dumb enough to still be carrying a gun—assuming he was even carrying one last night outside Pam's place. So he could say that DeMarco had planned to assassinate him, but then what? Since DeMarco hadn't taken a shot at him or shown a weapon, he doubted he could get a conviction for attempted murder. What he could do, however, was dump him into Rikers after he was arrested and make sure the judge didn't turn him loose for a couple of days. A lot of bad things could happen to DeMarco in Rikers. In fact, Quinn could almost guarantee that DeMarco would die in Rikers.

The problem was the confirmation hearing started in a few days. If DeMarco was arrested and given the chance to talk to the media, he'd tell the press that Quinn had killed his father even if he didn't have any proof. He didn't want to deal with that sort of nonsense while the confirmation hearing was occurring. For that matter, he didn't want to deal with that issue after he was confirmed.

DeMarco had to go. He simply couldn't tolerate having the man out there looking for an opportunity to assassinate him again. He could ask Hanley to kill him but he wasn't certain Hanley would do it. Hanley would have no problem killing DeMarco if DeMarco was trying to kill Quinn—or if Hanley even *thought* DeMarco was trying to kill Quinn—but Hanley wasn't an assassin. Grimes, however, might be easier to convince. Grimes was more cold-blooded than Hanley and owed him just as much as Hanley.

Grimes had been one of his detectives for a brief period when he ran a squad, before moving on to command a precinct. He wasn't a particularly good detective because he couldn't relate to people; he couldn't schmooze and cajole them the way the good dicks did when they were trying to get information out of folks. What Hanley was good at was intimidating people, and sometimes that was better than schmoozing.

On one case, Grimes forced a woman to lie on the stand to put away a scumbag who they knew was guilty but couldn't get the evidence against him needed for a conviction—then Grimes committed perjury when he testified. Quinn knew what Grimes had done and wasn't bothered by it at all; in fact, he'd been impressed with how far Grimes had been willing to go to put the shithead behind bars. Unfortunately, a cop who'd worked with Grimes on the case was caught taking a bribe, and he decided to rat out Grimes to keep from going to jail. But Quinn saved Grimes. He went to bat for him and completely discredited the cop who was planning to testify against Grimes. After it was all over, Grimes came to him and said, "You ever need anything, boss, and I mean anything, you let me know."

So. Would Grimes kill DeMarco if he asked? Maybe. But if Grimes was caught for killing DeMarco, would he give Quinn up? Probably not—but Quinn didn't want to take the chance. He needed to find someone else to take care of DeMarco, someone who would kill the man without knowing who'd hired him. But how the hell could he arrange that? How could he hire an assassin without the assassin finding out his identity?

As he walked past the pond, he noticed a panhandler on the walk ahead of him badgering an old lady, asking her for money. The bum was big, a foot and a half taller than the old woman, and Quinn could tell she was frightened. Quinn quickened his pace and caught up with the bum.

"Leave that woman alone," he said.

The bum was taller than Quinn, too, and Quinn was six foot two. He was also filthy and Quinn could smell him from ten feet away, but he looked well fed for a man who wasn't employed. He turned and snarled at Quinn, "Get the fuck away from me or I'll give you a beat-down."

Quinn took out his badge case and by then Hanley and Grimes were standing next to him. "Get out of the park or I'll have these two officers beat the shit out of you, then throw you in jail."

"Hey, all right, fine," the bum said. "I wasn't doing anything wrong."

"You were harassing this lady. Apologize to her," Quinn said.

"I'm, uh, sorry ma'am if I was bothering you," the bum said and shuffled away.

"Thank you, Officer," the old woman said. She had no idea who Quinn was.

Quinn walked beside the old woman, chatting with her about the weather, until they separated when they came to a fork in the path.

Quinn suddenly knew how to get rid of DeMarco. It was funny the way the mind worked: when you concentrated on a problem, sometimes the answer would refuse to come, but if you stopped thinking about it completely and focused your mind on something else, then suddenly the solution would appear.

He took out his cell phone and scrolled through the contacts list until he found the number he wanted. Dr. William Layman—the same doctor who had helped treat Hanley's kid for cancer—wasn't immediately available so Quinn asked his receptionist to have the doctor call him. Forty minutes later, when Quinn was back in his office, the doctor returned his call.

"Bill," Quinn said, "I was wondering if you could do me a favor? There's a man named Anthony Benedetto in Flushing Hospital with lung cancer. Benedetto's an old-time mafia guy and I need him to testify on something and I need to know how long he's going to live. I could ask his doctor but I don't know the man and he'd probably refuse to tell me because he might be concerned about patient confidentiality. The other thing is, I don't know how competent his doctor is and I know you're very competent. So I was wondering . . . Thanks, Bill, I appreciate it and give my best to Ellen."

———————◆◆◆———————

Tony Benedetto had a private room at the Flushing Hospital Medical Center. DeMarco didn't know if the old man needed to be there or if he'd just gotten himself admitted so he couldn't be called to testify at Quinn's hearing. Whatever the case, there was an IV tube running into a vein in his right arm, oxygen was being pumped into his big nose, and a machine was monitoring his vital signs. Tony's eyes were closed but DeMarco could sense that he wasn't sleeping; his face was the color of cigarette ash and it looked like every breath was a major effort, as if there were hundred-pound weights pressing down on his chest.

"Tony," DeMarco said, and Benedetto slowly opened his eyes.

"Aw, shit. What are you doing here?" His voice was stronger than DeMarco had expected. Before DeMarco could answer Tony's question, Tony made a sound that might have been a laugh. "You know, Joe, you're the first person who's visited me since I was admitted. My fuckin' kid, after all I did for him, hasn't been here once and I can't even reach him. As for my so-called friends . . . well, fuck 'em."

"I'm sorry to hear that," DeMarco said, although he wasn't sorry. As far as he was concerned Tony deserved to die alone.

"So what do you want? I told you I'm not going to testify against Quinn."

"I'm not here to ask you to testify or make another video. I want to know what Carmine had on Quinn. You told me that Carmine 'owned' Quinn. What did you mean? What else did Carmine have on him beside the shooting cover-up? I figure since your kid's out of the can and since nobody's forcing you to testify, it wouldn't hurt you to tell me." DeMarco had almost added: *And since you're dying.*

"I don't know what Carmine had on him, and that's the truth. All I know is what I told you the other day, that Carmine said he owned him, which had to mean that he had something he was using to control Quinn or blackmail him or something. But even when Carmine was dying, he never told me what it was."

"Do you think he gave whatever he knew about Quinn to his daughter?"

"I don't know. How would I know that? All I know is his daughter thinks she's going to be a senator or a congresswoman or maybe the fuckin' mayor of New York. I don't know why she got into politics—she inherited a shitload from Carmine—but I guess she wants to make a name for herself. When I was young, women used to stay home and take care of their kids and their husbands. Now they all want to run the fuckin' world."

Tony suddenly grimaced and his back arched with a spasm of pain, then he started coughing and DeMarco thought he might be choking, too. One of the machines above Tony's bed started beeping at the same time. DeMarco thought about running down to the nurses' station to get someone to help him—but he didn't. "Rot in hell, you old bastard," he said as he left the room.

Tony felt someone poke him in the arm and he opened his eyes to see Brian Quinn, looking down at him dispassionately, not an ounce of concern or sympathy in his gray eyes.

"Well, ain't this my lucky fuckin' day," Tony said. "First DeMarco, now you. My two best friends."

"What?" Quinn said. "DeMarco was here?"

"Yeah, a couple hours ago. I started coughing up a lung and instead of helping me, he just walked away."

"What did DeMarco want?"

Tony said, "Give me some water. Put that straw up to my lips." Quinn did, an expression of disgust on his face. Tony took a couple of sips, then put his head back on the pillow and closed his eyes.

"Answer my question," Quinn said. "What did DeMarco want?"

"He wanted to know what Carmine had on you. He said he knew Carmine had something and whatever it was, he probably passed it on to his daughter."

"What did you tell him?"

"I told him I didn't know. And I don't know. I don't know anything."

———◆◆◆———

Quinn didn't speak for a moment, trying to decide if the old man was telling the truth. He suspected he was. If Tony had known what Carmine had on him, he would have used that information to get his kid out of jail rather than go through the ruse of making the video for DeMarco.

"I talked to a doctor," Quinn said. "Not your doctor, another one, a guy who's one of the best oncologists in New York. He figures you have less than two weeks to live."

"My doctor says I got a month."

"It doesn't really matter, Tony. The important thing is that you're going to be around long enough to do something for me, but not much longer after that."

"What are you talking about?"

"I want you to hire someone to kill DeMarco."

"Get the fuck out of here," Tony said.

"Listen to me," Quinn said. "If you don't do what I want, I'm going to find some reason to arrest your son again, then I'm going to throw him into Rikers and he's going to get beaten to death."

"We had a deal."

"The deal we had was that the drug charges against your idiot kid would be dismissed, and they were. But we're going to make a new deal. You're going to hire someone to kill DeMarco and if you do what I want, I'll leave your son alone. If you don't, some psycho at Rikers is going to pound his face into mush. You'll be attending your son's funeral before your own."

"Why? Why do you want me to do this?"

228

"It doesn't matter. What matters is that I know you have the connections to hire someone."

"Why don't you hire someone?"

"Because I don't want there to be any link between DeMarco's death and me. But if *you* hire someone and if that guy gets caught, he'll point the finger at you. The good news is, since you'll be dead in a couple of weeks, the trail ends with you. And if you were to point the finger at me, no one would believe you. I want you to set this up today."

"You want him dead before the confirmation hearing?"

"That would be ideal but I don't know if I can find DeMarco before the hearing. The fact that he visited you in the hospital today means he's probably still in New York but I'm going to have to run him down. After I do, I'll let you know where he is. So do you know somebody who can do the job, somebody you can get a hold of immediately?"

"Yeah, I can think of a couple of guys. But they're not cheap."

"Well, how much they cost is your problem. There isn't going to be any money trail leading from me to you."

"You expect me to use my own money?" Tony said.

"Hey, you can't take it with you, Tony. And I'm getting tired of repeating myself. If you don't do what I want, your kid dies. What's more important to you: money you'll never live to spend or your son's life?"

"Carmine always said you were the most cold-blooded son of a bitch he ever knew. He said you were worse than anybody he knew in the outfit."

"Carmine was right, Tony."

Tony could think of two guys he could use to kill DeMarco. Actually, he could think of two *dozen* guys, but only two who had any brains. One was a Creole named Hugo Lavolier, who lived in New Orleans, or at least he did before Katrina. Hugo had supposedly killed at least five people, and although Tony had never used him personally, he knew people who had, people he trusted who vouched for the guy.

The other possibility was a guy in Brooklyn, a Russian named Oskar Pankov that Tony had used once before. The Russian and his wife owned a hole-in-the-wall restaurant, a place that only served breakfast and lunch; Oskar was the cook and his wife waited the tables. And Oskar looked like a short-order cook. He was mostly bald, tall but not so tall as to stand out in a crowd, and although he was a skinny guy, he had a paunch. Tony guessed he was probably in his early fifties by now.

Tony didn't know anything about Oskar's background; no one in the Italian mob did. All he knew was that Oskar came over from Russia twenty-five years ago and it didn't take him twenty years, like it took the Mexicans, to become a citizen. He worked for a guy in Brighton Beach for a while—a slimeball involved in the sex trade—but after five years Oskar wasn't working for anybody but himself. And that was impressive. The Russian mob wasn't an organization that normally let a guy go off on his own; once you were in, you were in for life. But not Oskar. He freelanced for anyone he wanted to, and the Brighton Beach boys left him alone.

There were rumors that Oskar had been Russian military, one of those Russki special forces Spetsnaz guys, but that was just rumor. What wasn't rumor was that Oskar could shoot the balls off a hummingbird with a sniper rifle. The one time Tony used him it had been to get to a snitch being protected by federal marshals—a guy who was going to be a problem to a lot of people if he appeared in a courtroom. Tony figured the only way to get the snitch was to snipe him from a long way off, but Tony and his cronies didn't know anyone who could shoot a rifle. All the fuckin' wops they knew, none had ever been in the military and they didn't hunt, so Tony asked around and found the Russian. Oskar turned out to be really expensive, and three other guys had to chip in with Tony to pay Oskar's fee, but he got the job done: he made a shot from six hundred yards away and hit the rat right in the heart.

—◆◆◆—

Tony thought for a bit about how to contact Oskar Pankov, then figured, what the hell, just call the guy up. If someone later traced a call from him to Oskar, what would he care? He'd probably be dead by then.

He called Oskar's restaurant in Brooklyn, and a woman answered, probably Oskar's wife. For a couple of seconds, Tony listened to pots and pans being banged around and people talking in what sounded like Russian, before Oskar came on the line.

"What do you want?" Oskar said, although it sounded like *Vut do you vant?*

"Is that the way you answer the phone?" Tony said. "Vut do you vant? You don't say hello?"

"What do you want?" Oskar repeated.

"This is Tony Benedetto. You remember me?"

"Yeah, sure."

"I need to see you."

"So come to the restaurant. I'll make you a nice sandwich."

"I can't. I'm in the hospital. Cancer."

"That's too bad," Oskar said, although he didn't sound terribly sympathetic.

"I'm at the Flushing Medical Center in Queens. I'll make this worth your while."

"Okay. I'll come see you after the guy brings the meat for the restaurant."

33

After the futile visit to Tony Benedetto's hospital room, Emma rented a car and they drove back to D.C. together. During the trip, neither of them spoke much, and DeMarco spent the time trying to figure out what to do next.

He knew he wasn't going to try to kill Quinn again. He'd had one chance and Emma had screwed that up. The fact that she'd also saved his life, or kept him from spending the rest of his life in prison, was beside the point. He also couldn't figure out what Carmine Taliaferro had on Quinn—information that he'd most likely passed on to his daughter—and he couldn't figure out a way to force Stephanie Hernandez (née Taliaferro) to tell him what she knew. Only one thing occurred to him and that was to get Neil to dig deeper into Stephanie Hernandez's background, particularly her finances, and see if there was something there he could use to squeeze the woman. He was just about to say this to Emma, when she spoke first.

"I think the best thing you can do at this point is act as bait," Emma said.

"Bait?"

"Yeah. When we were at Susan's beach house, I said that I didn't think Quinn would have you arrested before his confirmation hearing because he wouldn't want you talking to the press. And I still don't think he'll have you arrested. But I think there's a possibility that he may try to do something to you before the hearing because he won't want to risk the possibility of you doing anything to cause him a problem."

"Like what?" DeMarco said.

"I don't know for sure. I suppose he could try to kill you. Not him personally but someone working for him. Or maybe he'll have a couple of his goons snatch you and stick you someplace until the hearing is over—which is essentially what he did with the teacher. Or I suppose he could send a couple of guys over to rough you up, like they did with Dombroski, to make sure you've gotten the message to leave him alone."

"I don't know," DeMarco said. "I kind of doubt—"

"I was thinking that if he does try to do something, maybe we can catch his people and force them to testify against him. I realize that's a long shot, but I can't think of anything else to do; and in order to catch them, you need to be available. You can't go into hiding."

"I wasn't planning on going into hiding," DeMarco said, offended she'd even think he would.

"Good. So you're bait. You stay at your place and hope we get lucky and Quinn tries something." DeMarco thought that over for a moment. He didn't like the idea of passively standing by, just hoping Quinn would do something. He wanted to play offense, not defense.

"It's too bad you dumped that gun I had into a sewer drain," he said, thinking it would be nice if the bait were armed.

"You won't need a gun. I'll get you some professional security—people who actually know how to shoot. And you need witnesses in case Quinn does do something."

"I can't pay for security. I'm unemployed. Remember?"

"Don't worry about paying them. I'll take care of that."

"I don't know," DeMarco said. He was already beholden enough to Emma.

Thinking that he was objecting to her plan, Emma said, "Well, do you have a better idea?"

"Only one. Get Neil to dig harder into Stephanie Hernandez's past to see if there's something there we can use to pressure her."

"I think that's probably a waste of time, but I'll do that. Neil's more inclined to follow orders when they come from me."

"Or what we could do," DeMarco said, "is kidnap Taliaferro's daughter and some of your DIA friends can waterboard her and force her to tell what she knows about Quinn."

"I assume you're joking," Emma said.

"Yeah. Sort of."

"And for your information, the DIA did not engage in waterboarding, at least not while I was there."

"Good for you. But if Quinn doesn't act in the next couple of days, I'll have to come up with a plan B. I can't play bait forever and even as rich as you are, you can't afford to pay people to protect me forever."

"Well, we'll worry about that later."

They were passing over the Delaware Memorial Bridge and DeMarco saw a boat approaching the bridge, fishing rods stuck in holders at the stern of the boat. He remembered one time when he was sixteen and he and his dad had gone fishing with one of his uncles in a boat about the same size. They caught a few fish that day but the thing that had made the day memorable was his dad let him have a beer, saying, "Don't tell your mother." It was funny how his tough-guy father had been afraid of his wife.

"I saw a movie one time," DeMarco said to Emma. "I don't remember the name of it, but I remember a guy in the movie was being used as bait so the cops could catch this bad guy. You know what the guy in the movie said?"

"No," Emma said.

"He said, *The bait always dies.*"

The morning after he returned from New York, DeMarco went out to breakfast in Georgetown—counter to Emma's order to remain in his house until his bodyguards arrived. When he returned to his house, he found two thugs waiting for him, sitting on the top step of his front porch. Well, *thugs* may have been a bit harsh.

Their names were Mike and Dave and they were both in their fifties, stocky guys about his size, and they looked tougher than horseshoe nails. They had big .45s in shoulder holsters.

After the introductions were made, the one named Mike, the apparent thug in charge, told DeMarco the plan as devised by Emma, the plan being pretty simple: DeMarco was to hang around his house, every once in a while poking his head outside the door so folks would know he was home, and if anybody tried to break in and harm him, Mike and Dave would shoot them.

DeMarco chose to occupy his time by filling out an online resume form, not sure how he could possibly spin being Mahoney's fixer into something appealing to a future employer. Under the section on *Special Skills* he wondered if he should put down *red fire axe*. Mike and Dave spent the time playing cribbage, periodically glancing out the windows to see who might be lurking about. Mike also informed DeMarco that as neither he nor Dave cooked, DeMarco was the designated chef.

Being the bait sucked.

34

The day after meeting with Tony Benedetto, Quinn was in his Manhattan apartment, packing for the trip to D.C. He needed to be in Washington several days before the hearing started because there were a number of people the White House wanted him to meet with, including half a dozen senators on the Judiciary Committee. He would have a long lunch tomorrow with the acting director of the FBI to receive an informal briefing on current issues facing the Bureau, followed by a meeting with the attorney general. Dinner was planned for one evening with the secretary of Homeland Security, a woman he expected to be working with closely. He wouldn't be meeting with the president again until after the hearing.

Unfortunately, his wife would be accompanying him. He wished he could have taken Pam with him but that obviously wouldn't do. And, he had to admit, Barbara was good in social settings with the politically powerful. She also seemed excited about the idea of living in D.C. and had already been in contact with a real estate agent there. She clearly had no clue about his affair with Pam. Well, maybe that wasn't true. She knew things weren't right with their marriage, and she might even suspect that he was having an affair, but maybe she was thinking that he would be faithful to her since he was being appointed to such a highly visible position.

During the confirmation hearing, he and Barbara would be staying at a friend's house in Georgetown. The friend and his wife were currently on an extended African tour—some sort of world hunger thing—and Quinn preferred to stay in a private home rather than a hotel. Grimes and Hanley would accompany him for security purposes and they'd live in the house where he and Barbara would be staying. Barbara wasn't happy about that, but with DeMarco on the loose, Quinn wanted his security people nearby.

He was trying to decide how many suits he needed to pack—two or three?—when Hanley called.

"DeMarco's back in D.C.," Hanley said.

"How do you know?" Quinn asked.

"He used a credit card this morning to buy breakfast at a place in Georgetown."

"I need to find out where he's staying, Hanley."

"I think he's staying at his own home. After I heard about the credit card charge, I called his home phone and he answered."

What the hell was DeMarco doing? Had he given up? Or had he just returned to D.C. to regroup? Whatever the case, it wasn't going to change Quinn's plan.

"What do you want me to do, boss?" Hanley asked.

"Nothing," Quinn said. "I think the guy's given up after what happened the other night. We're taking the shuttle to D.C. as planned this afternoon and if DeMarco tries something, you and Grimes will deal with him, but I doubt he'll try anything."

"Okay, boss," Hanley said.

Quinn finished packing, then walked into the living room, where his wife was on her cell phone with somebody. She was always on the phone. "Have you finished packing?" he asked. "We're leaving in two hours."

She cupped her hand over the phone and said, "Yes. I packed last night while you were doing whatever you were doing."

He wondered if that was a zinger. Last night, he'd told her he had to deal with a few urgent issues before they flew to D.C., but he'd actually been with Pam. "Good," he said. "I have to go out for just a moment, but I'll be right back."

"Where are you going?"

He ignored the question and left the apartment, and ten minutes later was using a public phone. He called Tony Benedetto's hospital room and when the old man answered he said, "He's at his home in D.C. You know who I'm talking about. Get this finished, Tony."

Tony started to call Oskar Pankov after he finished talking to Quinn, to tell Oskar what Quinn had told him: that DeMarco was at his home in Georgetown. Then something occurred to him. He'd already called Oskar once and a second call might not be smart, and it also wouldn't be smart to mention DeMarco's name or address on the phone.

He remembered the big stink a while ago about the NSA monitoring everybody's calls and emails, and although he thought the likelihood of somebody eavesdropping on a call he made was almost zero, why take the chance? One thing that Carmine had drilled into his head when he was young was that telephones were dangerous.

He thought for a couple of seconds, then called a guy he used to work with, a guy named Shorty for obvious reasons. Shorty had been able to pick any lock in existence before he got all crippled up with arthritis. He told Shorty to come to his hospital room, and because he owed Tony and because Tony said he'd pay him a C note to run an errand for him, Shorty showed up half an hour later. After Shorty stopped pretending that he gave a shit that Tony was dying, Tony handed him a sealed envelope containing a note that said DeMarco was at his home in Georgetown, and told Shorty to deliver it to Oskar's restaurant in Brighton Beach.

"My wallet's in that closet over there," Tony said. "Take out a hundred and get going." After Shorty left, he thought about checking his wallet to see how much Shorty had really taken from it, but no way did he have the strength to get out bed.

He closed his eyes and debated whether he should take more morphine—he had a little button he could push that would drip the dope into his veins—but he wanted to delay that as long as possible. The dope put him in some weird half-awake state where his brain didn't work and where he had memories of events he was sure had never really happened. The doctor also told him that he could push the morphine button as many times as he wanted—that the only thing that mattered at this point was minimizing his pain. And when the doc said this, Tony had thought: *Bullshit.* The doc was really telling him to push that fuckin' button until he overdosed because there wasn't anything else that could be done for him. Well, he wasn't ready to commit suicide yet.

He heard the door open and he opened his eyes to see who it was. He was expecting it would be one of the nurses just coming in to check on him—the nurses, he had to admit, had been really nice—but it wasn't a nurse. It was his damn kid.

"Hey, Pop. How ya doing?"

"How am I doing? I'm dying, you fuckin' numbskull. Where the hell you been? And how come this is the first time you've come to see me?"

Anthony Benedetto Jr. was a small man in his forties, his face prematurely wrinkled from booze and dope and because he liked to sit in the sun. Tony thought his kid's face looked like a white raisin, and the raisin got smaller every time he saw him. Also, every time he saw him, he couldn't help but think that it was his fault his son had turned into the loser-cokehead he was. If he'd spent more time with him, been more patient with him, maybe . . . The problem was, although he loved his son, he didn't really *like* him. He felt bad that he'd had to screw over a decent guy like DeMarco to save Junior's useless hide again.

Answering Tony's question, Anthony Jr. said, "I checked myself into rehab after they let me out of the can; I figured I'd better do that before I got into any more trouble." Before Tony could respond, he went on. "I still can't believe they're dropping the charges against me. Anyway, when I got out of rehab, I went by the house to see you and found out you were here. Mrs. Giacoma next door told me."

Tony hadn't told Junior about the deal he'd cut with Quinn to get the charges dismissed, only because he hadn't seen the kid since he'd gotten out of jail. And bullshit, he went into rehab. They don't let you out of rehab in just a couple of days, not unless you walk out. What Junior had most likely done—just based on the way he looked—was go out to celebrate after he got out of the can; he'd hooked up with some of his doper friends and had been on some kind of bender, snortin' shit up his nose.

"Anyway, I'm here now and I'm sorry I didn't get here sooner, Pop. Can I get you anything? Magazines, a book, something?"

Tony almost said: *A book! When the fuck have you ever seen me read a book?* But he didn't say that. Instead he said, "Just sit with me awhile. Okay, Anthony? Just sit here with your old man until he falls asleep."

Tony knew that after he died, Anthony Jr. would inherit quite a bit of money and all the property he owned, and then he'd lose everything gambling, or he'd blow it on dope, or the money would get taken from him by guys smarter and harder than him—and there wasn't anything he could do about that. All he could do was protect him from Quinn—and hold his hand for a while before he died.

"You remember the time," Tony said, "when me and you and your mom went down to Jersey and rented them horses?"

Anthony Jr. brayed a laugh. "You on a horse! That had to be the funniest thing I ever saw in my life. I thought you were gonna shoot that fuckin' horse."

35

Emma had no intention of asking Neil to dig into Stephanie Hernandez's past, and her plan to use DeMarco as bait was a ruse.

Emma thought it unlikely that Quinn would try to do anything to DeMarco before the confirmation hearing. After he'd been confirmed and was running the Bureau, then he might do something, but she figured DeMarco was safe until then. What she was really doing was making sure DeMarco didn't do something crazy, like go after Quinn again on his own. Boxing him up in his own house with Mike and Dave watching him would keep him pinned down until she could execute the only plan she could think of to get Quinn and to keep DeMarco out of trouble.

Emma had never met Mary Pat Mahoney before. She'd heard about Mahoney's wife from DeMarco, and based on everything DeMarco had said, she sounded like a decent woman. Why on earth she'd married Mahoney, Emma couldn't imagine. Well, that wasn't exactly true. She could imagine how a man with Mahoney's charm could have seduced her when she was young, but she couldn't imagine why Mary Pat had remained married to the reprobate for forty years.

When she arrived at the Watergate and told the doorman she was there to see Mrs. Mahoney, the doorman said, "And may I ask who you are, ma'am?"

Emma gave the doorman her name and added, "Tell Mrs. Mahoney this concerns a man named Joe DeMarco and that Mr. DeMarco is in trouble and needs her help."

"Joe's in trouble?" Mary Pat said when she opened the door.

"Yes," Emma said, "and I'm hoping you can help."

Emma liked Mary Pat Mahoney the moment she met her. Like her husband she had snow-white hair and blue eyes, but that was where the similarities ended. Mahoney had a good-sized gut and a broad butt; Mary Pat was slender. Mahoney had the eyes and complexion of a drinker, and he smoked, as well; Mary Pat seemed to glow with good health. Mary Pat was a vegetarian—Mahoney a meat eater. Mary Pat exercised daily—Mahoney considered lifting a tumbler filled with alcohol to his lips all the exercise he needed. She was also different than her husband in that she was kind and generous whereas John Mahoney, in Emma's opinion, was a selfish scoundrel.

"Please come in," Mary Pat said. "Would you like some coffee or tea?"

"No, I'm fine."

They took seats in the living room. It was nicely but not ostentatiously decorated. Prominently displayed were pictures of Mary Pat's three daughters.

"I'm assuming you know that your husband fired DeMarco," Emma said.

"What!" Mary Pat said.

Mary Pat had known DeMarco for a long time and a few months ago, DeMarco had saved Mary Pat's middle daughter, Molly, from going to prison for insider trading. So Emma knew that she and her husband owed DeMarco. One of the things Emma also liked about Mary Pat was that when she discovered her daughter was avoiding a prison sentence for a crime she'd committed—a crime that was partly due to Molly's gambling and alcohol addictions—she insisted Molly go to work for UNICEF for three years, about the amount of time she would have spent in prison.

"Why did John fire him?" Mary Pat asked.

Emma told her the story: DeMarco had recently learned that Brian Quinn had killed his father and he was planning to destroy Quinn's reputation during the confirmation hearing. However, when he went to Mahoney to tell him what he was doing—and essentially to ask for Mahoney's help avenging his father's death—Mahoney had ordered DeMarco not to do anything until he'd conferred with the president.

"In other words, your husband was considering the political ramifications of exposing Quinn, and Joe didn't care about the political ramifications. Then I'm afraid Joe lost his temper. He said he was going to reveal some of the things your husband had done in the past if he took any action that would hinder Joe's vendetta against Quinn."

"I see," Mary Pat said—but the look on her face said that if she had to choose between protecting DeMarco and protecting her husband, she would choose her husband.

"Congressman Mahoney naturally took offense at being threatened by Joe and fired him. And then things got worse after that."

Emma then explained how DeMarco had decided to kill Quinn, and almost succeeded, but fortunately she was able to keep that from happening.

"He was going to shoot the man?" Mary Pat said.

"Yes."

"My God. But I'm confused," Mary Pat said. "What do you want me to do?"

"Your husband can still help Joe if he wants to and I'm hoping you can talk some sense into him. When he fired Joe, they were both pretty emotional and I'm hoping the congressman has calmed down since then."

"I don't know," Mary Pat said. "John can be rather stubborn and he's not known for his forgiving nature."

"I know."

"And I don't understand how John can help Joe at this point, either."

Emma explained.

Mary Pat looked at her watch. "He's supposed to be home in an hour. I was just about to go for a walk. Why don't you come with me—John and Joe have told me some interesting things about you and I'd like to learn more. When we get back, John should be here and we can talk to him then."

———◆◆◆———

"What the hell are you doing here?" Mahoney said when he saw Emma sitting in his living room drinking tea with his wife.

Unlike his wife, Mahoney had encountered Emma several times when she'd worked cases with DeMarco. He didn't like her, because she was the sort of person—unlike himself—who always did the right thing and he couldn't control her.

"John," May Pat said, "why didn't you tell me you fired Joe?" Before Mahoney could answer she said, "Now sit down and stop being rude and listen to what Emma has to say."

"Humpf," Mahoney said, and walked over to a liquor cabinet and pulled out a bottle of Wild Turkey and poured two ounces into a glass without adding ice.

"Don't you think you've had enough to drink for one day," Mary Pat said. Emma had smelled the booze wafting off Mahoney the minute he stepped into the apartment and his wife apparently had, too.

"No," Mahoney said. "Especially not if she's here."

Mahoney sat down.

"Let me tell you what's been going on since you fired DeMarco," Emma said.

She then went through the whole story again for Mahoney: how DeMarco had gotten a video statement from Tony Benedetto that he'd planned to spring on Quinn at his confirmation hearing; how Tony had betrayed DeMarco and how Quinn had stolen the video from DeMarco's house; and then how Quinn had disappeared the teacher who could have talked about Quinn covering up Connors's death.

Mahoney's reaction to all this was to lift a white eyebrow in surprise and take another sip of his drink.

"Then after Joe decided he had no other choice, he got a silenced weapon from somebody and was about two seconds away from killing Quinn the other night," Emma said, and told him all that had transpired in New York.

"Jesus," Mahoney said. "I can't believe he'd do something so stupid."

"Quinn killed his father, Congressman," Emma said.

"Yeah, but . . ."

"And he's going to be the next FBI director unless you do something."

"Like what? What the hell am I supposed to do?"

"Do you know a New York politician named Stephanie Hernandez? She's the borough president in Queens."

"Yeah, I know who she is. She's a little pain in the ass who's always busting Chris Barlow's balls."

"In addition to being a ballbuster," Emma said, "she's also Carmine Taliaferro's daughter."

"You gotta be shittin' me," Mahoney said.

Emma then explained what DeMarco suspected about Stephanie Hernandez. When she finished speaking, Mahoney sat for a moment, finished the drink he was holding in his hand, then got up and poured another.

"For God's sake, John," Mary Pat said.

"So are you going to help DeMarco?" Emma asked.

"I don't know," Mahoney said.

"Well, I do," Mary Pat said. "You're going to help him and that's all there is to it. He's a good man and you owe him and you know it."

Mahoney glowered at the two women. He was being double-teamed and he didn't like it. His wife was bad enough but Emma . . . Emma was downright dangerous.

36

Stephanie Hernandez had no idea why John Mahoney wanted to see her. All she knew was that she got a call from his secretary last night and was basically ordered to come to Washington this morning. She could have told Mahoney to go to hell but knew it would be stupid to thumb her nose at the most powerful Democrat in the House without at least hearing what he had to say. She suspected he was going to tell her to quit going after Chris Barlow's head—and his seat in the House—and then he'd give her a bunch of bullshit about how her day would eventually come.

Mahoney scared her. She'd never met him face-to-face, but she'd seen him on TV. On TV, he was all bullshit and blarney, charming everyone, telling jokes, getting teary-eyed if he talked about the vets, acting like he was the champion of the common man. He was full of crap, and he usually looked like he was half in the bag. But she'd heard other stories, too, about how if you crossed him he'd stab you in the back—or maybe stab you right through the heart while he looked into your eyes. He was a tricky, vindictive son of a bitch and you didn't want him for an enemy unless you were willing to switch parties.

"You can go in now, Mrs. Hernandez," Mahoney's secretary said. She'd noticed the secretary had been a little cool toward her, not offering her coffee or anything, not apologizing that Mahoney had kept her waiting half an hour. She wondered if there was some sort of message in the secretary's behavior or if the woman was just naturally rude.

———— ✦ ————

Mahoney didn't bother to stand when Stephanie Hernandez entered his office. "Take a seat," he said, pointing to a chair in front of his desk, then he took a sip from his drink and just stared at her. She had small brown eyes, thin lips, and a combative square chin; she looked like the type that wouldn't back down in a fight. She was short—maybe five foot two—and broad-hipped. With the green pantsuit she was wearing, she looked like a shrub.

Mahoney was actually grateful she wasn't good-looking; he knew himself well enough to know he could be manipulated by good-looking women and sometimes the desire to get into their pants could distract him from what he knew he needed to do. That wasn't going to be a problem this time.

Mahoney waited until the silence became uncomfortable and she spoke first. "Why did you want to see me, Mr. Speaker?"

Mahoney was no longer the Speaker of the House. He'd lost the job a few years back when the Republicans took control of the House, but he'd been the Speaker for so long that people still addressed him that way.

"I wanted to see you because I know you've got something on Brian Quinn, and I want to know what it is."

"Quinn? The commissioner?"

"Yeah, that Quinn. And don't try acting stupid with me. You know damn good and well who he is, and I'm sure you're aware that he's been nominated to run the Bureau."

He could tell she didn't know what to say next; she was trying to decide if she should be polite or tell him to go screw himself. Before she could decide, Mahoney plowed ahead. "Your old man was a mobster up there in Queens and—"

She popped up from her chair like a jack-in-the-box. "That is a lie and I will not stand for—"

"Sit down!" Mahoney bellowed. She hesitated for a moment, then sat.

"It's not a lie. Your father was a goddamn guinea hood involved in loansharking and extortion and he made a fortune off dope. And every once in a while, he'd have someone whacked."

"I never had anything to do with my father's business," Stephanie said, not looking embarrassed, just defiant.

"I know you didn't," Mahoney said. "You went to college just like you were a normal person instead of a mafia princess and—"

"Goddamnit, I'm not—"

"—and then you started screwing around in politics, doing volunteer work and all the usual shit. The thing that's amazing about you, though, is that the money crowd up there loves you. You get donations from some of the biggest names on Wall Street and Park Avenue, and the person who's helped the most is Barbara Quinn, the commissioner's wife. So tell me how that happened, princess? How is that I've got pictures of you sitting at the head table at functions next to Mrs. Quinn when a person like her wouldn't ordinarily give you the time of day?"

"I have her support, you drunken buffoon, because she knows I'm an honest person and that I've done good things for my borough. She also knows that I'd represent the Seventh District better than that idiot Barlow."

That almost made Mahoney smile: Barlow was an idiot.

"Bullshit," Mahoney said, slamming his big fist down onto his desk, slopping some of the bourbon out of the glass. "She's supporting you because you're blackmailing her husband. I *know* this, Stephanie. I'm not guessing."

Actually Mahoney didn't know and he was guessing.

"What I don't know," Mahoney said, "and what you're going to tell me, is exactly what you have on Quinn."

"This discussion is absurd and I'm leaving."

"No, you're not," Mahoney said, "and I'll tell you why. I'm going to call the president and suggest that he withdraw Quinn's nomination. I'm going to tell the president that I know some things about Quinn that I can't prove, but should they ever come to light, the president will wind up with egg all over his face. I'll also tell the president that the reason I can't prove what I know is because this lady named Stephanie Hernandez won't tell me, and that I intend to make sure Mrs. Hernandez never holds another public office. How would you like that, Stephanie? Having both me and the president of the United States for enemies?"

"I'm telling you," Stephanie screamed, her face as red as Mahoney's, "that I never had anything to do with my father's business and the only association I've ever had with Commissioner Quinn is because of his wife's support of women's issues."

"Yeah, yeah," Mahoney said. "Let me give you a couple scenarios, Stephanie, and see which one you like better. You want Barlow's seat and it just so happens that privately I agree with you that Chris Barlow ain't the sharpest knife in the drawer. Now I could probably convince the DNC that you're the gal we want up there in the Seventh District and I could probably convince Barlow that it's time for him to move on. I'll come up with some kind of job for him over on K Street, something that will make him happy. So then you'll become a congresswoman and when you get down here, I'll do my best to help you out, and then, the next thing we all know, you're running for senator or governor or I could give a shit what.

"Scenario number two is, you keep lying to me about not having something on Quinn and I destroy your political career. The other thing is, and you may not know this—although half the fucking New York Police Department does—is that Quinn has a girlfriend and I wouldn't be surprised if he and your political meal ticket get a divorce.

"So I don't know, Stephanie. Maybe Mrs. Quinn will continue to stand by your side after she's the ex–Mrs. Quinn, but I doubt it. I'm thinking the only reason she supported you in the first place is because her husband made her, which he won't be able to do after the divorce."

Stephanie just sat there looking stubborn.

"Why don't you go take a walk around the Mall and think things over," Mahoney said. "If I don't hear back from you in an hour, I'll assume that you've decided not to become my new best friend—and the next congresswoman from New York."

It didn't take Stephanie an hour to make up her mind.

37

DeMarco's home phone rang, and he walked into the den to answer it. As he picked up the receiver, Mike—or maybe it was Dave—called out from the kitchen, "Hey! Don't stand in front of the window."

"Hello," DeMarco said, ignoring Mike.

"Get your ass over here," the caller said and hung up.

DeMarco was so stunned that for a moment he just stood there, the phone still in his hand.

"Hey! I told you not to stand in front of the window," Mike said, walking into DeMarco's den. "Are you trying to get killed?"

"Yeah, yeah. I have to go to the Capitol. My ex-boss wants to talk to me."

"Emma said you were to stay here."

"Well, Emma only thinks she's in charge of my life, and I don't need her permission. If *you* think you need her permission, give her a call."

"Don't be a smartass," Mike said.

"I'm going to shave and change into a suit. I'll be leaving in about fifteen minutes."

"We'll take my car," Mike said.

"How 'bout putting some of those dishes lying all over the kitchen into the dishwasher while I'm changing?"

Mike made a snorting sound that DeMarco interpreted as *Do I look like your maid?*

———◆◆◆———

Oskar Pankov strolled past the target's house in Georgetown. He was on the other side of the street from the house, and as he walked, he studied the place without being obvious about it. He wished he had a dog to walk so he could stop and let it shit, which would have given him more time to exam the house. He could see the target through one of the windows, talking on the phone—and he was beginning to think that maybe the easiest thing to do would be to shoot him through that same window. He had no idea why Tony wanted DeMarco dead; it didn't matter to Oskar.

He didn't see the two men DeMarco had with him, but he knew they were inside the house, too, and he suspected they were both armed. He knew one of them was armed for sure because when he had come outside earlier to get the paper off DeMarco's front porch, Oskar—sitting in his car, just a few houses away—had seen the gun in the shoulder holster the guy was wearing. Tony hadn't said anything about DeMarco having bodyguards and Oskar was going to call Tony and raise the price they'd agreed to. An urban kill was risky enough even if the guy didn't have protection.

If DeMarco left his house, Oskar could follow him and see if an opportunity presented itself. He'd brought a silenced pistol with him in case he had to take a close-range shot—like maybe if the guy was in an underground parking lot or in an elevator by himself—but now, since he knew DeMarco had bodyguards, he wasn't going to do anything like that. He didn't really want to use the pistol, anyway. He'd always preferred to use a rifle because he was better with a rifle, and because a rifle put distance between him and the target, which gave him a better chance to escape and not be seen.

If DeMarco went to a meeting or to a restaurant, maybe he could find a place where he could pick him off. The problem with doing that, however, was that he probably wouldn't have much time to pick a good spot to shoot from. In the past, when he'd killed with a rifle, he'd usually picked his spot days in advance, devised a way to conceal himself, and figured out multiple routes for getting away. The other problem with trying to snipe DeMarco anyplace public was that there were cameras all over Washington. America was turning into a fucking police state and if he shot DeMarco near any government building, he'd have no idea if he was being videoed while he was taking the shot. He'd end up like those two evil little Chechen pricks who bombed the Boston Marathon; the smoke had barely cleared before their pictures were all over the news.

Yeah, the best thing to do would be to shoot him right in his own house when he passed in front of one of the windows or the next time he came outside. So now he had to find a place to shoot from, which wasn't going to be easy in a densely populated neighborhood.

Oskar decided to walk all the way around the block to get back to his car. If he passed in front of DeMarco's house again, and if DeMarco's security people were worth a damn, they would notice him. As he was walking, studying the neighborhood, he wondered how things were going at the restaurant. His brother-in-law was substituting for him while he was in D.C., and although the man wasn't a bad cook, he was incredibly slow. He knew all his regular customers would be angry having to wait so long for their orders and his wife would be a nervous wreck by the time he returned. Maybe he would call his wife when he got back to the car and tell her to take a few of the more complicated dishes off the menu.

He'd just reached his car when two things happened simultaneously: his cell phone rang and DeMarco and the two hardcases protecting him stepped out of DeMarco's house. The security guys immediately looked in Oskar's direction, so when he answered the phone, he turned his head slightly and used the hand holding the phone to partially obscure his face. He noticed that one of DeMarco's bodyguards looked a lot like DeMarco: he was DeMarco's height and had the same build, but his hair was gray instead of dark. He'd better make sure he shot the right guy when the time came. He quickly got into his car, hoping DeMarco would think he was just someone who lived in the neighborhood.

Only two people had the number of the burner phone he was using: his wife and Tony Benedetto. "What do you want?" he said to whoever was calling.

"It's Tony," the caller said. "Why the fuck do you answer the phone like that?"

He was glad Tony had called. He didn't know what the old wop wanted, but this would give him a chance to tell Tony the price for killing DeMarco had gone up substantially.

———————◆◆◆———————

As DeMarco and his escorts were leaving the house, a cell phone rang and Mike and Dave spun in the direction of the sound; Mike actually reached for the gun in his shoulder holster.

"Jesus, relax," DeMarco said.

DeMarco barely saw the guy answering the phone, just that he was a tall, balding guy. He didn't recognize him, but then there were a lot of people in the neighborhood he didn't know; people were always moving in and out as the politicians played a never-ending game of musical chairs.

"Where did you park your car?" he asked Mike. "I don't want to be late."

Quinn glanced at his watch, wondering what was keeping Hanley. He was meeting with two senators this morning at the Russell Building, with a third at the Dirksen Building, and then would have lunch with the acting director of the FBI over at the Hoover Building. He didn't want to start out the day being late for his first meeting.

One thing he didn't like about staying in his friend's town house was that the place only had a small one-car garage and his friend's car was parked in the garage—which meant that Hanley had been forced to park the rental car on the street, and he may have had to park a block away. Georgetown was a pain in the ass when it came to parking.

His wife, however, liked the town house and the neighborhood; she especially liked being close enough to be able to walk to the shops in Georgetown. While Quinn was in meetings today, a real estate agent was planning to show Barbara some large homes in Arlington and in Northwest D.C. off Embassy Row, but Barbara was now talking about looking at town houses in Georgetown instead. He felt bad about the fact that she was probably going to put down money on a house or town house, and a couple of months after that, he was going to divorce her. He'd tried to talk her into renting a place until they got to know the area better, but Barbara's financial people were telling her that the real estate market for upscale homes in the D.C. area was good and improving, and she could probably sell whatever house she bought for a profit. Oh, well. He'd tried.

Hanley finally arrived with the car. "I'll see you this evening," Quinn said to his wife. She was on her phone—as always—and she just waved at him. Grimes stepped outside before Quinn and looked around, then nodded to Quinn and he left the house.

On his way to Capitol Hill, Quinn thought about the questions he'd most likely be asked by the senators in these private meetings this morning. He wasn't worried about the first two meetings; those sena-tors liked him, and one was from New York and he knew the man well. His third meeting, however, was with Senator Beecham of Georgia, a man who intensely disliked the president and was inclined to oppose whomever the president nominated. Aw, he could handle Beecham, although the man was so damn old he probably wouldn't be able to remember whatever Quinn told him.

38

DeMarco had no idea why Mahoney wanted to see him. He was hoping that Mahoney had decided to forgive him and was going to offer him his job back—but the way he'd sounded on the phone made that fantasy seem unlikely.

When he arrived at Mahoney's office, Mavis coolly said, "He's waiting for you." Mahoney's secretary had always liked him—but Mavis was loyal only to the man she'd served for more than thirty years.

With Mahoney was a short, broad-hipped, dark-haired woman DeMarco didn't know. The woman looked unhappy and tired. Mahoney looked unhappy and hungover.

"This is Stephanie Hernandez," Mahoney said.

Jesus! Taliaferro's daughter.

"The other day," Mahoney said to DeMarco, "your pal Emma came to see me and told me that Mrs. Hernandez might have some information that would, uh, demonstrate that Brian Quinn is not the man who should be our next FBI director. I subsequently spoke to Mrs. Hernandez and she confirmed what I was told."

DeMarco knew what Mahoney was really saying: he was saying that Emma had told him that Hernandez had something that had been given to her by her father, and she'd used whatever she'd been given to blackmail Brian Quinn to advance her political career. DeMarco had no idea what Mahoney had done to force the woman to cooperate, but it was apparent that he was now treating her as some sort of ally.

DeMarco, however, had no interest in participating in whatever game Mahoney was playing. "What do you have on Quinn?" he asked Hernandez.

She hesitated, and looked over at Mahoney.

"Go on, tell him," Mahoney said. "He's not going to be a problem for you. All he wants is Quinn."

"I have photographs of Quinn killing your father," Stephanie said. "My father gave them to me."

"What! How did Carmine manage to get pictures?"

"I don't know. All I know is that before my father died, he gave me the photos and told me to hide them someplace where Quinn wouldn't ever find them. And right after my father died, Quinn got a warrant to search my house, my father's house, and all the businesses we own. He'd convinced some judge, who was a crony of his, that my dad had hidden information that could be used in an organized crime case. The warrant was bullshit. He was looking for the photos.

"His people just *ripped* my house apart and they disrupted our businesses for more than a month. Anyway, after the search, I met with him. I told him that he was never going to find the photos and he'd better stop harassing me or I'd give them to the FBI. I told that shithead the truth: that I wasn't a criminal like my father, that all I wanted to do was work for my community and I would appreciate his help."

"In other words, you blackmailed him," DeMarco said.

Stephanie Hernandez jumped up from the chair where she was seated and shouted, "Fuck you! It wasn't blackmail. Don't you dare call it blackmail. I never asked for a dime from him or his snooty bitch of a wife. All I wanted was for him not to get in my way and maybe give me a few endorsements."

Bullshit it wasn't blackmail, DeMarco thought, but why argue with her.

Mahoney said, "Calm down, Stephanie." To DeMarco he said, "Mrs. Hernandez is a little tired. Yesterday, after I met with her, she had to go back up to New York, get the pictures, and bring them back here. So she's tired and understandably distraught."

"What happens next?" DeMarco asked Mahoney.

"The first thing that's going to happen is, I'm going over to the White House and tell the president that he needs to immediately withdraw his nomination of Brian Quinn. Right after that, Mrs. Hernandez is going to become a hero. She's going to go see the acting director of the FBI and she's going to tell him that she was cleaning out her garage or her attic or some fuckin' place, and she ran across these pictures. Being a good citizen, she felt it was her obligation to come forward with this information immediately and, because of who Quinn is, she felt the only one she could go to was the head of the Bureau. The Bureau is then going to arrest Brian Quinn. At the same time, the Bureau is going to question Tony Benedetto before he dies and try to get him to repeat the story he told you."

"Quinn's going to say the photos are phony," DeMarco said.

"You don't understand," Mahoney said. "These are old-time photographs with negatives. They're not digital. They couldn't be Photoshopped. I mean, Quinn can claim they're phonies, but the wizards at the Bureau will be able to prove they're not."

"I want to see them," DeMarco said.

"Aw, Joe, what's the point? Do you really want to see your dad being killed?"

"I want to see them," DeMarco said again.

Mahoney shrugged and pushed an envelope toward him. "Don't touch the negatives," Mahoney said.

DeMarco opened the envelope. There were three identical sets of eight-by-ten photographs in the envelope, each set consisting of ten photos. In a small, clear envelope were the negatives.

The first photo showed Gino DeMarco walking down the aisle of what appeared to be a brightly lit warehouse, and standing behind Gino was a young Brian Quinn pointing a pistol with a silencer at Gino's back. Both men were dressed almost identically in work clothes and hard hats. The next photo showed Quinn shooting his gun at Gino while Gino appeared to be spinning around, turning to face Quinn. The photo captured the gas or flame or whatever it was escaping from Quinn's gun as it was fired.

DeMarco figured that whoever had taken the photos had used one of those cameras that advanced the film really fast, because the next series of photos showed Gino firing at Quinn and Quinn firing back, then Quinn firing again as Gino just stood there. The last photo was Quinn standing over his father's body.

DeMarco had tears in his eyes when he looked back at Mahoney.

He wiped the tears away with the back of his hand and said, "I want to confront Quinn with this before he's arrested. I want to look him in the eye and tell him his life is over."

"I don't think that's smart," Stephanie Hernandez said. "He might run after you talk to him. You know, flee the country."

DeMarco ignored Stephanie; so did Mahoney.

"Yeah, okay," Mahoney said. He understood that this was something DeMarco needed to do. To Stephanie, he said, "Quinn's not going to run. He's so damn arrogant that he'll think he can beat the evidence."

"Do you know where Quinn is?" DeMarco asked Mahoney.

"No. All I know is he's running around town, glad-handing folks before the confirmation hearing starts. I'll have Perry track him down. Somebody must have his schedule. Perry will call you."

DeMarco nodded. "Can I get my badge back—I mean temporarily— so I can get in and out of the buildings up here?" He meant so he could go to the various congressional office buildings on Capitol Hill if he needed to find Quinn.

"Yeah," Mahoney said. "Mavis has your badge." Mahoney stood up. "Now, I have to get over to the White House so I can ruin the president's day." To Stephanie he said, "I'll call you as soon as I'm done with the president and I'll make an appointment for you with the guy you need to talk to at the FBI."

"I need a shower and a change of clothes," Stephanie said. "I've been wearing this suit for the last twenty-four hours." DeMarco figured Hernandez was thinking there might be a photo op in the near future and she wanted to look her best.

"Talk to Mavis," Mahoney said. "She'll help you out."

To DeMarco, Mahoney said, "Don't do anything stupid."

39

When Oskar Pankov saw the small FOR SALE sign on the house—showings by appointment only—he looked skyward and said a silent *Thank you.* He hadn't noticed the for-sale house at first because he'd focused primarily on the target's house. Oskar was actually an atheist; nothing he'd seen or experienced in his lifetime gave him any reason to believe God existed. Nonetheless, he was grateful to whatever or whoever it was that had decided to grant him this good fortune.

The for-sale house was vacant—he knew this because the drapes had been taken down and he could see the rooms were empty of furniture—and from two of its windows, he would be able to see the target's front door and into some of his windows. He would break into the vacant house, knock a hole in a window so it wouldn't interfere with the shot, and when the guy exposed himself, he'd shoot him. Nice and simple, nothing fancy.

Or maybe he wouldn't break into the house. The for-sale house could be alarmed and if it was, the alarm would sound and the cops would show up; he'd be able to get away before the cops arrived, but that would end any chance of him being able to use the vacant house for a shooting nest. So maybe the best thing would be to lie down in the rhododendron bushes on the east side of the vacant house and shoot from there. There were big rhodies all along the east side, and there was a space about two feet wide between the house and the bushes. The other good thing about the rhodies is that people in the house on the east side of the for-sale house wouldn't be able to see him through the bushes. The only drawback with this plan, other than lying on the ground for hours, was that he'd have to wait until it was completely dark to take up his position in the bushes.

He thought all that over and decided he would certainly be more comfortable and less likely to be seen if he could wait inside the vacant house until the man showed himself. And since they were selling the house, even if it had an alarm, the alarm most likely wouldn't be set because then they'd have to give the security code to a whole bunch of real estate agents. He doubted real estate agents would be showing clients the house after dark.

Nah, why take the chance? He could stand it, lying on the ground in the space between the bushes and the vacant house for a few hours. It got dark around 6 P.M. this time of the year, and if the guy went out during the day, most likely he'd be back before midnight. Oskar could take six or seven hours lying on the ground.

He remembered once when he was in the army, this enormously fat man he'd been order to kill in Georgia—that was the country of Georgia, not the American state. He didn't know who the fat man was or why he was killing him. All he'd been told was that the man would eventually come out of his house to feed his rabbits, and he was to shoot him then.

The shot had been easy—three hundred yards looking through powerful scope at a target the size of the Goodyear blimp—but it had been ten degrees below zero. He kept his hands warm but almost lost four toes to frostbite. He'd been nineteen years old then—a lot younger and tougher than he was now—but he could certainly lie on the ground for a few hours when the temperature would be above forty degrees and it wasn't raining.

There was a problem, however. Although killing the guy would be easy—almost as easy as killing the blimp-sized man in Georgia—he was going to have a hard time getting away, even shooting at night as he planned. He couldn't take the shot and then run out into the street in front of the vacant house and jump into his car, because the body-guards might see him—and shoot him. To make matters worse, there was no alley behind the vacant house. Instead, it butted up against the backyard of another house, and the two backyards were separated by a six-foot redwood fence. He was still in good enough shape at the age of fifty-three that he could make it over the fence, but scaling the fence would waste vital seconds. Hmm.

Okay, here's what he would do. He'd go to a hardware store and buy one of those short stepladders that fold up and are about eighteen inches high. Yeah, that would work. He'd be able to place one foot on the stepladder and be over the fence in an instant.

It was decided. Tonight, he would come back after dark, and the first thing he would do was place his stepladder near the backyard fence of the for-sale house. Then he'd lie down in the bushes on the east side of the house and wait for the target to either pass in front of a window or come outside. He'd take the shot—he'd only need one—drop the rifle, run for the backyard fence, step on the stepladder, go over the fence, run through the neighbor's backyard, and then run to his car, which would be parked on the street in front of the neighbor's house. If the neighbor came outside after he took the shot, well, then he just might have to shoot the neighbor with his pistol.

Now that he had a plan, he would go back to his room at the Mar-riott, rest until nightfall, then come back. If he couldn't get a shot tonight, he'd come back the following night. If an opportunity didn't present itself either tonight or tomorrow night—if the blinds in the house were shut or if the guy didn't come outside or pass in front of one of the windows—then he'd develop another plan. He wasn't going to rush the kill, no matter what Tony had said when he called.

40

Quinn had just taken a seat in Beecham's office. The old senator was staring at him, looking confused, as if he didn't know who Quinn was or why he was there. Quinn couldn't help but think that there really should be a mandatory retirement age for politicians. He was about to remind Beecham why he was there, but before he could say anything, Beecham's good-looking chief of staff, Amelia Sherman, walked into the room. She told Quinn that the president's chief of staff was on the phone and needed to speak to him immediately.

"You can use the phone in my office, Commissioner," she said.

She led him to her office. "He's on line two," she said and closed the door as she left the room. Quinn punched a blinking button on the phone and said, "This is Brian Quinn."

Without any sort of preamble, Horrigan, the president's chief, said, "The president is withdrawing your nomination. The confirmation hearing has been canceled. Go back to New York."

"What?" Quinn said. "What the hell's going on?"

"Just what I told you, Commissioner. You are no longer the president's choice for FBI director," Horrigan said and hung up.

Quinn sat there in the chair behind Amelia Sherman's desk for a minute, so shocked he couldn't move. He needed to understand what was going on. He checked his cell phone for Horrigan's number and called him back. The son of a bitch owed him an explanation.

"This is Brian Quinn," he said when a woman answered the phone. "I need to speak to Horrigan again."

"I'm sorry, Mr. Quinn, but Mr. Horrigan is not available," the woman said and hung up.

Son of a bitch! What the hell was going on?

He was going to drive over to the damn White House and demand to see Horrigan or the president. They couldn't pull this shit without telling him why. He opened the door to Sherman's office and the first thing he saw was DeMarco talking to Amelia Sherman.

DeMarco pointed a finger at him and said, "Go back inside the office. I've got something to say to you before you leave. If you try to leave before I talk to you, I'll beat the hell out of you."

"Behave yourself, Mr. DeMarco," Sherman said, but DeMarco ignored her and took a step toward Quinn.

Quinn wished that Grimes and Hanley were there. He'd told them to wait outside the building while he talked to Beecham. He hadn't thought that he'd need their protection inside a Senate office building with the U.S. Capitol Police all over the place. Before he could react, DeMarco was standing in front of him and then DeMarco shoved him hard in the chest, pushing him back into Sherman's office. DeMarco heard Amelia Sherman let out a small cry of surprise as he shut the door.

———◆◆◆———

"What in the hell do you think you're doing?" Quinn shouted. "I'll have your dumb ass arrested for assault."

"Sit down," DeMarco said, pointing to the chair behind Sherman's desk. When Quinn just stood there, glaring at him, DeMarco said, "Sit down, or I swear to Christ, I'll pound your face into hamburger."

Quinn reached for his gun—then realized he wasn't carrying a gun.

He took a breath, to center himself. He needed to remain calm. He didn't understand what was going on. He didn't know why the president had withdrawn his nomination, nor did he understand what DeMarco was doing here. He had to wonder if the two events could be connected, but he didn't see how they could be. A nobody like DeMarco would have no influence over the president.

"All right, DeMarco," he said, taking a seat. "Tell me what you want. And make it quick."

———— ◆◆◆ ————

It was amazing how Quinn was able to do that, DeMarco thought: instantly regain his composure and now act as if he owned the room and was the man in charge. He was pretty sure, however, that Quinn's composure would be short-lived.

DeMarco didn't sit. He opened the manila envelope he'd been holding in his left hand, pulled out the single photo in the envelope, and dropped it on the center of the desk. It was a photo of a young Brian Quinn with a gun in his hand standing over the corpse of Gino DeMarco.

DeMarco saw Quinn glance down at the photo, puzzled at first, and then he realized what he was looking at. He sat back in the chair and closed his eyes. DeMarco was sure Quinn had seen the photo before. At some point in time, probably right after Quinn killed his father, Carmine Taliaferro would have shown Quinn the series of photos of Quinn killing Gino DeMarco. He may have even given Quinn a set of the photos. When Quinn opened his eyes, he looked at DeMarco for a moment, then quietly said, "How did you get the picture?"

It sounded to DeMarco as if he was simply curious.

"John Mahoney forced the photos out of Taliaferro's daughter. I figured out that she had something she was holding over your head, but I didn't know what. Mahoney convinced Stephanie Hernandez that it was in her best interest to give up whatever she'd been using to blackmail you."

"I've always hated that woman," Quinn muttered. In a louder voice, he said. "So now what, DeMarco?"

"Right now Stephanie is talking to the acting director of the FBI, showing him all the photos. Then I imagine the Bureau, being the cautious folks they are, will mull all this over for a few days, have their experts confirm the photos are real, then they'll talk to a bunch of lawyers to see what kind of case they can make against you. Then they'll arrest your ass."

"I'll fight this, you know," Quinn said. "I don't know how, yet, but I will. I was a cop and your father was a criminal. I killed him during the course of my duties."

"You tried to shoot him in the back. The photos show that."

"Those photos don't show what transpired before I shot him. I'll say I chased him into that warehouse and he fired at me before I shot him."

DeMarco barked out a humorless laugh. "Come on, Quinn. How are you going to explain why you didn't report killing my dad if you killed him trying to make a legitimate arrest?"

"I don't know. Yet. But I'll come up with something. I'll beat this."

For just a moment, DeMarco almost believed that Quinn might be able to save himself—and he almost lost it. He started around the desk, intending to knock the smirk off Quinn's face, and maybe just keep beating on him until he was dead. But he didn't.

"You're through," DeMarco said. "And I'm the guy who brought you down." He didn't bother to add: with a whole bunch of help from Emma and Mahoney.

DeMarco had said what he'd come to say, and he'd gotten the satisfaction of seeing the look of defeat on Quinn's face when he initially saw the photo. He picked up the photo and turned to leave the office, but before he reached the door, Quinn stood and shouted, "Your father was a hit man! He was a killer! I don't deserve to go to jail for killing him. I've spent my entire life putting criminals like him in jail and protecting New York from terrorists. I don't deserve this," Quinn said again.

DeMarco thought for a minute about telling Quinn everything his father had meant to him and how Quinn was no better than the criminals he bragged about incarcerating. But what would be the point? All he said was "He was my dad. And fuck what you deserve."

41

Quinn walked out of the Dirksen Building, still stunned by what had happened. Hanley and Grimes were waiting for him on the steps, bullshitting with one of the Capitol cops. As soon as they saw Quinn, they walked over to him. Quinn figured that DeMarco must have left by a different exit; if Hanley and Grimes had seen him, they would have detained him.

"Where to, boss?" Hanley said.

"I don't know," Quinn said.

"Are you all right, boss?"

Quinn didn't answer. He was wondering if he should call Tony Benedetto and tell him that he'd changed his mind about killing DeMarco. Now there was no point in killing DeMarco. Well, that wasn't exactly true. Killing DeMarco would be very satisfying, but if DeMarco was killed now—and considering the photos Stephanie Hernandez was supposedly showing the FBI—he would be considered a suspect. Yes, it would probably be best to tell Tony to call off whomever he'd hired. He didn't, however, want to call Tony from his cell phone.

"Have you seen a pay phone around here?" he asked Hanley.

"A pay phone? Do you want to use my cell phone, boss?"

"No, I want . . . Never mind."

Quinn started walking, with Grimes and Hanley trailing behind. He didn't have any idea where he was going; he just needed to walk. He needed to think. He'd find a pay phone someplace along the way and call Tony.

Goddamn Tony. He hadn't told Tony to kill DeMarco before the confirmation hearing, but he thought he'd made it clear that he wanted the job done quickly. He couldn't help but think that if DeMarco had died a couple of days ago he wouldn't be in the situation he was in now because it would have taken some time for DeMarco to force Stephanie Hernandez to turn against him. Maybe he should tell Tony to kill Stephanie instead of DeMarco.

The person he really wished he'd killed, however, was Carmine Taliaferro. He should have killed that conniving old fuck right after he killed Gino DeMarco.

<hr />

Quinn could see Carmine, clear as a bell, when he met with him years ago, a few days after he'd killed Gino. He had gone back to see the doctor who had treated his gunshot wound, to make sure everything was healing okay, and Carmine had been sitting in the junkie doctor's living room wearing a baggy brown suit and those big black glasses he wore.

"What the hell are you doing here?" Quinn had said.

"How's the shoulder? You gonna be able to play tennis or whatever it is you play?"

"What are you doing here?" Quinn said again. "I told you I didn't ever want to see you again."

As if he hadn't heard him, Carmine said, "Anyway, I hope you're mending okay. Your health's important to me. You're important to me."

"Carmine, you've got nothing you can use to control me anymore. You can't tell people I killed DeMarco and Jerry Kennedy. Well, I suppose you could tell, but who'd believe you? I mean, they might believe you if you said you'd ordered me to kill them, but then you'd go to jail as an accomplice. And as for me accidentally shooting Connors, since you gave me the name of the witness, I can always take care of the teacher if she ever becomes a problem. So you have nothing, Carmine. From this point forward, you stay the hell away from me and just pray that all my friends in the department don't come after you."

And that's when Carmine had said, "I got something I want to show you, young Officer Quinn."

Quinn almost threw up when he saw the photos.

He remembered the night he killed DeMarco, how brightly lit the warehouse had been, but he hadn't thought too much about it. The story Carmine had given Gino DeMarco was that the warehouse was used for a high-stakes Saturday night poker game, and Quinn was one of the players. The warehouse was lit up, Quinn figured, to match the story—so the poker players wouldn't have to stumble around the warehouse in the dark to make their way back to the office where the game was played. When he saw the photos, however, he understood why every light in the warehouse had been turned on.

Quinn figured out later that the photographer must have been hiding up on the catwalk, partially hidden by the warehouse overhead crane or under the tarps stored on the catwalk. He positioned himself so he could look directly down at the main aisle of the warehouse—the aisle he knew Gino DeMarco would walk down. The photographer hadn't used a flash—Quinn would have seen a flash going off—and Quinn didn't hear the clicking noise a camera makes as the film is advanced because of all the noise on the pier.

He never did find out who took the photos—the photos that could prove he was a murderer—the photos that Carmine had used to squeeze him for years. Whoever it was, the guy had to have been a pro.

He did everything he could to find the photographs and the negatives after Carmine died—but he never could. Then Carmine's pushy bitch of a daughter shows up after he executed a search warrant on her house and tells Quinn that he and his wife are going to become her political guardian angels. The fact was, supporting Stephanie Taliaferro Hernandez hadn't been all that painful and from everything he could see, she was actually a fairly decent politician.

And maybe that's why she sold him out—because she was a politician.

———◆◆◆———

Quinn walked over to the National Mall and started walking in the direction of the Lincoln Memorial. He noticed that the Washington Monument appeared to be fully restored after the earthquake that had occurred in 2011. It had taken them forever to repair it.

One thing he was going to have to do was stop seeing Pam. He hated to do it—he really did love her—but in order to save himself, he needed Barbara's influence. And he really needed her money. Whichever lawyer he hired to defend him would have to be one of the best in New York, and it was going to cost hundreds of thousands of dollars to defend himself against a murder charge. He was somewhat worried that Barbara might not stand by his side—but not too worried. Barbara had always been an extraordinarily loyal person and her reputation would be damaged almost as much as his if he were found guilty.

As for his defense, the obvious tactic was to impugn the photos. If experts could demonstrate how the photos could have been manufactured, it wouldn't be hard to make a case that his enemies—like people in the mafia—had tried to engineer his downfall. Yes, with his reputation, any decent attorney should be able to get him acquitted if it could be shown that the photos might not be real. And he was going to have more than a decent attorney and he'd buy all the experts he needed.

Another possibility was the one he'd mentioned to Joe DeMarco: admit that he'd indeed shot Gino, but he did so only in self-defense and while trying to arrest Gino. That was going to be tougher to sell to a jury. Like DeMarco had said, how would he explain why he didn't come forward immediately and admit to killing Gino that night if the shooting was in the line of duty? Maybe what he could do was . . .

Ah, a pay phone. Over there, by the Hirshhorn. He'd always liked the sculpture garden in front of the Hirshhorn Museum, particularly the famous *Burghers of Calais* by Rodin. Rodin's human figures were so real he could imagine them coming to life and talking to the tourists in the garden.

"Boss!" Hanley called out.

He'd actually forgotten Hanley and Grimes were trailing along after him.

"I'm just going over to use that phone, Hanley."

"Boss, aren't you supposed to be over at the Hoover Building for lunch?"

Quinn laughed. "Not today, Hanley, not today."

"Boss, are you sure you're all right?"

Quinn just waved a hand—a mild quit-bugging-me gesture. He picked up the phone, then realized he didn't have any change and he'd probably need three or four dollars to call New York. He called Hanley and Grimes over—they didn't have any change, either—so he had to wait until Hanley could get change from a street vendor.

"Tony, do you know who this is?" Quinn said when Benedetto answered the phone.

Tony didn't answer, but Quinn could hear him breathing.

"Tony! Goddamnit, can you hear me? Do you know who this is?"

"Yeah," Tony finally said. He sounded really weak, like he might die any moment.

"I want you to call off the hit on . . . on you-know-who. Do you understand?"

"Yeah."

"Tony, are you sure you understand?"

"Yeah."

Shit, Quinn thought after he hung up. Tony had sounded so out of it that he couldn't be sure that Tony had understood a thing he'd said. From this point forward, he needed to make sure that he had people around him constantly in case DeMarco was killed. He needed credible alibis.

———◆◆◆———

Tony hung up the phone, wondering who had just called. He'd been hitting the morphine pretty heavily; he was having a hell of a bad day.

———◆◆◆———

Quinn walked for almost two hours on the Mall, and while he walked he came up with a plausible way to explain why he'd killed Gino De-Marco in that warehouse and never reported the shooting. In order to make it work, he would need the cooperation of one man, his first mentor in the department, the man who'd been the chief of D's when he was still a rookie. Leo Boyle was eighty now but still sharp, and he loved Quinn like a son—not to mention that Quinn had done a lot for Leo's grandson when he joined the force. Yeah, he might have to sweeten the pot in some way, but Leo would most likely be willing to commit perjury to save him; Leo wouldn't care that he'd killed a thug like Gino DeMarco. He'd still prefer to impugn the photos, but if he couldn't . . .

It was time to go see Barbara. He would tell her how he was being framed, and then they'd fly back to New York the next morning. Before they left D.C., he'd call Adam Morse and ask Morse to represent him. It was almost funny. He'd always despised Adam Morse for his ability to convince juries to acquit the criminals he represented; tonight he'd ask Morse to meet him for lunch tomorrow to discuss strategy.

He turned and said to Hanley, "Get the car. I want to head back to the town house."

"Boss, the car's all the way back at the parking lot near the Russell Building. Remember?"

"Oh, that's right," Quinn said. It would take Hanley at least half an hour to retrieve the car. "Well, see if you can get me a cab, then you go get the car and Grimes will go with me." At this point, he preferred Grimes to Hanley because Hanley kept asking what was bothering him.

Barbara wasn't at the town house when he arrived. She must still be out looking at real estate. Quinn drank only sparingly and hardly ever had a drink before six in the evening—but now seemed like a good time for one. He prowled the town house until he found the liquor cabinet and filled a tumbler full of scotch. Excellent scotch.

Barbara finally arrived and he was a bit drunk by the time she got there. As soon as she saw him, she said, "Have you seen the news? Brian, what's going on?" She wasn't talking—she was *screeching*—and she looked wild-eyed. Barbara, with all her money and her pampered upbringing, was a woman who rarely lost her composure.

"What did they say on the news?" Quinn asked.

"They said, he said . . ."

"Who? Who made the announcement?"

"The president's press secretary."

"So what did he say?"

"He said the president has withdrawn your name for the FBI job."

"But did he say why?"

"Not really. All he said was . . . I was watching at the Four Seasons, having a drink with the real estate agent when the news came on. My God, Brian, it was humiliating. I didn't know what to say to the woman."

"Barbara, calm down. What reason was given for the president dropping me?"

"All he said, all the press secretary said, was something like 'Certain information has come to the president's attention, information that is currently being evaluated that has caused the president, for the time being, to reconsider Commissioner Quinn's appointment.' A bunch of gibberish like that. Brian, what's this all about?"

"Sit down, Barbara. I need to tell you something, something that happened when I was young." He took her hands into his and looked deeply into her eyes. "I need you, Barbara, more than I've ever needed you before."

42

DeMarco had told Mike and Dave it would be too much of a hassle to get them passes to come into the Dirksen Building and that even if they could get in, they wouldn't be able to carry weapons. So what use would they be? He'd told them to wait for him on the steps on the north side of the building and, to his disappointment, they were still there when he finished with Quinn.

"I'm not going to be needing you guys anymore," he said. "You can take off."

DeMarco figured that no way in hell was Quinn going to make a run at him after Stephanie Hernandez showed the FBI the photos. If DeMarco was killed, Brian Quinn would be the prime suspect—and Quinn didn't need to be a suspect for more than one crime at a time.

"Yeah, well," Mike said, "we're not exactly working for you. We're working for Emma. So she needs to tell us if it's okay for us to take off."

DeMarco was in too good a mood to argue with him and tell him that it was *his* decision and not Emma's regarding whether or not he needed their continued protection—which consisted of them primarily sitting around his house, eating his food, and playing cribbage. All he said was "Then I'll give Emma a call in a while, but right now I'm heading over to the Monocle for a drink. I feel like celebrating. You can tag along if you want."

"What are you celebrating?" Mike asked.

"Karma," DeMarco answered.

Yep, Brian Quinn might still be alive, but he'd eventually pay for what he did. Or at least DeMarco was pretty sure he would pay. It would probably take two or three years with a legal system that moved slower than slugs could travel, but in the end, Quinn would go down. He was concerned, of course, because Quinn was bright and slippery and well connected—and because his wife was so goddamn rich—that Quinn might be acquitted. But DeMarco didn't think so.

The Monocle restaurant—a well-known watering hole for the denizens of Capitol Hill—was only a few blocks from the Dirksen Building and it was too nice a day to take a cab, so they walked. As they were walking, Dave suddenly tensed up and said, "Hey, Mike! That guy over there, across the street, the guy in the tan jacket? Is he the one we saw this morning near DeMarco's place, getting into his car?"

DeMarco looked over at the man they were talking about. He was pretty sure it wasn't the same guy; although he was tall and balding and wearing the same color jacket as the man they'd seen near his house, this man was younger. Mike apparently thought the same thing because he said, "Nah, I don't think it's him."

At the next corner the man in the tan jacket turned and headed west and Dave said, "Yeah, it probably wasn't him."

DeMarco almost said, *Probably?* He was going to tell Emma that in the future, if she thought he needed bodyguards, to hire people with twenty-twenty vision.

In the Monocle, DeMarco ordered a vodka martini. Mike and Dave ordered draft beer; apparently drinking beer on duty—as opposed to the hard stuff—didn't violate whatever sacred oath they took as bodyguards.

DeMarco looked up at the television over the bar as he waited for his drink; CNN was on, the sound muted, and captions were running across the screen too fast to read, but DeMarco saw enough to understand that the maniac who ran Iran was up to something screwy again.

His martini arrived, and as he was sipping it, it occurred to him that he needed to call his mother. He didn't want her to be surprised when the news broke that Quinn had been arrested for killing Gino DeMarco. Dealing with her husband's death had been hard enough the first time; he wished there was some way he could spare her from having to go through it all over again. Maybe the best thing would be to call his Aunt Connie first, give her the news, and ask her to stay with his mom for a couple of days. Yeah, that sounded like a plan.

"How long we gonna sit here?" Mike asked.

"Until I'm through celebrating. Just relax and drink your beer."

At that moment, he looked up at the television and saw the CNN guy's lips moving and on the caption were the words *Brian Quinn* and *FBI director*. "Hey," DeMarco said to the bartender, "would you mind turning on the sound for just a minute?"

The bartender's expression made it clear that it would be a major inconvenience for him to pick up the remote and hit a single button, but he did, and at that moment the president's wimpy press secretary appeared behind a podium and told the nation that the president had decided to drop Brian Quinn.

DeMarco raised his martini and made a toast: "Here's to John Fitzpatrick Mahoney."

"What?" Mike said.

DeMarco sat there a moment longer, noodling things over as he finished his drink. *What the hell?* he thought to himself. *What do I have to lose?* He took out his cell phone and made a call. "Is he available?" he asked.

"Yes," Mavis said. "For exactly twenty-two minutes."

"I'll be right over."

It was time for DeMarco to go beg for his job back.

"I'm heading over to the Capitol. You guys can come along if you want."

"Can we go inside the building this time?" Dave asked.

"Sure," DeMarco said. "You just go over to the visitor's center and get in line with all the rest of the tourists."

Mahoney was on the phone when DeMarco walked into his office. He glared at DeMarco briefly, then said into the phone, "All right, Stephanie, and thanks. I'll talk to Barlow in the next couple of weeks—I gotta figure out what to do with him—then after I talk to him I'm going to send you a guy who'll help with your campaign."

He put down the phone and said to DeMarco—or maybe he was talking to himself—"She's going to be a real pain in the ass. I know I'm going to regret getting her a seat in the House." Then he said to DeMarco, "What do you want?"

"I, uh, just wanted to thank you for what you did."

Mahoney just stared at him, his small blue eyes boring into DeMarco's. DeMarco was about to open his mouth and go into the spiel he'd prepared, telling Mahoney how he was sorry that he'd lost his temper and threatened him, how he shouldn't have done that even though he'd been understandably upset, and how if Mahoney . . .

Mahoney opened the center drawer in his desk and pulled out a key and tossed it to DeMarco. It was the key to DeMarco's office—the office of the *Counsel Pro Tem for Liaison Affairs*. The office where the red fire axe resided.

"Get the fuck out of here," Mahoney said. "But if you ever pull something like that again . . . Go on, beat it."

As DeMarco walked past Mavis's desk, a smile on his face, he remembered what Jake had told him the first time he met Mahoney: *"I thought that went pretty good."*

———◆◆◆———

Now DeMarco really felt like celebrating and he also realized that he hadn't eaten lunch and he was starving. He called Emma so he could shed himself of Mike and Dave but Emma didn't answer her phone, which didn't really surprise him. Emma viewed her cell phone primarily as a one-way communication device.

DeMarco decided to treat himself—and Mike and Dave—to an early dinner at a sports bar in Georgetown. Once they arrived, Mike and Dave proceeded to drink more beer, and DeMarco got the impression that they weren't pacing themselves. DeMarco, not being a big beer guy since beer usually gave him a headache, decided to stick with vodka martinis.

At one point, while waiting for his next drink to arrive, he called Emma and this time she answered. He gave her a recap of all that had transpired with Mahoney and Brian Quinn. She'd already seen the news conference announcing that Brian Quinn would not be occupying the big chair in the Hoover Building.

"I appreciate you hiring Mike and Dave to watch over me," he said, "but I don't need them anymore. Quinn's not going to do anything now."

"Probably not," Emma said, "but I want them to escort you home and make sure there's no one lurking around your house. Plus it sounds like you're in some bar and about three sheets to the wind."

"Hey, I'm celebrating." He didn't bother to say that Mike and Dave were probably as drunk as he was.

"Whatever. Put Mike on the phone and I'll tell him what I want him and Dave to do."

"Thanks, Emma. For everything." Then he added, "You saved my life."

———◆◆◆———

By the time DeMarco got home, it was dark outside. Dave made a tour around the exterior of the house, looking, DeMarco assumed, for evidence that somebody had broken into his home. Mike stood next to him while Dave was searching, glancing casually about the neighborhood. DeMarco wasn't too sure about Mike's powers of observation since he knew how many beers the damn guy had had; he'd paid for the beers.

Dave returned from his walk around the house and Mike took DeMarco's house key, pulled out his .45, and opened the front door. DeMarco rolled his eyes—and prayed that Mike wouldn't shoot something in his house, like his TV set, when Mike saw his own reflection in the screen. Mike punched in the code to DeMarco's alarm, flipped on a light, then proceeded to walk through the house, flipping on more lights, while Dave and DeMarco waited by the front door; DeMarco just wished this charade would end as he desperately needed to take a piss.

"All clear," Mike called out.

DeMarco fast-walked toward the bathroom—to discover the door closed and Mike inside the room.

43

Oskar Pankov looked outside his hotel room window. It was almost dark and it would be completely dark by the time he arrived at the vacant house in Georgetown. He hoped he could finish the job tonight and wouldn't have to hang around any longer. He hated to sleep in any bed other than his own.

He dressed all in black—black baseball cap, black shirt, black Windbreaker, black jeans, black Reeboks. Even his socks were black. Lastly, he put on black leather shooting gloves; to keep from leaving fingerprints on his weapons or in his rental car, he wouldn't take them off until the job was finished. That afternoon, he'd wiped down the rental car and both his weapons—the rifle and the pistol—as well as all the ammunition. He knew he was going to have leave the rifle after he made the shot and he might have to leave the rental car as well if something went wrong. He'd used a fake ID and credit card to rent the car, so he wasn't worried about anyone tracing him through the car.

He took one last look around the hotel room to see if he'd forgotten anything, then took a piss. Experience had shown, particularly as he'd grown older, that it was always prudent to take a piss before a job.

Oskar parked his car in front of the house that abutted the back of the for-sale house. From the backseat of his car, he took a canvas shopping bag that contained his short stepladder and a rectangular case that looked like it might contain a musical instrument such as a saxophone. He walked around the block until he reached the front of the for-sale house and looked casually around. There was no one on the street that he could see.

Moving swiftly—not like someone sneaking around—he walked directly up to the gate on the west side of the house, opened the gate, and passed through it. He acted like a man who belonged. He walked to the backyard fence, placed the stepladder at the base of the fence, then walked to the east side of the house. Going down on his belly, he crawled into the space between the house and the rhododendron bushes on that side of the house.

He opened the case, took out the rifle parts, attached the barrel to the stock, and attached the scope. Now, if someone had seen him and called the police, he might be arrested for trespassing and for having a rifle and an unregistered pistol. Of course, if the cops arrived, he would leave the weapons in the bushes and stand up to greet them, hands in the air, and hopefully they wouldn't find the weapons. If they did, they'd still have to prove they belonged to him. What he would not do was shoot the policemen.

Lights were on in the house across the street but Oskar didn't see anybody in the house. Fifteen minutes passed; the cops had not arrived and he still hadn't seen anyone in the house. Thirty minutes later, a man walked into a room and picked up the phone. The man was perfectly framed by the window and clearly visible through the scope on the rifle.

Oskar smiled. He'd be sleeping in his own bed tomorrow night, next to his warm, fat wife.

DeMarco dialed his Aunt Connie's phone number. He was going to ask her to go visit his mom tomorrow, so she'd be there when he told his mom about Quinn. As he waited for her to answer—he hoped she was home—he stood in front of the window, looking at the house across the street.

———◆◆◆———

Oskar Pankov pulled the trigger.

44

The doorbell woke him at 6 A.M. Although his bodyguards had left the night before, he really wasn't worried about his safety. Nonetheless he looked through the peephole before he opened the door, and saw a man and woman standing there, both wearing suits.

He thought about going back to his bedroom and putting on some pants, but said: screw it. They woke him up. Wearing only boxer shorts and a sleeveless T-shirt, he opened the door partway and said, "What do you want?"

"FBI," the woman said. "We're here to talk to you about the assassination of Brian Quinn."

"What!" DeMarco said.

DeMarco excused himself and went to put on some pants. The male FBI agent accompanied him.

The agents were named Crawford and Blanchard, Crawford being the female, and they were polite and formal and as serious as a couple of heart attacks. They informed him that Brian Quinn had been killed the night before, about 8 P.M. He'd been standing in the den of the house in Georgetown where he'd been staying, talking to a big-shot New York lawyer on the phone, and someone shot him through the heart. He died before the medics arrived and his two security people, New York cops named Hanley and Grimes, hadn't been able to find the shooter in the dark. This morning the FBI found a rifle in the bushes in the house across the street from where Quinn and his wife had been staying.

They pissed DeMarco off immediately when they said they wanted to talk to him about Quinn's *assassination*—the word making it sound like Brian Quinn had been a head of state as opposed to the cold-blooded killer he was. They pissed him off a second time when they said they were there because they'd been informed that Quinn had *allegedly* killed DeMarco's father. They knew this because Stephanie Hernandez had talked to the acting director of the FBI the day before and had shown him the pictures of Quinn killing his dad.

"There's nothing alleged about it," DeMarco said. "Quinn killed my dad."

"Be that as it may, Mr. DeMarco," Crawford said, "can you tell us where you were at eight P.M. last night?"

Fortunately for DeMarco, he had not one but two alibis, Mike and Dave, decorated military veterans. Thank God Emma had insisted that they escort DeMarco home the evening Quinn was killed, and then hung around to drink the last four beers in his refrigerator.

DeMarco suggested to Crawford and Blanchard that they might want to talk to Tony Benedetto. Benedetto would confirm that Quinn had killed Gino DeMarco and would also be able to give them the backstory on why his father was killed.

In response, Crawford said, "We're not investigating the death of your father, Mr. DeMarco. We're investigating the death of Commissioner Quinn."

And DeMarco realized at that moment that Quinn would never be exposed publicly for what he'd done and would go to his grave as some sort of hero.

———◆———

Tony asked one of the nurses to turn on the television and put on the news. He was too weak to pick up the remote or even punch the button to turn the TV on. He was almost too weak to smile when he saw the news; he'd never imagined that one day he'd be so weak he couldn't move his lips.

The guys on CNN were going on and on about Brian Quinn. He'd been assassinated in Washington, D.C., last night. The FBI claimed they had no leads except for a rifle that had been found. The White House refused to tell the media why the president had decided to withdraw his nomination of Brian Quinn; the president's press secretary just said that the president had been given some information regarding Quinn that had caused him to reconsider the appointment. And now that the commissioner had been killed, the president saw no reason to share that information with the media because the information had not been substantiated and could possibly damage the reputation of a man who had served the city of New York in an extraordinary manner. The only thing the president cared about was that whoever was responsible for Quinn's death be found and brought to justice.

"Well, that ain't going to happen, bozo," Tony said out loud to the president's press secretary. "Not unless God decides to let me live."

In a way, Quinn was dead because of God. Tony, a lifelong Catholic who rarely attended church, had never believed that you could make a confession at the last minute and God would forgive a lifetime's worth of mortal sins. God would never make things that easy. But Tony decided that before he croaked, he was going to do one last thing that was good instead of bad: he decided to spare DeMarco and have Oskar Pankov kill Brian Quinn instead. He'd always liked DeMarco—and he'd never liked Brian Quinn.

It had been easy to find out where Quinn was staying in D.C. Tony still had connections in the NYPD, connections he'd inherited from Carmine Taliaferro. However, it had cost him a hell of a lot more to have Quinn killed because Oskar knew that the FBI and the entire New York Police Department were going to hunt for Quinn's killer forever, so Tony had to pay him enough to make the risk worthwhile.

But now he could die in peace and with almost a clean conscience—and at that moment, and for once with perfect timing, Anthony Jr. walked into the room with Father Mazzini, the pastor of St. Sebastian's. Although Tony still didn't think a last confession would save his old ass from hell, what did he have to lose?

Agents Crawford and Blanchard did decide to visit Tony Benedetto, but the reason had nothing to do with the death of Gino DeMarco. One of Quinn's security people, the cop named Hanley, informed them that the commissioner had made a call from a public pay phone the afternoon he was killed—and this was strange since Quinn had a cell phone. Crawford and Blanchard checked outgoing calls from the pay phone and saw one call was to a hospital room where an old mobster named Tony Benedetto was staying, and they decided to ask Tony about the call.

However, when the agents entered Benedetto's hospital room, they found out that Tony Benedetto had died a short time before they arrived. His son, Anthony Benedetto Jr., was in the room weeping quietly, clutching his dead father's hand. The agents tried to question Anthony Jr., but he was so distraught it was impossible.

———— ◆◆◆ ————

Anthony Jr. didn't know why the goddamn FBIs had come to see his dad; he was just glad when they finally left. Still squeezing his father's bony hand, he said, "I'm sorry, Pop. I'm sorry I was always such a fuckup."

Anthony Jr. was scared. His dad had always been there for him and had always protected him as best he could. He hadn't realized until after the old man died how much comfort he'd taken in knowing he could go to him if he had a problem.

He'd been a *great* father—and fuck the FBI.

———— ◆◆◆ ————

Although she didn't let her friends see it, Barbara Quinn was surprised to find that she wasn't really grief-stricken that her husband was dead. She was sorry, of course, and shocked by the way he'd been killed, but she wasn't . . . well, she wasn't *crushed* by his death. In an odd way, and she knew this was somewhat ghoulish, she was actually looking forward to his funeral. She knew it would be a grand event, block after block of blue-clad policemen marching in his honor, the bagpipes playing as they marched. Her husband deserved that honor and she, as his wife, deserved it, too.

The thing was, although she'd never admit it to anyone, her marriage had been over for years. For the last three years, she'd been having an affair with an architect she'd used several times when she'd remodeled the cottage in the Hamptons. She didn't know if she would marry him or not, but she did know he was the kind of man she needed: someone warm and artistic and spontaneous. Someone who could make her laugh.

Brian had always been so cold and calculating, it had been like living with an android.

But God rest his soul, and she hoped they put his assassin to death.

———————◆◆◆———————

Pamela Weinman was inconsolable. She hadn't left her apartment or stopped crying since Brian was killed. She wasn't sure how she was going to be able to carry on without him. She didn't want to carry on without him.

She was also angry. No explanation was ever given as to why the president had withdrawn his nomination and, in spite of all his accomplishments and the good things Brian had done, he died with his reputation somewhat tarnished.

A great man like Brian Quinn didn't deserve that.

———————◆◆◆———————

Agents Blanchard and Crawford sat in a room with thirty other agents poring over the files of people Brian Quinn had arrested in a twenty-five-year career in law enforcement. It was going to take them months to review all the files.

The FBI had only four pieces of evidence regarding Brian Quinn's assassin: a partial footprint from a Reebok tennis shoe, a shell casing that had no fingerprints on it, and an old Remington hunting rifle that could have been purchased at a yard sale, a gun show, or any one of a million stores; the serial numbers had been obliterated. Lastly, they had an eighteen-inch stepladder that, just like the rifle, could have been bought anywhere.

Crawford and Blanchard really wished they could have talked to Tony Benedetto before he died because of four phone calls that couldn't be explained. First was the call Quinn had made from a pay phone to Tony's hospital room the day Quinn was killed; why would Quinn call a retired, dying mobster? To gloat? Second, Tony had made a call to One Police Plaza, but the call went to a multiline phone in a room where twenty detectives sat, and all the detectives denied speaking to Tony. Third was a call to an untraceable cell phone, another dead end. Finally there was a call Tony had made to a Russian lunch counter in Brighton Beach a few days before he died. Brighton Beach was infested with Russian hoods.

When they talked to the owner of the restaurant, who was also the cook, he said he didn't remember the call. He said maybe it was a wrong number, and Crawford and Blanchard figured it could have been a wrong-number call, as the call was less than thirty seconds long. Nonetheless, they checked out the cook at the restaurant, a guy named Oskar Pankov, and as near as they could tell he was just a cook. He certainly looked like a cook.

Oskar had been in the Russian army when he was practically a kid, then immigrated to the United States and became a citizen. He didn't have a record in Russia or in the United States, and NYPD's organized crime guys had never heard of him. When they asked Oskar where he was the night Quinn was killed, he said he was at home. Where else would he be? His wife, his brother-in-law, and an old babushka who lived in Oskar's building—a woman who barely spoke English and might have dementia—all backed up his story.

They'd keep digging into Oskar's background—maybe talk to some retired organized crime cops who were around when Oskar first came to this country—but Blanchard was about 90 percent certain he was clean and Crawford was ready to agree with him.

Oskar Pankov placed the tongue sandwich on the counter in front of the old man, one of his regulars, a guy who came in three, four times a week for lunch. The old man's name was Sergei and it looked as if a strong wind could blow him away, but Oskar knew Sergei had survived one of the worst gulags in Siberia for sixteen years, which meant he was tougher than a wrecking ball.

"How you feeling, Oskar?" Sergei asked in Russian. "You weren't here the last time I came in and your wife said you had a cold."

"I'm doing better," Oskar said. "By the way, I wanted to tell you since you come in so often, that I'm thinking about closing the restaurant in November and going down to Mexico to catch some sun, maybe do a little fishing. Martina keeps complaining we never go anywhere."

"You're going to be gone a *month*?" Sergei said. He said this like a child who was being abandoned and would have to fend for himself.

"Yeah, I came into a little money recently." Oskar winked and added, "Made a long-shot bet, something I don't usually do."

"You're not thinking about closing the restaurant, are you?"

"Oh, no, I'd never do that. All I know how to do is cook."

<hr />

DeMarco had wanted to take his mother out to a nice place to eat but she didn't want to go. She said she didn't feel like getting dressed up, plus she had a lasagna she'd made just the day before and it was going to go to waste if they didn't eat it. His mother's lasagna was to die for.

DeMarco didn't know why, but he just had the urge to see his mom. He'd decided he wasn't going to tell her about Brian Quinn—there was no point opening up all those old wounds. Her husband's life had been a mystery to her, as was his death, and he'd decided to just leave things the way they were. But he wanted to see her; he just wanted to spend a little time with her.

She was at the stove putting a pie into the oven; she'd started making the pie five minutes after he arrived. He looked around the kitchen. She hadn't changed a thing in it—not even the appliances—since his father had remodeled the room twenty-five years ago. There was a little nick in the countertop Joe could barely see from where he was sitting because when his dad installed the countertop his router had slipped as he was trimming the Formica. The little nick drove his mother crazy—she'd complained to Joe about it dozens of times—but she'd never said anything to Gino, because if she had, he would have replaced the whole sheet of Formica, which cost a fortune back then.

"You remember when Dad remodeled this kitchen?" DeMarco said.

"Oh my God! I'll never forget it. I was cooking on a propane camp stove for three months down in the basement. I tried to get him to hire a professional to help him but I couldn't get him to do it. Talking to that man was like talking to a rock."

But she was smiling when she said this.